A Tender Age

AF729144

Also by Chang-rae Lee

My Year Abroad

On Such a Full Sea

The Surrendered

Aloft

A Gesture Life

Native Speaker

A Tender Age

Chang-rae Lee

Summit
Books

London · New York · Amsterdam/Antwerp · Sydney/Melbourne · Toronto · New Delhi

Summit Books

First published in the United States by Riverhead Books, an imprint of Penguin Random House LLC, 2026
First published in Great Britain by Summit Books, an imprint of Simon & Schuster UK Ltd, 2026

SUMMIT BOOKS and colophon are registered trademarks of Simon & Schuster, LLC

Copyright © Chang-rae Lee, 2026

The right of Chang-rae Lee to be identified as author of this work has been asserted in accordance with the Copyright, Designs and Patents Act, 1988

1 3 5 7 9 10 8 6 4 2

Simon & Schuster UK Ltd, 7th Floor, 199 Bishopsgate, London, EC2M 3TY

For more than 100 years, Simon & Schuster has championed authors and the stories they create. By respecting the copyright of an author's intellectual property, you enable Simon & Schuster and the author to continue publishing exceptional books for years to come. We thank you for supporting the author's copyright by purchasing an authorised edition of this book.
No amount of this book may be reproduced or stored in any format, nor may it be uploaded to any website, database, language-learning model, or other repository, retrieval, or artificial intelligence system without express permission. All rights reserved. Enquiries may be directed to Simon & Schuster, 199 Bishopsgate, London, EC2M 3TY or RightsMailbox@simonandschuster.co.uk

Simon & Schuster Australia, Sydney
Simon & Schuster India, New Delhi

www.simonandschuster.co.uk
www.simonandschuster.com.au
www.simonandschuster.co.in

The authorised representative in the EEA is Simon & Schuster Netherlands BV, Herculesplein 96, 3584 AA Utrecht, Netherlands. info@simonandschuster.nl

Simon & Schuster strongly believes in freedom of expression and stands against censorship in all its forms. For more information, visit BooksBelong.com.
A CIP catalogue record for this book is available from the British Library

Book design by Amanda Dewey

Hardback ISBN: 978-1-3985-6294-3
Trade Paperback ISBN: 978-1-3985-6295-0
eBook ISBN: 978-1-3985-6296-7

This book is a work of fiction. Names, characters, places and incidents are either a product of the author's imagination or are used fictitiously. Any resemblance to actual people living or dead, events or locales is entirely coincidental.

Printed and Bound in the UK using 100% Renewable Electricity at CPI Group (UK) Ltd

FSC www.fsc.org MIX Paper | Supporting responsible forestry FSC® C013604

A Tender Age

A life can catch up to you.

It's a wonder, really. One morning, maybe you woke up too early, the span of years will collapse and meet you in full. There's no great thwack. Hardly even a jolt. You could follow the usual motions of the day.

But here you are, resolving to pay more attention. You need to pay more attention. Otherwise, you can easily misplace your everyday fortunes, the fact, say, that you have a loving spouse who is inordinately talented and impassioned; children who have grown up to be wry and kind, and for whom you'd give your life without pause; work that is consuming enough but not ruinously; friends to share food and drink with, and to tell silly stories. Still, I don't always cherish things as deeply as I should. I try as hard as I can and continue to fail. I want to be *here*, even if I'm often dreaming. Each moment is a singular moment, particular in its coordinates, the countless dimensions in which those coordinates can be observed and measured a marvelous conspiracy that fixes us in a way that will never be repeated.

And yet we can't help but keep going back to old times, futilely scratching at a spot. It doesn't matter how significant a certain event or instance was, sometimes the barest irritation will draw incommensurate attention and the skin can go raw before you realize it. Lately, I can't seem to help but linger on this time or that, those tender ages rife with curiosities, and go over in serial fashion what I might have done or said to defuse a tricky situation or take a more principled stand or else assuage my frustrated heart. So many chances, ceded. What remains are these disparate patches of existence that end up knitting vaster and less randomly than you would have ever imagined.

The other day, for instance, I was suddenly thinking about the circumstances of how our girls got our dog. It's no big thing. We met him when he was three months old, while we were on a vacation in Florida. Old friends happened to live there, a family with a boy and a girl the same ages as our daughters, and during an afternoon visit with them the wife casually mentioned that they were looking for someone to adopt their new puppy. Our girls were playing tug-of-war with the dog, a black-and-white toy terrier and Shih Tzu mix, squealing as he wrenched at the snout of the armadillo plush toy and made his tiny throaty growls, and when they heard her say *adopt* they both cried out, "Please, Momma, please!" They knew not to entreat me, as I was firmly against having a pet—we traveled too often, was my rationale—but my wife, whose neck instinctively flushed with their joy, let out a long sigh and met my eyes, and I understood what had now become the inevitable. The puppy was undeniably cute, with wistful, floppy ears and a corkscrew tail that shook like a rattler's, and he seemed sweet-mannered besides, and so with genuine curiosity and a last hope for a reprieve I wondered aloud how they could possibly give him up. *Our other dog is super jealous* was one response, *The puppy sheds too much* was another, both somewhat lame justifications that of course only ensured that we would take him.

After lunch, while our families took the dogs for a walk, my friend and I had a smoke and whiskey on his back deck, which overlooked the waterway. We'd known each other since childhood, but he'd been transferred away from the New York area just after our first children were born, and we exchanged news of the old gang, the comings and goings of jobs and moves, half joking about our sudden-onset middle age and various physical diminishments. The usual breezy stuff that precedes the more real turn in the conversation—raising kids, paying school fees and mortgages, the sex after many years of marriage—which in turn signals the conversation's near end. All fine. We could hear our families entering the house—my friend's son, oddly, had a habit of hooting like an owl—and we clinked our tumblers, finishing them off.

"Hey, thanks for taking on the little guy," my friend said. "Better for all."

"Except me," I said. "I'll be the one picking up his shit."

"At least they'll always be one-handers," he said. "I bought him for Colt. I hoped he would stop bothering Pepper." Pepper was their other dog, an adult Pekingese.

"Well, looks like Pepper always fights back."

His face seemed to shade, and I was going to pursue it, but then everybody came out with ice cream sandwiches, and we watched the fishing boats and pleasure yachts pass by. It was a perfect way to end a good visit. When we departed the girls had their new puppy and all his accompanying gear and food and treats, and back at our vacation rental, they immediately filled his food and water bowls and knelt beside him as they coaxed him to eat. But the "little guy"—as yet renamed—had trouble. He surely was hungry, but it was all he could do to simply approach the bowl. Every time he got within a muzzle's length he'd suddenly recoil, as though the food might leap up and snap him. The girls initially found this humorous, but he really wasn't going to get close enough to eat, and when my younger daughter nudged him forward he began whimpering, literally digging his heels into the carpeting. He lost it and peed. Eventually we figured out that if one of the girls held him in her lap he'd accept the dry food; he was still anxious but gently plucked the kibble from their fingers, which made them very happy.

Pu-chu, I must admit, has been a fine dog. He's feisty and barky with strangers, but soon enough he'll be extra friendly, even clingy and docile. He's certainly never bitten anyone.

The girls are no longer living at home so it's just the three of us. My wife is by far his favorite, he never leaves her side, although when she's out he'll sometimes come around and curl himself up next to my desk chair. It's true that he sheds a lot, faint sprays of white fur perennially dusted about the house. I complain when I vacuum but don't really mind.

And he eats almost like a normal dog once you get him going. Just before he'll attempt the first jawful his gears grind, there's a stuttering in his neck, something blocking him from finally reaching it. After a couple taps of the index finger next to the food on our kitchen floor—Pu-chu still can't abide a bowl—he'll break the chain and gobble as quickly as he can, his claws skittering on the tile the moment he's done as he scrambles away. We have theories as to why he eats this way. All of them feature Colt, the little boy who hooted, especially after we heard what his sister told our daughters, that her brother pretended his new pet was a special military type, born with astounding capabilities of strength and agility; that he'd perch the pup in the middle of a lemon tree, to see how he would get himself down; or that he'd start a small leaf fire on the driveway and compel Pu-chu by leash to leap it; or what my daughter later recounted witnessing the very day of our visit, that Colt placed him near the edge of their Ping-Pong table, quite a height for such a young toy breed, and then started slowly pushing him off.

They haven't been together since, but you can't help but wonder how Pu-chu would react if Colt, who by now must be college age, suddenly appeared in our kitchen. The scent of him would surely collapse the years. I'd like to think Pu-chu would growl, maybe even leap at him. But what's most likely, what's sadly fated for any warm-blood thusly forged during a seminal time, is that our little guy would do nothing, maybe not even move, his paws stuck in a cold glue of dread.

But then I like pretending, too. I imagine myself commandeering Pu-chu's stout little form, building up the spring in my hind legs, and instantly attacking the kid. I'd tear a chunk of ankle or calf, or at least viciously bark and growl, force a full retreat. To dispirit a certain kind you must be malign, become as bent as your nemesis. You must shock even yourself.

Only then can you be free.

When I was a kid there were some rough times. All of us go through it, a period when it can feel as if your life is a morass of poor timing and odd people that you can barely escape. Mine spanned the near-year that led up to my eleventh birthday during camp in the summer of 1976, a time when I was still a mere boy and had no yearnings to grow up or know anything more. My family was living then in a town north of New York City, a thirty-five-minute ride on the local commuter train, a town that was much darker-skinned and poorer than the surrounding villages and hamlets, which were and still are mostly white and wealthy. Those other villages had community pools with cordoned swimming lanes and multiple high-dive platforms. Their public high schools fielded complete symphony orchestras and produced not one but two musicals yearly. Their tidy parks and playgrounds were thick with mothers and au pairs and scrambling toddlers, and on the weekends, fathers who monitored the action or even horsed around with the kids.

In our 1970s town, the adults, for whatever reason, whether they were working a job or not, left us on our own, and to one another. This was suitable. We also knew very little else. Evidently there were some rich people in the area, a string of glittery beach houses on the Sound, and inland hillside enclaves of creepy Gothic mansions, but you never saw them except inside their big Cadillacs motoring quickly through our more typical neighborhood of low-rise tenements and modest one- and two-family houses. After the school day or during the summer we were always out on the double-parked streets playing some ball game or in our cruddy playground, with its rusty jungle gym, and splintery wooden swings, and riven, sticky asphalt you could pry up with your bare fingers.

My family lived in a sprawling redbrick rental apartment complex built after the war for the light industrial, service, and clerical workers who were saving up for their own houses in a better area. Our neighbors were Blacks and Puerto Ricans, working-class Irish and Italians, and some Jews who hadn't yet moved on, plus the legions of us new immigrants, from Asia and Eastern Europe and the Caribbean. The whole diverse lot of us, before diverse was an operative notion, made a mix that seemed natural and right despite how tense and fraught it could sometimes be. Were we all "friends"? I suppose we were. We were young enough—we ranged in age from eight to twelve—that the bonds felt fierce, like in a tribe, tourniquet tight, yet our tribe was fueled by constant disagreements, contentions, sometimes outright bloodletting, which made everything dire and fragile. Again, I rarely saw anyone's parents or guardians, or ventured into their apartments, and it was easy to believe that we somehow existed on our own as we tilted in our pastimes.

I should say that we were mostly boys, though there was a handful of older girls who infrequently played with us who were, depending on the activity, as vaunted and intimidating as the most athletic boys. One who stood out was named Katie Croker, a tall, angular blond-haired fifth grader who was rumored to have been left back one year and looked like one of those smushed-faced cats with a permanent glower, though it would be unfair of me to say that she wasn't also kind of pretty whenever she smiled, which was usually after she'd triumphed in one of the games. Her mode was to be aggressive and menacing, and most fearsome in one of our favorite games, Running Bases. It's a classic game where there are two catchers, each posted at a base, and everyone else, after three initial throws, running between them in a baseball-type rundown. If you got tagged you were out. The last remaining runner won, and then the two who'd been tagged first would have to be the catchers for the next round. I was good at the game, being swift and dodgy, and if I didn't win, I was usually tagged later in the rounds and rarely had to play catcher.

Katie Croker, while big and wiry and strong, wasn't terribly agile and thus regularly got tagged out early. This infuriated her, and she'd always try to knock the ball out of the tagger's mitt, or just totally bowl them over like she was rushing home plate. But it was when she played catcher that she was at her most terrorizing, her sparkly green eyes only going greener, the bulbous hull of her forehead a livid, shining white, and as she threw high into the air the third and final throw she'd shriek *Go!* and we'd sprint for our lives.

Katie Croker had a *rifle*, as we'd say, a whipping sidearm delivery that I swear generated Major League velocity. I don't know where her motion came from, but it was wicked, her ball seeming to rise as it missiled across the weedy apartment complex field, where it was heading nobody knew, including Katie Croker. Or maybe she did. We ran half ducking, shoulders to ears, moving in a herd in the illusion of safety, sometimes breaking off solo in a reckless dash, our necks and backs tensed against an impact that you feared would be lethal. One time my little sister wanted to play, and as we scurried, I had to shield her with my body as if we were under sniper fire, taking one in the thigh. Everyone got nailed at some point, in the butt or the kidney or the shoulder or how Gregory Fluss got it, beaned right in the temple, which was kind of scary when he didn't come to for a few seconds, and especially after we finally got him upright, when a nub of turd fell out of his shorts. We made him promise not to tell his parents.

After that we replaced the rubber-coated baseball we always used with a tennis ball—some wuss, maybe me, entreated the rest of us with this safety protocol—and although we were now spared the heaviest bruising and near-fractures, the actual pain of being struck was just as intense, for Katie Croker only threw harder, and at closer range, fueled with the fury of the thwarted. I dreaded that bright yellow felt. Once, she even caused Cleon Washington, our apartment complex alpha, to well up after she hit him square in the solar plexus. Cleon was a handsome, tall, soft-spoken kid who had his own tight crew and was a champ at every sport and game, and although he didn't always join in whenever he graced us, we couldn't help but saunter in his way and speak in his laconic style and attempt to impress him with our physical zeal, if not skills. He often sported a pick in his perfect halo of an Afro, and my mother was perplexed by my request for one, which she bought for me anyway, and which I'd futilely try to perch in my limp, straight hair. I'd never seen him so disenabled. When Cleon composed himself, he jumped up and shoved Katie Croker hard, and she shoved him hard back, triggering a collective gasp, and although I was terrified, I registered even then an unsavory, fetishistic surge at this particular tangle of humanity. Would he punch her? Would she punch him? Might they wrestle? Kiss?

It turned out nothing happened except for a stone-cold stare-down that verified why Katie Croker's presence in our games went unquestioned even though she wasn't anyone's friend, girl or boy: here was the baddest s.o.b. around, and even our playground king Cleon knew it. They both derisively chuckled, neither quite backing off, and maybe it was because there were never adults around to adjudicate that we often witnessed this sort of détente, at least between relative equals. The rest of us, we endured. To be a kid was to be bullied, no exceptions. Even Cleon had to deal with his much older brothers and their crew, hardened grown men they seemed to me, with aims and interests light-years beyond our conception.

At that point I had already suffered my own private miseries with Katie Croker, episodes she appeared to have completely forgotten but that rooted thick enough in my throat that sometimes I felt I could hardly breathe. I still think about those times, more often than makes any sense in the wider context of my life. This is the nature of certain youthful happenings, how they can become a knot in the flesh that every other occurrence must bypass in order for you to know yourself, in order for you to grow.

One unusually warm afternoon in early spring, Katie Croker surprised me while I was peeing in the shadowy hollows of the huge laurel bushes at the far corner of the complex property. No doubt she intended to do the same; everyone peed there, for while our apartments were merely a minute's sprint away, the distance might as well have been a mile, given how long we'd all hold it in, never wanting to stop playing. Plus there was a rusty drinking fountain at the playground whose water was sometimes lukewarm and metallic and sometimes ice cold and clean, and when cold like that in the summer was the most wonderful water you could ever have. Katie Croker hadn't really acknowledged me before that, I was just another boogery, lard-cheeked boy with grungy fingernails and hands, and to me she was the queenly eleven-year-old with the pinkish sun-kissed shoulders and scary diamond cat eyes, and when I realized she was watching me I tried to stop.

"Hey! Keep going!"

I shook my head, wincing as my stream flagged.

"I want to see!"

I didn't want her to see, but it was too painful to do otherwise, and I let go, startling us both with the furious flow coming from that tiny hole.

She whinnied in dark delight, and as I frantically tucked myself back into my trousers, scraping hard against the metal zipper, I realized I was crying, both from the pain at the tip of my already extra-sensitive member—it was as vulnerable as a just-birthed gecko back then, even the shower made it hurt—and the burning humiliation of her regard. And yet I was also sharply aware of my mother. It's funny how you can be stricken by the oddest point of focus in such moments, it's the same way in dreams, I could not stop thinking of how my mother would periodically run a bar of Ivory soap along the zipper of my winter coat, of my zip-up galoshes, the zippers of my shorts and trousers, as they always seemed to seize up and snag in my hasty hands. Had she not done so with this pair? I was desperate for that soap, that milky white bar I wished I could hold on to and cover my shame.

"Okay now, get lost," she ordered, pulling up the hem of her emerald-green smocked dress with the appliquéd sunflowers as she began to crouch.

I ran back to my mates pretending nothing happened. Like me they were infantile and clueless and ruled by sensation, and none of them noticed that I'd gone to the bushes, or that Katie Croker had been in there, too, or that she had now emerged and was gazing at me with her characteristic mouth hang, that diffident, lightless cave. Nor did they catch on to how she would regularly follow me into the laurel, where she would compel me to pee according to her whim, straight up in the air or zigzagging or splashing that mossy rock or, once, directly on the palm of her hand.

"It's so gross and hot," she said, her disgust only surpassed by my own. I was miserable, certain that what we were doing was wrong, maybe evil. Up to that moment all I knew was what any reasonably fortunate child knew, namely, the simple lessons of pain and pleasure, serial bouts of elation and disappointment and boredom, the sustenance of genuine attention and love, but now I was sopped by a piss-smelling fog of guilt that in my child's consciousness was condensing into the special muck of a novel psychic state: self-loathing.

Ah.

Then you're remade, the first of countless times. . . .

You'd think I'd learn not to drink so much water or resolve

to run up to our second-floor apartment and pee in private, but something about our encounters kept me heading for the pungent glade of the laurel bush. Yes, I was being dominated, I was being debased, thoroughly and abjectly humiliated, and yet there was a measure of exchange that I began to crave, if not enjoy. Of course, young children can have erotic feelings (and I certainly did), but I don't believe ours was some inaugurating and momentous psycho-sexual stamping. She simply needed me, a notion I in turn needed, and so I served.

Nothing lasts. Either she got bored with the exercise, or she began to resent my willingness in the role, and after a couple more hand showers, and a final command that I foul my own sneaker, Katie Croker left me to pee alone.

My given name, Jeon-Gi, with a hard *G*, was one she enjoyed deforming. She made fun of me with it, as some others did and would, though her taunts were oddly soothing and dulcet, if tinged with a maniacal lilt, these sly meowings of *Chun-ky, Chun-ky.* As skilled bullies will do, she was weaponizing a truth; for I was a chunky kid, bordering on fat from my one-a-day habit of a large Snickers bar, boxes of which my mother would stock for me as long as I ate the food she made, which I happily did. She and I were a tight pair that way, coconspirators in a plot to ensure my full indulgence, in every way, as I was her first born and only son. In ensuing years I'd become uncomfortably aware of the expectations behind all that spoiling—to be number one in my studies, in my sports, in even my citizenship, such as being class president—that I wanted very much to realize for her and lavishly envisioned for myself but could never achieve given my natural laziness and lack of resolve, much less talent.

But in those first few summers at the apartment complex, I only knew a princely feeling, its herald my mother's velvety ring of a voice calling from our kitchen window that looked out onto the playground and abutting patch of field.

Jeon-Gi-ya! Jeon-Gi-ya!

Wa-suh chum-shim muh-guh!

Come and eat lunch!

More beckoning words didn't exist; no matter what was transpiring in our games I would sub myself out, or simply quit, my mates grumbling but also jealous, as none of their mothers ever summoned them, or came out bearing snacks (as she sometimes did, with my sister Ella in tow), potato chips or Ritz crackers. We'd crowd around her, and she'd unpeel the brown wax paper from the baton of Ritz and let each of us take a few. I had to wait until the end, for in this instance they were our "guests." Katie Croker seemed to disappear whenever any adults came around, there was something of the stray cat about her, but she watched us from the periphery as we munched the crackers and drank the lemonade or iced tea my mother would pour from a big red-plaid-colored

Thermos into paper Dixie cups that we would then nest in a stack in her hand before sprinting off. I would instantly reimmerse myself in the play, never thinking twice about my mother's kind and solicitous efforts, but Katie Croker must have been paying attention because one day while my buddies and I were combing the high grass at the far boundary of the complex grounds for grasshoppers (to suffer as conscripts for a long-jump contest), I heard a distant murmuring of "*Jeon-Gi-ya, Jeon-Gi-ya . . .* "

Naturally a warm current uncoiled through my body, but the summons confused me, as I had just been inside for lunch. I looked to our narrow kitchen window on the second floor. Like most of the others on this south façade it was shaded and shut tight against the summer heat. I heard the calling again, this time more clearly, and I drifted toward it. There was a timbre of injury to the voice, one more mental than physical, as if something were oppressing her. My mother was an innately sturdy, resolute person, but living in a foreign place with few friends and no other family and not speaking the language was steadily dissolving a vital part of her. This was one thing I was painfully aware of, even then. How surprisingly fragile she was, collapsible.

As such I was constantly afraid for her, which made me afraid, too, the fear forming me to be a sometimes-brutal little boy. Most people didn't notice. My brutality was the colder variety, the kind that you had to peer closely to see but that was startling when you did.

Still, here in the playground, here at the apartments, I was one of the pliables. So when I found the source of the calling to be none other than Katie Croker—she had positioned herself in a service stairwell leading to the basement of our building, deviously bouncing her voice against the red brick—I stood before her as she reprised her uncannily accurate mimicry of my mother, though now it was with a sneer, making it seem as if the most loving and important person in my life were taunting me. I was miserable and angry and yet utterly useless; I simply stared down at the grass-stained white rubber toecaps of my brand-new sneakers and began to whimper.

"Why are you crying?" Katie Croker rasped. "You have nothing to cry about, you know that? You're a spoiled brat. Spoiled!" She was the one getting animated now, sounding more like a grown-up than a girl of eleven. "You just play your little wuss games with your little wuss friends and have snacks brought to you. You think everybody gets that? You think it's *normal*? Do you?"

I didn't know what to say. I probably did think it was normal, for I knew nothing outside of our parochially secure if periodically beleaguered immigrant existence. The only times I felt something off was when my father or mother encountered some misunderstanding out there in the abstruse, backward world of our town's streets and shops and offices, but I was still young enough to uphold them as being infallible, or at least never wholly at fault. Our life—or more accurately, my life—was happy enough. It was as it was meant to be. Of course I couldn't explain any of this to Katie Croker, much less articulate it to myself. All I knew was that I couldn't bear to displease her more, or have her think me a selfish, bratty boy, so with frantic grasping childish logic I unzipped my shorts and poked out and tried to pee for her.

"Stop that! God! You're so gross! In fact, you're *revolting*!"

I didn't know what "revolting" meant but the word hotly stabbed me where I was softest. My tiny piddler shrank even more, practically retracting itself. And now Katie Croker was dragging me by the elbow up the stairs and down the meandering paved walkway that snaked along the straight long side of my Building A. I enjoyed leaning into those curves on my bicycle, but they seemed needlessly tortuous now. Where was she taking me? Only the other buildings of the complex, B and C, lay ahead. Katie Croker lived in B, and rumor had it that she lived only with a father, or maybe only with a brother, whom nobody had ever seen but was much older and even meaner than she. Either way it was too weird and scary a scenario to think about, especially for a coddled kid like me. Yet sometimes I couldn't help but imagine their evening meal, taken under a weak bulb, a severe, empty-feeling table. Even now, as she dragged me forth, I should have been in a full-on panic, but a part of me wondered: What did the Crokers eat? And who was cooking it? I felt a sadness thinking about their probably cold dinners; I pictured a bologna sandwich, something I liked, but this one was crude and hastily put together, a tongue of pinkish meat flaring out from the white bread, like a dead animal's. I had shown my mother how to cut off the crusts like Gregory Fluss's mom did, my sandwiches now even more perfectly edged and square than his, for this was the way my mother liked things, too.

Katie Croker stopped us short. Her broad, curving forehead loomed bright, like the sheer face of an unscalable granite peak. And yet she no longer appeared as angry with me. She released my arm. Maybe she was done with the tormenting, done with our dirty little rituals, done, at last, with finding me so abjectly intolerable.

"You know any curse words?" she asked.

I nodded. Along with our ready currency of racial and ethnic slurs, I'd recently picked up some foul new terms from the gang, bathroom stuff, sexual stuff, all rankly misogynistic and homophobic, and none of which I understood.

"Let's see."

I let out an exhilarating string of fucks and shits and faggots and dykes and assholes and pussies and tit-lickers and cocksuckers, epithets that were clearly impressive and deeply pleased her.

"Okay, call for her."

I didn't know what she was asking. "Call who . . . ?"

"Who do you *think*?" she said sharply.

I realized then where we literally stood, which was directly below the kitchen window of my family's apartment. Katie Croker knew more about us than I could ever dream to know about her.

"Call for your mother, like you always do. When she looks out, you're going to start cursing."

I pled for mercy, any reprieve, I promised I'd do anything else, reminded her that my mother didn't understand much English anyway, but Katie Croker wouldn't budge. She said if I didn't comply, she'd find my father (who did speak some English) next time he was out with me on the playground and tell him what we did in the laurels, that it was all my idea, and that I'd even made a poop for her. This last bit was a horrid, disgusting idea, for I was very private about that, even at home, sneaking off during our evening TV viewing and cracking the small, frosted window to try to dissipate the bad smell, and my chest began to shudder with the reality of what I was about to commit. I could hardly breathe. My mother was the world. I loved my father and my sister to death, but it was my mother who spun and wove the fabric of my existence, she was the one who darned it, smoothed its rents, let it waft and unfurl.

I couldn't gather my full voice. So Katie Croker marshaled it for me, her pitch and accent dead-on.

"Um-*mah*! Um-*mah*!"

I peered up, squinting against the high summer sun reflected in the windows, and saw the silhouette of my mother's head craned out, the fall of her straight shoulder-length hair half shrouding her face.

"*Gu-reh, mo-yah*?" *Okay, what is it?*

Katie Croker nudged me with her sandaled foot, her eyes glacial. Staring down at my sneakers, I began to mumble.

"Louder," Katie Croker said. "Uh-mah can't hear you."

And then she did hear me, at first not comprehending the improbably melodious tune of my rank litany; her expression as always was eager and expectant, curious as to what unusual phrase or practice her American son had learned today. I functioned as the bearer of novel tidings, the family herald of the realm *Out there.*

"Again," Katie Croker commanded.

I finally stopped when my mother said my name. *Jeon-Gi-ya.* . . . She uttered it softly though not kindly; it was as if she were saying it to test it, weigh the truth of its sound. I could not meet her gaze. Whether or not she understood any of my hideous performance she had heard enough. She shut the kitchen window. I started to cry, first meekly, and then in great gasps. Like a comrade, Katie Croker gently cupped my shoulder and said, "Good."

For the next week or two, or maybe it was merely a few days, my mother and I kept our distance from each other, or whatever distance a young boy and his mother could achieve in a cramped tenement apartment. She went about her daily chores and activities, and I must have spent most of my time in the bedroom I shared with Ella, who tended to stick close to her. Maybe I read the books we borrowed from the R. I. F. van that stopped by every couple weeks, or played demolition derby with my Matchbox cars, or assembled plastic scale models of the World War II warplanes that I was obsessed with at the time. I was bad at making them, they always turned out slightly skewed and jalopy-esque, the joints overglued, the insignia decals rippled from being too hastily applied. When I got hungry, I loitered about our thrift-store dining table, picking at the chipped Formica, and eventually she would put out food for me, my favorite a bowl of watery rice along with some pickled daikon and deli ham that she would cut up so I could make spoons of it. I ate quickly and didn't ask for seconds.

For obvious reasons I avoided the playground, telling myself it was too hot and sticky outside. A late summer heat wave was blanketing the tristate area, and the complex grounds were mostly deserted, even after school, when kids were usually raring to play. Luckily my father had recently installed a small AC unit in our bedroom window, and I pulled my desk chair right up to it and pressed my forehead against the fan grate and awaited the compressor to kick in and spew icy air. I don't believe my mother informed my father about what happened, nor would she speak to me about it, either then or ever. Every now and then I think about that moment and I wish that she had, maybe a good sharp scolding or her letting me know how deeply I had wounded her would have set me straighter, or girded the flimsy struts of my character, but all that's left to me is how that brilliantly brutal girl fathomed each of our most dismal shames and through them smashed us both.

That would turn out to be the final episode with Katie Croker. I'd like to say that I stood up to her, that I cowed her or got her respect by besting her on the field or playground, or that I told her the truth of who she was, namely, that she was the most miserable person in the world. But no, sometime soon afterward she went to stay with a relative in another state, and by Halloween we realized the Crokers had moved away altogether. The last time I saw her was before she went to her relative's, she was a few kids ahead of me in line for the Good Humor truck that made its weekend afternoon stop right by our playground, and my heart was stalled with what she might say or do to me, I couldn't even think about which ice cream I wanted, and by the time the white-suited Good Humor man handed her her bar—Strawberry Shortcake—I was already withering inside. She peeled the paper from the bar and took a bite, strangely, from a lower corner, as if to quickly disable it. She stared at me. I was ready for anything, which is to say that I had completely given up. But she simply walked by me while gazing straight ahead, passing as closely as another being could without touching, my atoms oscillating, and when I finally gathered enough courage to look, she was gone.

I don't know if my mother sensed something different in me after that, maybe a certain easefulness, a certain calm, but the murk between us soon dissipated and we emerged back into our natural state of devoted union in which against all better judgment she hopelessly indulged me. Once again, I was spending most of my free time outside with the revolving gang of kids who lived in the complex, my mother monitoring my sister's play with other toddlers on the jungle gym while she fitfully chatted with some American moms, my father present every other weekend, when he wasn't taking on fill-in shifts at the hospital, and he and I would play catch or shoot baskets. And yet in the evenings, after supper, there was a new friction in my parents' talk. Friction perhaps not between them but around them, for what I could understand—they only spoke Korean with each other and although I spoke it, too, my vocabulary was and would forever be fixed at that elementary level—they were discussing what it meant for me and my sister to grow up in this apartment complex, this town, which of course meant our new country. My mother had a habit of speaking about us—whether in praise or in lament (though much more often in lament)—when we were within earshot, if only loudly enough that you had to strain, even concentrate, to hear her. One night she was complaining to our father about how my sister and I were starting to talk for her out in the playground, or at the stores, which was our job whenever we got a panicked nod from her, though admittedly sometimes we did so without her prompting, sometimes even talking over her when she attempted to make herself understood but fumbled.

"They're starting to act like the other children do with their parents, as if they're equals or friends."

"It's the way of all children, isn't it?" proposed my father. He was a physiotherapist for amputees and other profoundly disabled patients at the Bronx Veterans Administration hospital, working extra hard to keep up because of his barely adequate English fluency, which was somehow not disqualifying. Otherwise, he was well suited for the job, friendly and attentive to detail and in fact very comfortable working with his fellow therapists and the medical staff. He was much more adaptable than my mother, if not half as fierce or resolute.

"Not for our children," she told him. "We need to train them to be more respectful, to recognize the position of elders. You know I can't do this alone. You must help me."

"Of course I will. But we can only do so much."

"How can you say that? We can do everything!"

"We *will* do everything!" he said. Often when they spoke it sounded as if they were arguing, so I could never be sure how to feel. "It's never a question of that."

"Then what is it a question of?" my mother asked, exasperated. "Are you going to tell me again that we can't resist the weather? That it's too powerful? Well, I don't think I want to hear that idea anymore. We can prepare them. We can fight. And I think we should go to church more regularly. Reverend Hahm's wife said as much to me the last time we went."

My father didn't answer or at least give her an answer I could hear. Likely he acceded to whatever she wanted, for although he was a traditional Korean man and our sole provider, he was not the head of the household. He could flare with anger, even explode, but the instances were rare and he would quickly become remorseful and apologetic with her, with us; there was a genuinely deep well of kindness in him, a kindness that I think delivered him from what might have been an otherwise insecure, defensive nature. I know, because I see myself in him or, more accurately, see bits of him in me.

Over time they would conduct countless forms of this conversation, usually predicated by something I or my sister said or did that stabbed at my mother's sensibilities. I suppose she felt that if she promptly addressed each instance, they would less likely accrue into something habitual, ingrained. But my father's analogy was right. You can't shield yourself from the larger, atmospheric effects. The influence was all-encompassing, inescapable, the shifts in all of us, like the retreat of a glacier, imperceptible to the eye, but ultimately dramatic and permanent.

We ended up going to church again regularly, at least whenever my father wasn't on Sunday call. We drove in our faux-wood-paneled Ford LTD Country Squire station wagon across the Whitestone Bridge to Flushing, Queens, to a Gothic-styled Presbyterian church that leased the afternoon service slot to Reverend Hahm for his growing ministry. My parents were happily secular people, which is why their attendance had flagged, and would serially flag again, but they badly craved hearing their native language, even if it came in sermons and hymns, and eagerly awaited the post-service tea hour, as Ella and I did, when Mrs. Hahm and the ladies rolled out samovars of coffee and tea and trays of cut melons and homemade dduk. I didn't love dduk, and yet I always took a sticky square of whatever variety looked most appetizing in the hopes that it might taste better than I remembered.

While our parents socialized, my sister and I played out in the parking lot with the other kids, all recent Korean immigrants like us, and although you'd think we'd instantly bond, there was always a momentary whiff of contempt before the start of our games, everybody sizing one another up as being fresher off the boat, more foreign and weird. These were critical determinations, often coming down to the strangeness of some kid's sneakers or shirt or haircut. I don't recall any of the sort of taunting and name-calling we had at the apartment complex, but there was patent discrimination, the ones who couldn't yet speak any English usually picked last for dodgeball or stickball, at least until they'd proven their skill. The friendships were fleeting, necessarily occasional, as there were always church newcomers and samplers and those moving away. I could never keep track of the other kids' names, and I was always reminding them of mine, and it wouldn't be until the following summer, at a camp session sponsored by our church and a few others, that I'd get to know any Korean kids intimately.

But back home at Cove Gardens, and without even realizing it, I had completely acculturated to the tumult and machinations of our gang, even if that meant suffering the not-so-random bout of terror and misery. Yes, I was very young, and I knew nothing else, and yet if given the choice by a higher power to switch to any other way of life I'd have instantly declined. I loved our tireless roamings, the constant clatter we couldn't help but make, I came to associate the saltiness of the sweat that would stream from my scalp and down my face in viscous sheets with a breathless, bellowing joy.

The gang had grown, too, in the few years since we'd moved in, or perhaps I was simply older and more aware of how things really were. Along with Cleon and his running mates, there were the Irish-heritage kids and the Italian-heritage kids and the Jewish Joshuas, plus a gaggle of other kids whose names I can't quite remember but who I'm sure were companionable. I am grouping us now as I grouped us then, which is vaguely ethnically and/or familially, the only ways that made any sense to me. I would have been happily grouped with another Oriental—this the only polite term by which I knew myself—but there were no others around our age and so I had to bear alone any diatribes, epithets, stereotypes, all flung about with great bluster and ignorance in the context of our bristling group friendship. The few times when being Oriental was to my benefit were when there was a question of numbers (like comparing baseball teams starting rosters' individual batting averages, which I studied daily in the sports section of the newspaper) or doing math, which I was assumed to be good at. To be honest, I was only ever good at basic math but was swift in my calculations and recall, and this helped me gain the confidence of a popular boy like Paul Dipinto, a cheerful, voluble kid who still used his fingers to figure out 3 + 4 and entrusted me with his $1 or $2 or sometimes $5 bill (his dad owned a deli and regularly gave him cash) to pay the Good Humor man for him and myself and account for the correct change, which perhaps the Good Humor man didn't always return. I would pay Paul the twenty-five or thirty-five cents I owed him for my ice cream bar and then give him the change, but one time I accidentally shorted him by a dime—I found it on the sidewalk after he skipped away obliviously scooping at his Screwball—and after that I would slip ten or twenty-five or even forty of his cents in my back pocket. I liked Paul and Paul liked me but because I loved ice cream and because I could, I skimmed him most every time.

Soon enough I was constantly afraid he'd confront me, ask me how I could do this to a friend, and I had plenty of excuses ready, but they were lame ones, and he never did. And the funny thing about it was that I ended up thinking him pitiful because of what I was perpetrating, I saw him as being too trusting and weak, that he had no idea of how things truly were, which I did, and was thus doomed to being taken advantage of again and again. Even as his esteem of me grew I began to despise him.

I suppose these harsh feelings came from my own unvoiced fears about myself and my place with the Cove Gardens gang. Playing with them was my daily nourishment and joy, and yet after Katie Croker departed for good, which I was sure would mark the end of my troubles, there would be several serious disturbances to come, and for that whole, following year. The initial run of disturbance came in the form of two different boys in my orbit, one episode building upon the other and ultimately leading into the experience that would change everything for me: a stint at a summer camp.

The first boy was in fact a good friend in the gang. Joshua Messing was a sharp, wisecracking, curly-brown-haired boy whose tenth birthday I'd been invited to the year before and who was invited to mine a month later. He was admired for his ballsy, aggressive style of play as well as the many jokes he told and puns he made with his distinctively husky voice, which from a boy his age made him sound almost like a grown woman, if that makes any sense. And perhaps because he sounded like a grown woman we couldn't help but pay attention to him, if not heed him, which was usually fine because he told funny stories and enjoyed cursing and conversationally deploying anatomical insults that we loved learning, as in "Your smile is like a rectum." He had older sisters and so could extemporize with brio about various types of tampons and bras, and he could belch and fart at will, often to punctuate whatever joke he was telling. We all liked him immensely, and he enjoyed being the center of attention.

My problem with Joshua Messing stemmed from the perception that he and I were the smartest kids in our gang and the playground, which certainly wasn't true (Cleon Washington was the smartest, in every way, including, it was known, by his report card), and this notion somehow cast us as rivals despite the fact that very little of our Cove Gardens activities had anything to do with brains. I didn't want or need to be rivals, nor did Joshua, but the idea of our tangling for any supremacy wormed deep in his head and he began insulting me, though without the usual verve. He'd made good-natured fun of my sometimes "garbage can" breath (if I had eaten kimchi at lunch) and the "pukey colors" of my trousers (an inexpensive Sears brand my mother bought me called Toughskins that came in scar red and pus yellow and death-mask blue and which were decidedly not tough-skinned, as I eventually split every pair in the crack), but one day during a water fountain break from Running Bases I saw him mugging antically for a couple boys while making slanty eyes with his fingers. Then they saw me and snickered, Joshua turning and facing me for a long second before dropping his hands. He didn't say anything or try to pretend that he was doing something different.

The next day I had planned to ask him about it, but I couldn't, mostly because I had convinced myself that he wasn't specifically targeting me, and thus it didn't matter. Besides, I could almost understand why one wouldn't want such eyes; for who really would? I'd been asked both innocuously and maliciously whether I could see through mine, enough so that I once spent an entire afternoon opening my eyes as wide as I could, to see if that made any difference, resulting only in a bad headache. A few days later, in the middle of a three-on-three basketball game, I forcefully nudged him under the hoop to give myself space to shoot when he shoved me hard and knocked the ball from me, crying, "Offensive foul, Chinky Chow!"

The game stopped. Joshua appeared as surprised as any of us, craning around as if the words had been blurted by someone on the periphery. Certainly nobody protested, I think because they, too, were startled, and naturally curious about what would happen. I was struck silent, as I still am when challenged. I'd been called names before, but always by someone outside our gang. We'd all done it to other unfamiliar kids. A present-day onlooker would be appalled by the infinite variety of racist and ethnic slurs we lobbed at one another back then that we didn't fully understand but employed with the most casual élan.

Yet to have it lobbed at me intramurally, and by a good buddy like Joshua Messing, made my gut feel like it was packed with wet sand, too heavy even to vomit. Finally, Cleon, who'd been flipping baseball cards with Berto and Juany courtside (he preferred to play hoops with an older, infinitely more skilled group of boys), picked up the loose basketball and zipped it to Joshua and muttered, "Just play the game, punks." John Wayne would be Cleon if John Wayne could ever imagine being that cool.

The rest of the game, after a brief interlude of distracted play, got vigorous and testy, and not just between me and Joshua. I had finally unfrozen, tapping a sudden lava flow of aggression, and Joshua could do little else but respond; when either of us had the ball we drove ferociously to the basket against the other, shoulders and elbows leading, ankles flared to trip, and tried to score right away. Thrilled by our warring, our respective teammates took up the vibe and kept feeding us the ball, and by the time I scored the decisive basket the contest had become so intense and consuming that Joshua and I couldn't help but slap each other a hearty low five, if with our gazes averted. He seemed to have gotten the message that he had crossed the line. But I wasn't ready to forgive him. Instead, I felt the compulsion to act upon my little world and thereby alter it, whether for better or worse. So, when Joshua asked me if I'd form a fresh squad with him after mine lost our next game, there was no hesitation.

"Sure thing, kike."

I'd never uttered such a word before, though apparently I was aware of it. I had no idea what it meant. But you could tell by Joshua's expression, one I instantly recognized, that a special button had been pushed, a button that powers everything down, momentarily untethering him from gravity and time so that he was floating distressingly free, to be batted about like a cheap party balloon. It simultaneously pleasured and frightened me, to see such raw, just-birthed astonishment in someone else.

"*What'd* you say?"

"Nothin', kike."

He pushed me hard, and I pushed him hard back, and then he jumped me, clawing at the back of my neck and ear as I tried to wrest my head from his armlock while weakly rabbit-punching him in the kidneys. Kids were shouting, "Fight, fight!" and I could hear Berto and Juany cackling as we flailed and tangoed in our clumsy baby-cub tussle. Finally, someone pulled Joshua off me. It was Cleon.

"You gotta settle this right," he said, holding Joshua by the collar with one hand and stiff-arming me with the other.

"Let's get 'em in the Ring!" Juany suggested, and it seemed everyone else cried out in assent.

"You want to do this?" Cleon asked us. "The Ring" was a kind of fight club that Berto and Juany would arrange for kids who had serious beefs with each other or maybe just felt like fighting, with Cleon serving as the referee who kept the time for the three brief rounds and then adjudicated with them as to who won if the result wasn't obvious. This didn't seem odd to any of us, as there was often some kind of semi-organized spectacle going on, like jumping trash cans on bikes or a demolition derby using grocery shopping carts, neither of which I would ever do because I was too scared. But fighting with Joshua Messing was not something I could decline with everyone standing by, and especially with Cleon asking.

I nodded, as did Joshua, both of us unable to muster any new slurs or brave words.

"Juany will set it up," Cleon announced. "You punks, be ready."

That evening my father got home early enough to eat with us, and as usual he asked me and my sister numerous questions about our day. He was always curious about our activities and games, what new friends we'd made, what their surnames were, if they were newcomers like us how long they'd been in the country, this mostly because he was a generous and good father but also because he grasped somehow that each day was another step in what would be our long and wandering march. Yet he must have sensed something askew in me that night, for he asked how I was feeling, checking my forehead with his hand.

"I'm not sick," I said. "I feel fine."

My mother wondered aloud if I'd eaten a second ice cream during the day, which I had, something I was doing more often of late, courtesy of the unwitting Paul Dipinto.

"Well, I'm glad you're so energized," my father said. He and my mother always spoke to us in Korean, and we always replied in English. "You like it here, yes? Better than the apartment in Manhattan?"

"Much better!" I practically shouted. "The playground's bigger, and the fields are great."

"Seems like the children here are very friendly and fun," he added. "Not like at that city school."

I didn't have to answer. They knew I'd had difficulties at my city elementary school, P.S. whatever, though for different reasons. The school was echoey and dark and crowded, like an underground train station, the halls smelling sharply of ammonia cleaner, the stairwells of cigarettes and piss, with some of the boys so tall and mature they seemed bigger than my father. At least once a week one of them "asked" to see my lunch money, all of twenty cents, and plucked it out of my hand with a smile. One day, when my stomach felt especially hollowed out, I tried to steal a chocolate milk and got caught by the cafeteria lady. When my mother arrived at the guidance office she was ready to holler at me, and I told her what happened and started crying in her arms. After that, my parents decided to move to the suburbs for the better schools, even if they could only afford the decidedly run-down, urban-style tenements of Cove Gardens. I knew they'd moved here for Ella's sake, too, but if I felt any responsibility, it was to assure them that they'd made the right decision. This was my one filial resolve.

It was partly why I wasn't telling them about my conflict with Joshua or the developing situation with Tommy Reilly, a kid who was not a part of our games but posed an increasing threat. What I couldn't know was how the combination of these two conflicts would soon launch me into the pivotal summer of my life, that astounding, tender age.

My parents were mostly happy enough and loving in their marriage, but in those early years, with no other family and few friends as foils, they only had each other as vessels for unloading their frustrations. Their arguments, which seemed to occur more frequently once we moved to Cove Gardens, were more like dueling catalogs of grievances, grievances not primarily with something private and personal but with their respective professional and domestic worlds, like a patronizing senior colleague for my father, or rude and impatient shopkeepers for my mother. Then they would blame each other for not understanding, or caring enough, and sharper words would ensue. I didn't want to add anything to their burdens, not my nasty little back-and-forth with Joshua Messing and the fight we were going to have, and certainly not the encounters I was about to have with Tommy Reilly, who was frightening enough that he seemed to be more a wraith than an actual person, much less a stocky, baby-teeth-missing, ginger-haired kid just one grade above me.

Tommy wasn't part of our gang, or anyone else's. He lived in the uppermost building of the apartment complex, in C, which we referred to as the Fort, as it was perched on an exposed granite rise that had a commanding vista over the grounds and, from its five-story-high rooftop, a brief stretch of sandy shoreline on the Sound and the old hulking pier from where my father and I would sometimes fish. I underscore where Tommy lived because that's how I mostly saw him, positioned on high, gazing down at the rest of us like we were mere crawly creatures that were riddling his realm. Something was profoundly wrong with him, I can see that now, but back then the many ornate ways that he was haywire appeared to be a pure, hard menace.

I first met him at our elementary school, which happened to be only an eight-minute walk (or three-minute sprint) from the west side of Cove Gardens, the route passing through a man-sized tear in the cyclone fence that opened onto an often-marshy stretch of cattails that then bordered the baseball field of the school. The U-shaped school building framed the baseball diamond, and before and after the school day there was usually a group of us running around the bases, home plate to home plate, vying for the fastest lap, the time kept by a kid who had an official stopwatch, lanyard and all. I never won but I came in third or fourth regularly, sometimes second, which stung less than you'd think because (if he was there) the winner was always Mehm, a wispy Turkish kid who ran in these rhythmic, almost slow-motion-looking strides that kicked up no dirt, his fisted hands held high in front of each shoulder. He crossed home plate at full speed and had to sort of drop-kick the backstop fencing to stop himself. Anyway, it was very lightly raining that day so most of the usuals weren't there, Mehm included, just me and Stopwatch Stu and a couple tubby younger kids I knew I could beat. It had been raining steadily the entire school day, so the dirt-only diamond was loamy and soft and home plate was totally submerged in a muddy puddle, with a tributary of it snaking down the third base line. With a stick Stu drew a plate in the mud alongside the puddle. The little porkers huffed through their laps, their footing giving way at various points, and then I ran mine, vigorously but prudently, slowing and widening my turn before each base so I wouldn't slip and fall. When I touched Stu's triangular home plate I knew there was no contest.

Then this kid who was my height but oddly muscular in a way that prepubescents really shouldn't be appeared in the backstop. "My turn now," he said, wiping his nose with his wrist. His orangey hair nearly matched a color in his brand-new Miami Dolphins jersey, the number 39 spangly and bright. He got down like a sprinter in the blocks right next to the puddle and dropped his blue-jeaned knee right in the muck, which made me shiver. I wasn't some clean freak, to my mother's daily dismay I got plenty dirty myself, but certain kinds of soiling could reach deep into me and tickle a madness. Take eating fried chicken, for example; our family loved Kentucky Fried Chicken, and my father took us once a month as a treat and to give my mother a break, but I avoided eating the drumsticks, despite how much I wanted them. The other pieces I could hold with only my fingertips getting slick, but the drumstick beckoned to be grabbed like a baton and ferally gnawed, and if I was hungry enough or badly frustrated or feeling guilty about something and craving punishment, I'd take a drumstick from the bucket and force myself to eat it full palm until I couldn't endure it a second longer. Afterward I'd rip open every accompanying Wet-Nap and frantically degrease my hand. The same awful ache skewered me, watching this kid so carelessly soiling a clean knee of his jeans. Stopwatch Stu squeaked *Go!* and he bolted, his back sneaker gouging a foot-long trough in the mud. Unlike Mehm, his arms furiously pumped as he ran, and it seemed certain that he would spin out, but his stockiness and short, powerful strides centered him as he pounded around the bases. He kept gaining speed, and as he turned for home, I knew we had no chance.

I expected that he'd skid on the drawn plate or maybe slow down and triumphantly stomp on it, knowing he had time to burn. Instead, he kept coming, low to the ground, rocketing down the third base line as though a catcher were there with the ball already in his mitt and had to be bowled over. And whatever any of us had in mind was instantly erased by how he finished, which was to slide chest first into the submerged home plate, sending out plumes of brown water like a ferocious little seaplane landing in a swamp. I don't know if Stu ever clicked his stopwatch because nobody bothered to ask. We were stupefied. I was perhaps the most blown away, watching this kid hop spritely to his feet as if nothing had happened, the front of his new jersey and his jeans thickly mortared with infield mud.

Still, being mere kids, all of us were naturally panicked by the thought of how the boy's mother or father would react when he got home. But Tommy—Stu asked him with hushed awe what his name was—simply cracked a grin and like a prizefighter stuck his nose in his own armpit while tapping at the bulge he was making of his bicep. He could have been the model for one of those manic, hyperactive cartoon characters who is blissfully self-unaware and so both ridiculous and winning, and maybe this blinded me to what I should have seen as the scariness of his performance and instead made me feel a tingle of envious admiration.

Which was why, afterward, I didn't run away from him when Tommy came up alongside me while I was walking home. The late spring sun had broken out and his clothes were still sodden, you could smell the live funk of wet earth on him, like he'd crawled up from the depths. He didn't say anything until we passed through the opening in the fence onto the Cove Gardens property.

"Where are you from?" His voice was harsh and nasally, delivered from the throat, like a kid version of the Burgess Meredith portrayal of the Penguin in *Batman*, which was my favorite TV show.

I pointed to Building A. I didn't have to ask him where he lived, as I now recognized him as the kid who sometimes hung out, always solo, up on the rocky crags of the Fort, mostly just sitting and watching, sometimes hopping from ledge to ledge. The Fort was just up to our left, mine straight ahead on the far end. Tommy, I could recall, sometimes had a long stick in his hands with a pointy-looking tip that might well have been an actual spear.

"I mean, where do you come from?" He peered hotly into my face. "Are you Chinese?"

I shook my head, though knowing from experience how this exchange would go; he would now ask if I was Japanese; I'd say no; then what was I, he'd wonder; "Korean," I'd say; he'd ask "What is that?," to which I'd offer "Kind of in between," not knowing exactly how or why or what that meant; to which he'd murmur "Korean," usually in a confused, skeptical tone.

Tommy, however, would do none of this.

"Uh-uh," he grunted, touching his dirt-caked knuckles to my chest. "You look Chinese."

"I'm not," I protested, if weakly.

"I already figured that you are," he said, totally confusing me, and then with his thumb he pushed me, not hard, not angrily, but squarely enough on my sternum that its force radiated through the rest of me.

He grinned again, a half-pained smile that back then I was certain meant he thought I was okay and was maybe sorry for not believing me but that I see now was his unconscious way of checking his basest impulses, or at least decelerating them.

"Later, alligator," he said, without a speck of friendliness or irony. He walked away, then bounded the concrete steps that led up to his building, taking them in twos, then threes, his exhalations whistling through his missing teeth.

I was still curious about what would happen when he appeared at home sopped like that in muddy water, but once I got home myself and my mother asked how the school day had been I told her nothing much had gone on. In fact, I had blocked out this very odd boy and the rest of the episode, stress-napping during the 4:30 movie on Channel 7 despite it being "War Week" featuring WWII films like *Flying Leathernecks* and *Air Force.* I loved those movies for the very reasons they were made, namely, to highlight American war machinery and the righteous fight against tyranny, even if some of the maniacal "dirty Japs" piloting the opposing Zero fighter planes looked like my father and my nightmares had him grabbing at his face with black blood gushing between his fingers after getting shot up by a square-jawed American ace. Watching those films made me flush with patriotic fervor but also a lingering ache of wondering how much of the enemy I was harboring within.

While I kept my eye out for another appearance by Tommy, I began to hear rumors about him from kids in the playground. Someone knew someone's brother who dated Tommy's older second cousin who lived in Building B. It was true that he had no friends in the complex. He'd only moved into Cove Gardens the year before, and never came down to play, at least not with others. His parents (or maybe grandparents) owned several gas stations and were always out dealing with their employees and picking up large volumes of cash, which was why Tommy was kind of wild, having essentially raised himself, and why he wore expensive pro sports jerseys and brand-new Pumas and had cool stuff like a medieval battle-ax, which Gregory Fluss swore he saw him splitting a pumpkin with up on the ledge. Like everyone else I scoffed at that but stayed silent about his slide into the mud puddle at school.

It was the heart of spring, a couple months remaining in the school year, and I was occupied enough by homework and chess club and piano lessons and Little League practices and my extra reading—my teacher and my mother and I decided I would enter as many reading competitions and library groups as possible, to make certain that I would fully master English—that my after-school playtime got shrunk to brief games of catch or flipping baseball cards with some of the Cove Gardens gang. I was also getting ready for my fight with Joshua Messing, jumping rope, shadowboxing, doing sit-ups and push-ups, even staring at myself in the mirror and picturing my face bruised up but steely and valiant. The fight, though, kept getting delayed. We both had plenty of excuses. He had Hebrew school on Saturdays, on Sundays we went to the Korean church in Queens, we both had birthday parties and family outings and there were rainy days when nobody wanted to do anything. Joshua and I were still together in the context of the gang but interacted without warmth or spontaneity. I suppose we were doing what we could to maintain the hard feelings, even if we really didn't want to, neither of us willing to be the one to say we were backing out of the fight.

One day after school, just as I had emerged on the Cove Gardens side of the cyclone fencing, I heard a rustling behind me in the chronically neglected, weed-choked ground. Then something ticked to the side of me, closer. I was alone and had the impulse to run, but the full-color illustrations of the *Snakes of North America* book I was obsessed with popped into my mind, particularly the one of the deadly eastern coral snake, its banded coloring of crimson and black and sunflower yellow an underworld version of a candy corn. I'd read that it was native only to the coastal Southern states, but I was suddenly sure that one had slithered all the way up here to Westchester County, New York, to lie in wait for me. Stalled, I scanned the thickets of choke grass and clover, listening for any movement, but I could only hear the tiny sawing of bumblebees alighting and hovering. I took a step, then another. Nothing. I felt silly for being such a wuss when I felt a sting on the back of my calf and then watched as a fat drop of dark red blood emerged from the center of the fresh welt. A wave rippled my vision, and I was already getting short of breath, my brain afire with the fact that the coral snake's venom was the second-most deadly after that of the western rattler.

Another tick in the grass, and almost simultaneously a cracker-sized shard of stone ricocheted up from the hard dirt and glanced off my hip. I instinctively flashed with anger for

Joshua, but I looked up and saw Tommy Reilly positioned on one of the rock ledges. He was bent on one knee, in a shooter's pose, exactly like that of some of my green plastic toy soldiers, from which he was pulling back the long band of a slingshot and smiling wide. I wanted to run but I couldn't; it seemed I had no limbs. Then he launched it. The stone, a little white-hot comet, flew in a tight, mean line across the expanse. It must have been a pure animal reaction because something instructed me to tip my head slightly to the side, and I tracked the stone as it traveled soundlessly past my temple, a disturbance registering only in my deepest inner ear.

That's dangerous! I wailed, this sounding of my own fear getting me scrambling, that and Tommy's gargly cackling at my panic. I ran half crooked, my neck and back tensed against an imminent strike. I don't know if he shot any more stones, but I could hear him, joyous. When I got home, I went straight to the bedroom I shared with Ella, who was playing teatime with her dolls. I told her to get out. She protested, saying that it was already set up, but I shouted at her and she calmly collected the teacups and plates and fake cakes in the straw tray she kept it all in and left, her face soured. She could endure a lot from me. Because my father was home early for dinner that night, my mother made Japanese-style beef curry, one of his favorites, which made everyone happy but me. I hated the bodily aroma of that starchy, yellow-brown sauce, which looked exactly like the diarrhea that poured out of me when I felt sick or maybe ate too many American cheese slices or an entire can of Chef Boyardee. I was not picky, there were only a few things I refused to eat, said Japanese-style curry and the lima beans in Campbell's vegetable soup and any kind of cake icing. On the curry nights I always had the omu-rice my mother would prepare just for me and sat alone at the half-folded-down table in the kitchen, while my family ate a few feet away in the dining area, but on that night I made a big deal about it. I shut the swinging door between us while petulantly complaining every few minutes about the strong odor.

Shut that racket, my father finally and sharply yelled in Korean. As noted, he rarely raised his voice, so I finished my meal in silence, counting out the peas in my fried rice. Later, my mother came into the bathroom while I was brushing my teeth and sat on the seat of the toilet. She checked my hair to see if I needed to wash it and casually asked me if something was wrong. I shook my head, keeping the tooth-brush working vigorously and long enough that she simply kissed me goodnight and left. I slept poorly that night, between the nightmares I couldn't remember but which had my heart thump me awake, and my sister's gentle but unsteady breathing—she had caught a cold—that kept me breathless myself, waiting for her next exhalation. As for what Tommy Reilly had done, I was obsessing not about him so much as the staggering potential of what he'd done. What if one of those sharp-edged stones had hit me directly? I could have been blinded, or somehow injured in the brain, and requiring assistance forevermore like those poor kids I sometimes saw at the public pool, their disfigured limbs exposed for all to see as they were cradled the whole time by an adult. I never snickered at or made fun of those kids like others did, not because I was a good person but because I always thought of my father holding me or Ella that way, trying to stay patient and keep smiling.

Heading to school in the morning, I took a different route to the hole in the fence, widely skirting the playground and basketball court, all the while scanning the airspace and ledges of the Fort for any suspicious movements, projectiles, ginger-hued hair. Nothing. Once I was through the fence I realized I had to hustle to make the first bell and ran hard, my book bag walloping my kidney, though the exertion conveniently served as mental cover for my fear. For it was scarier not seeing any signs of Tommy, whom I didn't happen upon that day in the building. After school I didn't stick around and went straight home, retracing the morning's roundabout path. My mother was surprised to see me back so early, but she didn't show any outward concern. Instead, she fixed a snack for me and my sister, a salami and pickle sandwich, and watched as I idly nibbled at my half. I didn't finish the unusually full glass of chocolate milk she poured for me, either, something she normally dispensed like a lifeboat ration. While I was loitering in the living room over my inane math homework, I heard a clamoring from outside: *J.-G.! J.-G.!* I peeked over the sill and saw it was my friends Husik and the other (nicer) Joshua, shoulder to shoulder, heads craning. This is how we summoned one another, a pair or bunch of us energetically chorusing to get a friend to come down.

"You don't want to go play?" my mother wondered aloud as she was dusting the TV.

"I don't know. I have a lot of long division to do."

They sang again, *J.-G., .J-G.!*

"It's a nice day, and it will probably rain tomorrow," she said, peering down as well. "I was planning to take your sister to the swings. You can do your homework later, if you want. Who knows, maybe the ice cream man will come."

At this my sister squealed and quickly put her sandals on. I had no appetite for ice cream, but hearing my initials cheered with gusto like that made me want to sprint around with my buddies. Normally the prospect of having my mother and clingy sister out there with me would have me feeling put out, but now the prospect offered me comfort.

When we did get outside, I subtly corralled Husik and Joshua to play Matchbox cars in one of the large, open-ended concrete barrels that was set on its side, right in front of the swings where my mother was pushing my sister. We would zip them up the curve, seeing who could get his car to go around the farthest. I didn't love the barrels, as little kids like my sister sometimes squatted and whizzed in there, but there were times you sought privacy. As we slung our cars up the side of the barrel I kept an eye out for Tommy Reilly, though I'd never once seen him on the fields or courts or playground.

In truth I was distracted, and Husik and nice Joshua, getting annoyed at my lackadaisical play, started trying to ram their cars in the barrel for fun. It was a peerlessly sunny afternoon and there were plenty of kids running about, including Paul Dipinto, who had recently soured on me, likely because he'd gotten wise from his new best friend, Joshua Messing, to my embezzling. I don't know how Joshua Messing got wind of any of it, but this was the state of our relations, a cold war that was turning hot again.

Meanwhile my mother was pushing my sister higher and higher. Ella was a daredevil, naturally much braver than I. Always leaping about, she once sliced open her scalp on the corner of a glass coffee table and had to get stitched up under our living-room floor lamp by the friendly and talkative Mr. Sagwala, a surgical nurse who always wore a paprika-colored turban and lived three doors down the hall. Now it was the sight of her at her apex—nearly level, it seemed, with the crossbar of the swing set before she suspended weightless and then fell practically straight down, whiplashing at the bottom from the breathtaking speed—that compelled me to emerge from the barrel.

"What are you doing?" I cried as I approached them, hands splayed at my sides. I was as appalled as I was impressed, surely a preview of what a parent experiences near daily in certain early (and then teen) years of their children's lives. But my astonishment was directed not at Ella but at my mother, who I couldn't believe would allow her to fly so wildly and high.

"She's gonna fall off!"

My mother assumed I was kidding, then realized I wasn't. She motioned for me to come to her.

"Jeon-Gi-ya, what's the matter?" she asked, letting Ella's momentum naturally wane. I blocked her hand when she tried to pat my head, but I didn't move away from her. In fact, I drifted closer.

"*You must pay more heed*," I seethed, parroting the long-suffering vexation of our elementary school's principal, Mr. Brescia, a beefy man with heavily pomaded jet-black hair whose diesel-engine thrum of a voice could have narrated historical or political documentaries but was relegated to the ceaseless cajoling and admonishing of us.

My mother had trouble keeping up with my ever-expanding English vocabulary and phrasings but could instantly register my insufferable carriage. It was an unequal power that I learned to deploy selfishly and wantonly, often to unsettle or misdirect her and thus either gain an advantage or veil myself.

She now regarded me as she often would, my insolence making her face go pale and clayish. Once again, she would be assailed by the one person she allowed and could hurt her great pride most. I didn't feel triumphant, though; I was dizzy, in the wrack of an unmooring, and I pressed my face into the girding of her ribs, her soft bra cup padding the crown of my head. She's gone now, has been for much of my adult life, and although I've secured my modest chunk of this world I would trade it in an instant for a few more hours with her.

She checked my forehead. "You're a little warm," she said, and whether she was being truthful or not, I believed her. "Let's go in. I'll make some bibim naengmyeon." It was one of my favorites. Expecting ice cream, Ella moaned in protest, but as usual my mother privileged me. Ella let herself bound off the swing, flying a few yards and landing hard and bracing herself with her hands, then deftly hopping to her feet. Back then there were no rubberized safety surfaces, just an expanse of rough, crumbly asphalt, and she always sported some fresh scrape or gash on her palms or knees. My mother asked if she was hurt, but Ella defiantly sprinted off toward the apartment entrance, drawing us forth.

Husik and nice Joshua were still playing in the barrel and so I let my mother clasp me around the shoulder as we trailed her. I always grew sleepy in her embrace, drained by the perfect heat of it, and I tipped myself heavily against her torso, convinced that I was genuinely feverish. I even half closed my eyes as we strolled. But then a sharp glint roused me, a disc of light flickering across my mother's chest and shoulder; it shivered back and forth, then blinded me again. Shielding my eyes, I peered out to the middle of the playfield and saw Tommy Reilly, his face folded by a queer smile, a round vanity mirror swiveling in his hand. My mother never noticed because he was now only targeting me, spotlighting my path as we walked, and after several steps I couldn't take it and broke from her and ran.

Upstairs, I could hardly swallow. My mother wondered aloud why I wasn't enjoying the bibim naengmyeon, and I insisted I was but couldn't do more than knit through the noodles with my chopsticks. Meanwhile Ella was in full feed mode, slurping them down like the raccoon I'd once seen feasting on watermelon rinds near the Cove Gardens dumpsters. My sister learned early on to make the best of whatever she got, to always just move on. I, on the other hand, expected things to come to me easily, and when they didn't, I readily gave myself over to the muck of my frustrated thoughts, allowing the foulness to seep in wherever it had a path and then fill my gut with bile. I ate what I could, but then had to run to the toilet and let it pour out of me, the stink so sharp and sick-smelling I almost threw up.

I was glad the next day was a school day, as I could simply run there and back and in between keep my head down during class. The following day I did the same. I was planning a repeat for the next day, Friday, and was relieved to hear from my mother at breakfast that we were spending the weekend in New Jersey at our family friends the Lims (even though I didn't like having to play with their too-friendly, babyish kids), but after school, just as I passed through the hole in the fence, a voice called out.

"Bruce!"

It was Tommy, standing at the base of the Fort.

"My Bruce!"

There was no one else around but even if there had been, I knew he was addressing me; periodically I'd get called "Bruce" (as in Bruce Lee) by both friends and strangers alike, in both friendly jest and as a taunt. It was pointless to try to correct them or argue, plus sometimes it was advantageous to allow them to attach to me the specter of deadly inborn skills; my hero Cleon even once took me aside and asked if I was good at kung fu. I smiled and didn't answer. With Tommy, though, it was different. There was an energy about him that seemed completely out of control. I desperately wanted to flee, but everybody knows you shouldn't run from an aggressive animal, in fact you had better make yourself bigger somehow and stand your ground or even face the beast and advance. Was that still true if the animal had been patiently waiting for you?

He tossed something that landed near my feet. I froze, simply trying not to look at him.

"Come on, champ, pick it up."

It was a brushed gunmetal "ninja" star, five-pointed and surprisingly heavy, the kind martial arts actors hurl at their foes and that certain cracked, undersupervised kids like Tommy Reilly had in their armory along with other quasi-illegal things like nunchucks, M-80s, and brass knuckles. But this throwing star was especially sinister, it could feature in a sadistic underworld rite, the knife-sharp inside edges of its hollow star-shaped middle painted a glossy bloodred.

"You've thrown 'em before, right?"

I tried to shake my head, but my body was vibrating with what it already understood would happen next: Tommy held up another ninja star and waved it.

"Doesn't matter," he said, taking a step toward me. He lifted his shirt. His torso was just like a G.I. Joe's, hard-looking and defined, not to mention a pale putty color. "I'll let you go first." He touched a point of his star to his heart. "If you get me right here, you could kill me instantly."

I don't know what frightened me more, the imminent duel he was proposing or the spellbound tone of his pronouncement. I was pretty good at throwing baseballs, but my right arm didn't feel like my own, it felt numb and detached, a phantom appendage that might as well have been as gelid and dead as a packaged raw chicken wing.

Tommy advanced another couple yards, the distance between us maybe the span between the mound and first base. He set his feet, taking up his notion of a hero's stance, his bared chest puffed out, his teeth clenched, ready to be skewered on the cross of his own dark design.

"Hey!" he yelled. "Let's go!"

"I don't want to," I peeped, hardly audible even to myself.

"Yeah, you do!" he commanded.

It was then that I thought of Katie Croker and what she'd made me do to my dear mother, and in my panicked, shelter-seeking logic I began to curse, not at Tommy but at myself, in Korean no less. I cursed from the position of my father, who never actually got cross with me when I committed a genuine wrong (and instead sat me down and soberly explained why he was disappointed in me), but would merely faux scold and gently noogie me with his index knuckle if I did something bratty like stuff his tobacco pipe with roasted peanuts to dissuade him from smoking too much: *Who do you think you are, you rascal son of a bitch!* Those were the very best of endearments.

Of course, Tommy had no idea of what I was saying, or why. He let his shirt fall back down. The foreign sounds made his face crimp, like somebody right next to him had farted. I could see the disgust building in him, this stiffness in his brief stretch of thick terrier-like neck, and although I might still have been gibbering, I had bent my head low in full submission to my fate, this last dazed moment in the abattoir.

"What you standing there for, little man?"

It was Cleon, accompanied by Berto, heading for the court with a shiny new red-white-and-blue ABA basketball under his arm. I started to whimper and reached out to Cleon as if for a lifeline, but Berto barred me from him like I had the plague.

"Yo, don't let him touch the ball! Punk is bleedin'!"

My first thought was *What is he talking about?*, but then remembered reading wartime accounts of soldiers getting shot and blown up and losing limbs and not even realizing they had been injured for several minutes. I quickly scanned myself and to my shock there were a couple drops of bright red blood on the white rubber toecap of one of my sneakers. The web of fine, radiating splatters made my stomach bottom out. I crumpled to the ground, listing against my book bag. Tommy had nailed me and nailed me good.

"Hey," Cleon said softly, kneeling by my side. "What you got there? Come on, now."

I would have hugged him around the neck right then, wishing that he was the solicitous, protective big brother I always longed for, but Cleon flinched at my momentum and firmly grabbed my wrist with one hand and with the other carefully pried the ninja star from my fingers.

"Damn, J.-G., what the hell you doing with this?"

For some reason I cried, "I found it!"

He tested the points with his fingers.

"This shit is *sharp*."

He wasn't complimenting me; I had been gripping the star so tightly that I'd cut my index finger on one of the edges. I looked back toward Tommy, but he'd disappeared. As noted, Cleon and Berto, along with Juany, were the royals of the playground and courts, Cleon the crown prince, and his friendly address to me had likely made Tommy bolt. Meanwhile Cleon slipped off his red terrycloth wristband—Julius Erving was his favorite athlete, and he patterned himself in his style, from the Converse high-tops to the fly threads to the willowy Afro—and had me press it against the weeping slash.

"I'm sorry," I blubbered, short of breath with the gaining realization of what could have happened. "I'll get you a new one, I promise. I will!"

"No sweat, slick," Cleon said. "We're cool. Just heal up." He gave the star to Juany, who inspected it closely before slipping it into the back pocket of his jeans shorts.

Juany said, "You still gonna fight, right? Get in the Ring? Or you gonna pussy out?"

"I'll fight," I insisted, though my words sounded like they were someone else's unconvincing promise to himself. "I'll heal up. I'll be ready soon."

"Go easy, champ," Cleon said, as he and Juany headed to the courts. "Peace."

When I got home, I went directly to the bathroom and dabbed on the antibiotic ointment my parents always seemed to be applying on us and put a bandage around my finger. As much as I wanted to keep it, I threw the blood-stained wristband in the wastebasket, covering it with toilet paper. While she served me and my sister an after-school snack of Danish butter cookies and milk, my mother asked what happened and I said I had accidentally nicked myself with the paper cutter at school. She used the occasion to remind me that I should be extra careful in everything I did, as usual expanding on the precept that we were alone in this country, that we couldn't count on anyone to help us if something went wrong, which someday it no doubt would, and that if I wasn't fully prepared, making sure I was as competent and strong as possible, the worst misfortune would befall me. I would have normally ceased hearing her, this the perennial hit on our family radio station, but that day her litany called to me with stark and resounding newness. I couldn't help but keep turning through the possibilities. What if Cleon and Berto hadn't been on their way just then to the basketball court? What if Tommy had launched, as he had with the slingshot, an unannounced first strike? How would I have shielded myself, or struck back? All I had was my pussy Batman book bag with its matching plastic pencil case and batwing-shaped rubber erasers. I didn't even have a pair of kiddie safety scissors.

Meanwhile Ella was explaining to my mother the reasons why the teacher had sent a note home with her, namely, how her friend Stacy played kitchen with a new girl during free time at school and only allowed Ella to join them for the cleanup part and made her put away all the pots and dishes and then still the two of them wouldn't let her put her mat next to theirs at nap time, or later share their paints during arts. All this was driving me mad; I didn't care about her drama with stupid Stacy and the new pretty friend, and I didn't care about the teacher's note, which I refused to read over (as I would regularly) for my mother in order to clarify its full meaning. I had my own troubles. The cut didn't actually hurt anymore, if it ever had, but I'd wrapped the bandage too tightly and my finger throbbed so hard that the pressure seemed like it was backing up into the rest of my arm, my shoulder, then into my chest, and I must have looked like an old man suffering angina, pressing my fist against my heart to try to quell the ratcheting tightness.

Finally, I snapped at Ella, telling her that she should just forget about Stacy.

"She's my best friend!" Ella hollered back.

"What kind of best friend is that?"

"She can braid my hair!"

"Wow, that's super."

"You don't know anything about anything!"

"Yeah, I know you're not Stacy's favorite."

Ella shoved me, making me spill some milk on the table. For her, this was practically homicidal aggression. Our mother yowled—she reviled every kind of mess—and ordered me to do my homework. She and Ella would walk to the nearby convenience store for a loaf of bread.

"When we get back, you're going to clean up your bedroom together," she decreed. "And if you do a poor job, you'll clean the bathroom as well."

Ella stuck her tongue out at me, and as they left the apartment, I covertly flipped them the finger while I crossed my arms, a move I'd learned from an unruly kid in my class who did it to the teacher whenever she reprimanded him for talking during the lessons. I felt sordid and foul and instantly wanted to take it back, but once I was alone the shame soon hardened into an ingot of rage, rage not for them but for the situation with Tommy Reilly, which in addition to petrifying me revealed the truth of how little control I had over my own life. I might as well have been one of the ants and beetles that my friends and I regularly surveilled with a magnifying glass, the articulations of their antennae and joints and the filigreed armor of their bodies wondrous enough to make them seem sacred and yet they were nothing under a hard thumb or the lasering ray of the lens, the scent of burnt carapace vaguely fishy and grim to inhale but quickly gone.

I began to rue that Juany had pocketed the ninja star. Tommy would come again for me soon, maybe even the next day on the way to or from school. Would Cleon have Juany give it back if I asked? Or would Juany and Berto simply mock me and say I would only hurt myself with it again? I picked through the bin of my sports equipment in our closet to see what I could use against him or protect myself with, the most useful gear being my football helmet and shoulder pads, but I certainly couldn't walk to school suited up like that, or stroll into class wielding a baseball bat. I required something that could fit in my book bag, something swiftly deployable, something decisive and fierce, something super scary.

I headed to the kitchen. I often found myself there, either because I was hungry or bored or simply wanted to watch my mother at work, her shapely hands always purposeful, efficient, artful, or ruthless depending on the task, and I knew every tool she stocked. In the drawer next to the utensil drawer was where she kept it, beneath a large serving spork and a pie spatula. The Knife. She had other knives on the counter, a typical chef's knife and a filleting knife and some small paring knives she used for fruit, but the Knife had to remain tucked away, I always thought, because it was especially dangerous. It was a stainless-steel carving knife with a cream-colored plastic handle and had its own cardboard sheath (illustrated, in fact, with miniature drawings on its use and care), the blade at least ten inches long and double-edged, honed on one side with a wavy scalloped finish, the other a jagged, geometrical toothing like a lumberjack's saw. I'm still uncertain what one was supposed to cut with such acute serrations. Cords of gristle? Hides and bone? The first time I saw it, when my father brought it out for our inaugural Thanksgiving celebration in this country, I startled, being both afraid of and for him. He used it to carve the bird and then slice the American roast beef my mother would sometimes make, nothing tough enough to withstand its terrible teeth.

I had furtively handled the Knife before, the blade throwing sunlight about our kitchen, its menacing flash suspending my breath. I'd place it back exactly as it was, shivering ever so. Now my mind was ratcheting, torquing the screws of a thousand rageful thoughts as I unsheathed it. The Knife was in fact quite cheap, surprisingly bendy and light and, a kid could think, made just for him. I gripped the handle tighter and tighter as I pictured pressing it against Tommy's freckled, stout neck. Would he wail and shake? Or would he beg for mercy, press his hands together or bow his head, or maybe both? The main question was whether I wanted him to be scarred for life or simply dead. Regardless, he must suffer in some profound way. Soon I couldn't sense any distinction between my sweaty palm and the plastic handle, only a palsy from exerting such intense, steady force trickling up into my wrist and forearm. I slashed and stabbed at the air. I thought I could almost taste the dense tang of blood, this evil syrup that was fuel for my fury. My lips were chapped, and I wiped my mouth and realized my fingers were tipped with actual blood. I'd broken through the cracked skin of my bottom lip; in moments of stress or excitement, just like my mother, I'd involuntarily bite it, and the more intense the feeling the harder I'd bite down, not even conscious of it. There'd be indentations, sometimes pronounced, but I'd never drawn blood before.

I understood then what I needed to do. Instead of putting it back I replaced the other implements that had been atop it and shut the drawer. It was possible that my mother would use any of these tools, the pie spatula, the hand-crank blender, the tenderizing mallet, in the next day or so. Yet I was calm. If she found me out, she found me out. I resheathed the Knife and went to the bedroom, where I slid it between workbooks in my school bag. Tomorrow would come soon. I strapped the bag on my shoulder and stood before the mirror hung on the back of our door, closing and opening the flap, startled, if for a moment, to see what I looked like, this steely, dead-faced boy.

That was late spring, my fifth-grade year. I wouldn't complete the school calendar, for I was suspended immediately for what I did. My final day of attendance ended with a midday meeting my parents and I had with the principal and guidance counselor, a meeting in which I was not included but instead was made to sit with Ella in the waiting area of the principal's office, the secretary chatty and kind to my sister but a stone statue to me. Oddly, the door to the principal's office was left ajar, and I heard the guidance counselor, a portly Black lady with a huge and shiny hairdo, say that there would be "a long probationary period," and that I needed a "thorough psychological evaluation." I didn't know what those things meant, only that after the conference my parents were stunned enough to walk us in perfect silence straight to our station wagon. Inside the car my mother again didn't speak, which to me was an unsettling circumstance, as she usually couldn't keep from broadcasting the run of her thoughts whenever she got stressed. My father also didn't say a word, and for some reason drove the long way back to the apartment complex through the neighborhood of large shoreside homes that ringed the point. He turned in at the harbor and parked in the lot in front of the boatyard.

My father suggested that my mother and Ella go see the sailboats, and while the two of them went to the docks he walked us out onto the public pier, where he and I sometimes fished for porgies. We loved how my mother prepared them, salted and pan-fried. It was a weekday so there was only one fisherman out, and my father surprised me by approaching him and asking if he'd caught anything. The fellow, an older white man in a fish guts–stained tank top and a faded Yankees cap, must have thought we were out-of-town visitors and began ticking through the whole angling history of the area and how back in the day you could just drop your line in and catch stripers and bluefish but now the water was too busy and polluted and only good for pesky garbage fish like cunner, which were bait-stealers. I don't know how much my father understood but he didn't rush the fellow and listened to everything the man said, and during a natural pause in his monologue thanked him for talking to us. He headed us toward the end of the pier and there we leaned on the railing as we looked out over the soft churns of the seaweed-colored waters.

"Jeon-Gi-ya," my father said, clearing his throat. It was a tic of his, perhaps analogous to my lip biting, but what I always appreciated about him was how he grew more deliberative and professorial whenever things got serious or worrisome, at least when it had to do with his children. This is not to say that I couldn't find him daunting, even scary. Though rarely, he could sometimes get rageful. But that day he was especially placid. "You know, I've been wondering about something."

I must have looked quite cowed when I nodded, for he mussed my hair.

"I'm a little confused. This boy, he is a friend of yours?"

"I guess so. I don't know. He was."

He stifled a snort. "But you were friends with him, yes? The guidance counselor told us your teacher reported that you regularly played together at recess."

"We used to. But not anymore. Not for a while."

"But he isn't your enemy, right? You don't hate him."

I didn't answer.

My father nudged up the bridge of his eyeglasses, another habit of his. Many of the photographs of him in our family albums catch him in this move, his index finger covering his nose. "You know, I won't be mad. You can tell me. This boy did something, yes? I think he must have done something to you. You can tell me anything, you know. You're my son."

I didn't answer, or couldn't, this last bit of what he said stamping at my heart, if a good stamping, maybe like the physiotherapy he gave to his patients at the VA hospital. I was crying then, silently, the tears dripping from my cheeks, and he pulled me into his chest, letting me blot my face on his dress shirt. He waited until I had composed myself and with his arm around me walked us back to the car where my mother and sister were waiting for us, the understanding being that I would clarify things once we got home, that the whole disturbing episode would be fully elaborated.

It ended up that I didn't explain any further. My mother, whom I expected to begin yelling at me and outlining the likely permanent damage I'd done to my future, retreated to their bedroom, my father closely trailing her. They shut the door, and although I couldn't hear her, I knew she was crying because of the way my father was consoling her, telling her to calm herself, to breathe deeply, his lowered voice resonant and gentle. Ella, as usual, continued about her own focused way. No one told her what I'd done but she understood it was something so awful as to be literally unspeakable, and this seemed to be satisfying enough for her; she went and organized her dolls and their accoutrements in our bedroom, a task she did daily.

I drifted into the kitchen. I didn't have to look in the drawer, knowing that the Knife was someplace else, someplace locked away and official. I was neither thirsty nor hungry, but out of habit and a mournful feeling I poured myself a tall cup of milk. The glass bottle—there were still weekly deliveries of milk to one's door back then—was nearly empty, and although I didn't love milk, mostly drinking it out of a sense of duty to my mother, who was constantly pushing it on us, I drank what I poured and then poured myself the rest, soon gulping that despite a hint of sourness that made me gag. On the last sip I gagged harder and threw up all of it in the sink. This seemed like a suitable punishment, disgust and misery for the undeniable disgust and misery I was causing my parents, now and in the future, because some part of me knew I was powerless to do otherwise.

What my parents didn't know was that the boy in question was not the one I had brought the Knife for. Neither they nor the school officials knew the first thing about my troubles with Tommy Reilly, or that he and I even knew each other. This is what occurred: on the first school day after Tommy had hurled the ninja star at me, I had carried my knife-laden book bag with the expectation that he'd accost me on the way there or back. I was certain I was ready, even if I had slept poorly and the chalky spit was blood-tinged when I brushed my teeth in the morning for how harshly I went at myself. My mother complained about how I'd idly poked at my over-easy egg and made a mess of it, as well as the half nibble I'd taken of the fried Spam slice, the rest of which I gave to Ella, who could never get enough of it. It would turn out to be a warm early May day, but I had chosen a long-sleeve shirt to wear, some part of me seeking any measure of protection, and by the time I reached the main schoolyard filled with kids madly shouting and sprinting around before the first bell, I was perspiring so heavily that I had to blink away the sweat from my brow. I was breathing too heavily and felt faint, and I realized I was already spent, that I was beginning to lose my nerve.

I moved to the cooler, shadowed corner of the asphalted yard with my hand under the flap of the book bag, gripping and regripping the handle of the blade. Unless he was tardy or out sick Tommy should have been there, but I couldn't find his squat form in the mosh. It was then that a boy named Osvaldo approached me. It was Osvaldo's first year at the school, and I knew from our class that he was clever and conscious about his image but because he wasn't too sporty or charismatic he wasn't yet popular, though he desperately wanted to be. He was slight and stump-shouldered and waddled, and if he'd had gray hair you would have thought he was a senior citizen from behind. Like me he was ambitious, but he could get pushy, constantly seeking any opportunity to better his standing. For example, since I was our grade's playground monitor for that month, a position I'd earned from reading and writing reports on the most books during a springtime contest, he'd been lobbying me daily so that I'd choose him as one of the two kickball or dodgeball captains. I don't know when or why this clearly flawed mechanism had been instituted by our teachers—perhaps there had been arguments, even physical tussles, over captaincy—but there it was, and Osvaldo, who detected something corruptible in my character, had begun bribing me with candies like sourballs or lollipops. Nothing was stipulated, nothing was promised, and like mobsters we inked the pact with an oblique look, a wrinkle of the nose. He was savvy and didn't simply pick the best players first but also those with whom he wanted to curry some other favor, like

Pat Pinsky, who was hopeless at sports and was usually picked last but who always brought a bagful of delicious cookies from his parents' bakery and headed the model rocket club. Osvaldo's problem was that he couldn't stop nudging, and even after I chose him to be a captain twice in one week, he kept on me, treats in tow, finally offering the newly available Bicentennial commemorative quarters, which I palmed for a few days without making him captain in order not to attract scrutiny but also, I admit, to remind him who was boss.

"Hey, J.-G., check out these cool new ones I got!" Osvaldo displayed a handful of shiny quarters. He was all smiles and syrup, but no doubt had been stewing all weekend about my welching on our cads' agreement. I couldn't care less. I could only focus on the background behind him, searching for Tommy as I tested the ferociously jagged edge of the blade inside my book bag. It was no longer that I wished to ward him off, to scare or intimidate him. That now seemed an infantile idea. No. He had to be torn open like the odd raccoon or stray cat we sometimes found curbside after a foggy or rainy night, their bellies garishly flared. I could almost feel the teeth of the blade tip chucking into the flesh of his raised palm, the splintering of the hard point of his shoulder. And I saw it, as before, pressed against his bared pale neck, but this time the knife cut in, if bloodlessly, Tommy's beady eyes disbelieving right up to the moment I held his detached head by the hair, just like the palace executioner had done with John the Baptist's in a biblical movie I'd watched with my parents.

"You can have all of them, okay?" Osvaldo said, trying to push the coins into my hand. I didn't want them. I was going to make him a captain later at recess anyway, but I didn't say anything and he kind of freaked out and tossed them, the quarters weakly caroming off me and scattering on the asphalt.

"These are yours!" he cried, scrambling to pick them up. "I have some for Joshua."

"*Messing?*"

From his knees Osvaldo nodded, his oldish boyish face crooked with long suffering. "He knows! He said he'll tell Miss Stavros if I don't keep giving him the same." Miss Stavros was our teacher. "So if you don't want them, I'll just give him yours!"

I was livid already and hearing this should have been an accelerant, but just then I noticed Tommy Reilly entering the schoolyard. I felt some vast piece of me fall away, like an ice shelf calving. Was it seeing him now as quarry? Was this how a predator self-vanishes? For as I drifted toward him, numb save my grip on the knife handle, I was awed by the momentum, to be so utterly discharged from myself. I felt so pure and free. But who was this with him? There were the grownups beside him, a couple who were of similar age to my parents, a woman with blond hair thickly flowing down to the narrow waist of her flared-bottom blue jeans, a man with long hair, too, but curlier and dark, like his brushy handlebar mustache. He had his arm around the woman, both of them lean and willowy and dressed like hippies in their colorful dyed muslin tops and not seeming to belong to Tommy at all. Walking a half step to the side of them was a beefy older man in a crisp white short-sleeve dress shirt and slate-colored trousers, a cap tucked under his arm. He looked like a bus driver. Or was he *their driver*? It was rumored that they had a lot of money. He opened the metal entrance door for the couple—the woman's face looked flushed, puffy—and as he turned, I saw a holstered handgun studding his hip. Tommy kept his head bent low as the man ushered them into the building.

You would have thought that it was a vindicating sight, that I'd be thrilled to witness a cowed Tommy and his parents having to be escorted into school by a policeman. But for what? No one else knew of his terrorizing of me, nor were there any reports of other kids being bullied. The very idea that there might be others—I hadn't allotted room for anyone but myself to be a victim—somehow made my shame only sharper, more caustic, and not because I cared an iota for them. It was that the mantle of my martyrdom was suddenly stripped away, leaving me exposed in a foolish fantasy of revenge. Weapon or not, I was still terrified of him and always would be: my plan was all an act, or more, an enactment of an act that would never be performed. I know. A coward revels in rehearsal. Still, I was shaking, and all I could do was walk away past Osvaldo, heading to the opening in the schoolyard fencing. I was ill and I had to get home. Osvaldo pushed at my back and without turning I batted him away.

"Hey!"

But it was Joshua Messing, standing close enough that I could smell his milk-laced cereal breath. Osvaldo was behind him, if not allied with him, curious about what might be unfolding.

Joshua poked me in the shoulder. "You think you're so smart. You think you got it all going, huh?"

Maybe I did think those things, because I needed to, but I didn't believe any of it.

"You're not fooling me."

"I don't care."

"Well, I'm choosing captains today," he decreed.

I started walking.

"And will until the end of school."

I turned and faced him.

"Fuck you, Josh."

"Yeah, FUCK YOU, J.-G.!"

He punched me hard in the chest, knocking me back a step. For a second I couldn't breathe, it was like my heart stopped, but then a flash of paleness crossed his face. I had already leapt at him, grabbing him by his shirt collar. My head was exploding with the iciest cold. They say I screamed, in Korean and English.

You wanna die? Ju-gu-leh? You wanna die right now?

Apparently, I was wielding the Knife, holding it high. I can feel it still, sometimes.

To this day I've never seen a person so scared.

The Messings, to their credit, ultimately agreed that a social rehabilitation program was the appropriate path for me. This after their initial shock and outrage, and demand that I be detained for arraignment and trial and possibly held at a juvenile correctional facility, all of which I was legally subject to, for even now, under the statutes of New York State, offenders as young as seven can be tried in the criminal justice system. I would turn eleven soon, that summer of 1976.

No one could blame them for wanting me locked away. Although Joshua and I were friends before we grew antagonistic, neither of us had ever visited the other's apartment, so I had never met his parents; they didn't know the first thing about me except that I had threatened to decapitate their only child with a ten-inch carving knife that I'd brought to school in my book bag. Joshua himself was unharmed, at least physically. While I was immediately suspended from school for the rest of the year, Joshua, I heard later, stayed at home the next school day and returned the following, but then didn't want to go anymore even though he knew I wouldn't be present. I heard later from some of the Cove Gardens gang that after what happened he didn't come out very often, and if he did would just play a quick game of HORSE and maybe get something if the ice cream truck came by, but at some point would slip away without a word. No one gave him trouble about it, you'd have to be a big jerk to do that, but in truth the rest of the gang was spooked by my actions and likely glad that I was out of circulation, too. The only one who came to see me was Gregory Fluss, who lived one floor above me, and who was returning a G.I. Joe I'd let him borrow a month before.

"I thought you might want him back now," he said, extending the action figure from where he stood on the far side of our doormat. He was examining me closely, as if checking to see if I was suddenly transformed, maybe sprouted nubs of horns or an extra eye. I took the G.I. Joe and thanked him, and Gregory's expression softened, and I told him he should come over later if he wanted, as my parents hadn't yet specifically forbidden that.

"I'm not sure," he said, leaning back a half step. "I have to ask my mom."

We stood idling for a bit. Before he left, he reached into his back pocket and gave me a piece of wrapped bubble gum. It was an awkward moment but one I appreciated. The gum, which I put in my mouth right after I closed the door, was misshapen and warm from being in his pocket, but I extracted every last molecule of its sweetness, chewing it long after it had turned hard and flavorless, this lump of useless putty that might as well have been how my only society now viewed me.

The big question is why I never told anyone about Tommy Reilly, when doing so would have clarified the situation to the public safety and school authorities and social service people, and to my and Joshua's parents, and made my life less fraught and complicated in the aftermath. Surely other paths would have opened, paths in which I would have been assessed and treated differently, in which I would have been swathed with benevolence and support and empathy, rather than handled at arm's length like some kind of novel biohazard. I can still see the reaction of the secretary at the first psychologist's office, the reflexive tightening of her lips when she realized I was *That boy* from J. F. K. Elementary School. At any point I could have spoken up. Yet it seemed right to me not to disclose Tommy's aggressions, even after it became known why he and his parents had been summoned to school that day: apparently he'd threatened two fifth-grade girls on school grounds, not with sling-shotted stones or ninja stars but with an actual pellet gun, an air pistol that he shot into the trees and then aimed at them as they were walking home. Somehow, I was certain that I wouldn't be believed, that I would be seen as simply claiming victimhood to excuse myself or at least rationalize my conduct.

Was I remorseful? I felt bad for causing everyone such unhappiness, but whether I felt remorse for the act itself was unclear. I didn't feel too sorry, if at all, about Joshua, for in my mind he deserved to have peed his pants just as he did right then in the schoolyard. In fact, I was almost liking him again, renewed by the idea that we were as allied as ever, now that we both knew what it was to fear so purely.

Tommy, it turned out, wasn't wholly at fault, if at all. He was also suspended immediately and processed through a similar series of assessments and evaluations, but we heard soon enough that he underwent care for a serious anxiety disorder, which was merely the first indication of what would be diagnosed in his later teen years as full-blown schizophrenia, complete with paranoid thoughts and visions. In this regard we were all fortunate that he didn't follow through with some truly harmful assaults. Tommy, of course, must have suffered more than anyone. Years later, long after we moved away, when Tommy should have been working his first job after college, Husik—whom I bumped into at a bar in the East Village—told me that he saw him pacing at a bus stop in White Plains, loudly haranguing no one in particular.

What happened for me in those subsequent weeks was a whirl of activity, courtesy of various criminal justice and social service and mental health officialdoms. You'd think that it would have been an overwhelming experience for a not-quite-eleven-year-old kid, a frenetic, enervating blur of prodding adults, packets of paperwork, the constant shuttling from office to office, then waiting room after waiting room, all of which it was, but the funny thing is that I can remember almost everything about that time, for it was the first (and only) period in my life when the world seemed to balance on the fulcrum of me. Somehow it didn't feel like I was being pressured by the unrelenting scrutiny, pinned down and pummeled by the multitude of testing, recommendations, directives. I didn't wither under the microscope. In fact, it was the opposite, a strange blooming was forced by all that trained heat, my child's need for simple, thorough coddling now become sharper, more desperate, until I could feel in myself every ravenous new contour.

Our first stop, at least after it was determined that I may have committed statutory crimes—felony threat and the brandishing of a weapon—was the fact-finding hearing at Family Court, when a county prosecutor and my court-appointed attorney presented the case to the presiding judge, a raven-haired middle-aged woman with glowing facial skin and bejeweled cat-eye readers who could have been Sophia Loren's only slightly less glamorous sister. The attorneys interviewed me and the two teachers who were playground monitors at the time, with the judge intermittently asking for clarifications. Joshua and his parents, citing his continued mental trauma, weren't present, but they submitted a statement saying they believed I should only be subject to probation and be given therapeutic supervision and care. They did acknowledge that Joshua and I had had a "minor playground disagreement" in the moments before, something I neither disputed nor would elaborate on, even after my attorney, an earnest, nasal-voiced, prematurely balding young man named Wohlers, asked me in several different ways whether Joshua or someone else had done something to me, even proposing a hypothetical situation with a nameless Oriental boy who was being bullied constantly. I shook my head. His unsatisfied and perplexed expression, so like the puzzlement of other adults who dealt with me, had the odd effect of rooting me that much deeper in my concealments. A primary struggle of childhood is the struggle to make oneself understood, but I found a special power in being indecipherable, leaving everyone grasping and unsettled.

The hearing proceeded, and according to the legal elements that the prosecutor was required to establish, namely that I, the juvenile defendant, had: (i) willfully threatened to kill or cause grave bodily injury; (ii) made threats orally or in writing; (iii) intended that my statements were to be understood as a threat; (iv) made it immediate, unconditional, and specific to the other person of the serious intention and immediate prospect of the threat being carried out; (v) that the threat caused actual and sustained fear for the life and safety of the other person; (vi) and that the other person's fear was reasonable under the circumstances, was clear and undisputed. The judge then made a "finding" that I had committed these crimes. This was when my attorney read statements he'd solicited from my current and previous two years' classroom teachers as well as both my Little League coach and piano teacher and even the R. I. F. van librarian, all of whom stated that this conduct was a shocking aberration from the hardworking, curious, and talented boy they knew and that there must be mitigating circumstances for why an otherwise well-adjusted and popular straight E student (E's were like A's at our school) had perpetrated such an act.

The Messings' statement and the airing of the supporting letters surely helped to save me, for instead of sentencing me to a locally notorious facility inhabited by older, already hardened juvenile offenders, the judge remanded me to the custody of my parents while we awaited my "disposition" into a host of interventional programs. I often wonder what might have been proscribed for me had I been a random Black or brown boy, or even my playground hero, the super smart and athletic Cleon. Would he have been locked up immediately under the same circumstances? Before closing the hearing, the judge had me approach her behind the bench, alone. My father had to nudge me twice to get me going. Up to then I was almost eerily unperturbed, yet in front of the judge I was terrified, ready to burst out in tears. From her imposing leather upholstered armchair, she stared at me icily over her sparkly framed reading glasses, the front of her robe waterfalling darkly onto the floor.

"I think you know this is your one chance, so I'm sure you won't mess it up." I can still hear the handsome reed of her voice, if bent through a thick New York accent. "But let me tell you one thing, young man." She leaned in close enough that I could smell both her fetching eau de toilette and the pepperoni pizza she'd had for lunch. "Don't always think yourself to be so great."

A funny thing to say, for sure, to a cowed child perp. It turned out that the judge was one of the few adults back then who was able to peer through all my seemingly paradoxical layers. Really everyone else was flummoxed, deeply confused by the vast gulf between how I "presented" and what I had done. After a physical examination and full complement of blood panels (all normal) and repeated queries as to whether I had been mistreated or abused (by other kids, a stranger, a relative, even my parents), they kept assessing and reassessing me, often with the exact same questionnaires and tests, to try to unlock some key clue to my extreme behavior. Because my father had to work, my mother took me to the appointments, sometimes with Ella in tow if it was outside school hours, and because of her poor English, after the first couple meetings she let me translate and ultimately speak for her while I was being evaluated, which essentially meant that I was speaking for myself.

For the first couple meetings, whoever was interviewing me had to explain through real-life examples most of the terminology of the psychosocial assessments such as Ritualistic

Behavior, which the first social worker described as being "if you need to tie and untie your sneaker laces five or ten times to get it just right," or "you have to have your milk poured exactly to the brim of your glass every time," both instances sounding not unreasonable to me, even if they were strange. And so it went, right down through the other markers of possible pathology, from Mood Swings to Panic Attacks, Sleep Changes to Excessive Worry, Hallucinations to Hyperactivity, et cetera, the one thing that we could confidently verify as being "Moderately Present" the "Change in Appetite" that my mother had noticed, as I wasn't asking as often for my usual second or third helping.

The item that had seemed patently outlandish to me was Suicidal Ideation—wait, hadn't I threatened to kill *him*?—but around the fifth or sixth assessment I began to question the question, asking myself whether the tiniest part of my rage was actually angled back toward me, and by the ninth or tenth intake, through a mixture of crankiness and boredom and the surreal but distinct sense of a materiality that can arise through repetition, I may have nodded at Mildly Present for the social worker with the clipboard, the momentary pulsing of his brow betraying his otherwise nonchalant posture. When we finished the assessment, he was acting like we were longtime friends and then excused himself, and after what seemed a very long time (but was probably just ten minutes) he appeared with a young Chinese American woman. She was likely a graduate student doing an internship at the social service agency and she was tasked to speak directly with my mother. But she was (and spoke) Chinese, and although my mother had learned a couple thousand Chinese characters during her education (a Korean newspaper would be rife with Chinese characters in those days), they could barely communicate with each other, much less discuss a topic as complex and delicate as inclinations of suicide, whether real or phantom. It ended up with the intern and me having a meandering, stilted conversation that I think now could have been about the mystery of existence, via exchanges such as:

Intern: What do you think about when you first wake up in the morning?

J.-G.: That I have to go to the bathroom?

Intern: I mean, other than that. What comes to mind?

J.-G.: I don't know. Maybe how tired I am?

Intern: Okay, good. But tired from *what*, you think?

J.-G.: (silent)

Intern: It's all right. Take your time.

J.-G.: Sleeping?

Despite how inconclusive this and the rest of the assessments were, there was unanimity among the professionals that they weren't going to take any chances. My parents were understandably fearful for me, and because of their language deficit and lack of knowledge about how the social service agency and other bureaucracies worked, they ceded me completely to various teams of professionals, officers, monitors, and even security guards, all of whom seemed fully poised, and even eager, to receive me into their respective realms.

This is not to say that other juveniles would have been treated less comprehensively, but the plain fact of it was that to every person who encountered me I presented a most unusual case. Again, I wasn't one of the many Black or Hispanic boys who were regrettably overrepresented in the client population, or some deeply disturbed white boy like Tommy Reilly, who at some point likely made his own way through the system; back then in their world I was a rare creature, akin to some tiny tree primate who foraged only at night, this clean-cut, soft-spoken, somewhat overcourteous Oriental kid who came from an intact and evidently loving, supportive family, whose parents weren't druggies or boozers—neither of them even drank alcohol—and didn't physically or sexually or even verbally abuse me; who was documented to be among the top students in his grade, as well as voted as its vice president; who pursued a variety of extracurricular activities and athletics; who attended church services regularly; who was a Cub Scout, with a full complement of badges of rank; who had delivered Christmas cookies with his Little League team to the large old folks' home downtown; and who consistently rated as low risk in personality trait screenings, as well as scoring in the top percentiles of various aptitude tests.

I must believe that it was my unflagging normality that lent extra fervor to their desire to uncover what was (or had gone) wrong with me, some one-off miswiring that intrigued and frustrated and ultimately energized their professional endeavors. Each of them employed a different approach or method to draw me out, among them play therapy and art therapy and, my least favorite, theatrical therapy, when I was asked to pretend to be one of the child models pictured in a spiral notebook, each sporting, in an overdone manner, a certain intense emotion, like fright or anger or elation. I was supposed to improvise why or how the kid got that way, and although I tried my best I could never get over the fact that I was acting, and that the psychologist knew I was acting, which made me feel silly and awkward. So I muddled through the range of emotions using the same imaginary scenario of an ice cream man having or not having the particular treat I wanted. Inevitably the psychologist asked me about the Ice Cream Man himself, but I couldn't understand what he was driving at and could only say that our ice cream man had hairy hands, which I noticed whenever he gave change from his belt-attached metal coin dispenser. The psychologist then gave me a box of crayons and had me draw us together. This was difficult for me as the ice cream man wore an all-white outfit and white cap—the white crayon had no purchase on the white paper—and after I outlined his figure in (a randomly plucked) scarlet red, the therapist seemed activated, following up with questions about the ice cream man's facial attributes, his stature, even whether I could recall anything of his body odor, none of which I was able to specify, which visibly deflated her, and I ended up with the sharp ache of having failed my therapist, my family, myself. If there was one thing I was reliably skilled at and took pride in it was the taking of tests, whether cognitive or academic or athletic.

Steadily, I improved at their practice. Things seemed to run more smoothly if I always said something, anything, even if I had no natural response, rather than remaining silent. It didn't seem like pretending or lying so much as exploring the budding branches of a particular thought. Showing some emotion was also effective in suggesting to them that we were on a fruitful path. Finally, I learned that if I asked questions of their questions, if I wondered, for example, whether I should rank the "three wishes" the social worker asked that I might make, or have him define what he meant by "best" when inquiring about my favorite times of the day (say, "happiest" or "easiest"), they seemed extra pleased. My eager, readily proactive participation only redoubled each professional's engagement with my case, and with me personally as well, a few of them remarking on how "hopeful for" and "fond" they were of me as our appointments were concluding for the day. I would give the slightest, humblest nod and let them usher me out to my mother and sister in the waiting room with a guiding hand on my shoulder, their enigmatic prize pupil.

It felt like there were scores of these sessions, though they probably numbered no more than a dozen. I grew fond of my interlocutors, too, and during those four or five weeks of assessments and therapies I came to see them as confidants, if not friends, sort of like priests one would confess to but outside any moral construct, implied or otherwise. I could say anything, and soon enough I did. One older social worker, a washed-out-looking man named Mr. Ricks whose hair and complexion were cousin shades of chalk, encouraged me to talk about any dreams that I could remember. Of course I did remember some dreams, they were typically nonsensical and disoriented, with the sort of embattled hero scenarios that a young boy might have, such as fending off a frenzied swarm of great white sharks with my bare fists alone but on the blacktop of a playground, which I recounted to him, after which we talked in predictable ways about feelings of insecurity, fear, being alone, et cetera. He sat up when I told him about another dream that was in fact more a fantasy I entertained, this one about being a human fighter jet, soaring fast and high and able to dive straight down and strafe an enemy that was fleeing like cockroaches in every direction.

"They're cockroaches, and not something else?" Mr. Ricks ventured. "Maybe people?"

I told him they were "definitely" cockroaches, because my mother was always trying to exterminate the ones that periodically marauded her kitchen. But then I said they could also be little ant people, ceaselessly gathering crumbs and other bits of food.

"How do you feel then, about shooting at them? These 'little ant people'?"

"I don't like them." Then something made me say: "I hate them."

Now he had to pause. "Can you tell me why? Listen, what if I said that they're just going about their activities. Their lives. Just like you are, like your parents and your sister are."

"That's what I mean."

"But I still don't understand what you're saying. What do you hate, exactly?"

"How everybody has to keep living their life."

He half chuckled. But then he got serious. "What else can we do?"

"I don't know," I said, the top of my scalp flaring at his use of *we*. I looked him right in the eye. "It just takes so much energy."

Mr. Ricks mulled this for a long moment. He didn't press me further, instead scribbling furiously in his notebook. He wrote for several minutes straight, his script flowy but messy. When he was done, we went out to the waiting room and he spoke to my mother at length about me in terms I only partly understood and that she couldn't comprehend at all—he never caught on that her English was extremely limited—and then talked about an innovative new program he strongly recommended that I was as yet too young for but that he would flag in my file for potential future participation.

"Good luck to you, son," Mr. Ricks brightly said as we left. "You'll be all right."

His confidence buoyed my mother, who at that point desperately needed any uplift, and made me feel like the session had been a triumph. I was learning something new about myself over the course of all these psychosocial assessments; I had evolved from being a cowed, fidgety boy who fumbled his words to an engaged client-partner sitting easefully in his chair while marking every reaction to the wide-ranging and indiscriminate volleys coming out of his own mouth. I had discovered the power of the provocateur, how one could, with a well-timed word or gesture, churn the waters.

Thus it was with a growing sense of command that I showed up for my next round of prescribed civic and therapeutic activities, which included a service day where I put out place settings of paper cups and plates and plastic cutlery at a local soup kitchen, a sculpting session in which I was tasked to mold something out of a mound of clay nearly my size using nothing but my hands, and an afternoon at a Marine-style obstacle course, which to me was the most fun but also odd, given that a number of the kids had physical handicaps like a withered arm or a useless eye, one boy unable to negotiate any part of the course because of his cerebral palsy. I did fine except for badly abrading my hands on a high climbing rope when I slid down a few feet from its top. Mostly I was glad that the many rounds of testing and assays and "conversations" finally seemed to have been exhausted, that I was getting back out in the world, as it were, meeting actual "civilians" again and strutting my stuff even if it was in tightly controlled environs. I was beginning to think that perhaps I preferred engaging with life this way, with circumscribed settings and cohorts and thus expectations, over the trivialities and inane bedlam of, say, the Cove Gardens playground, where you could utter or do anything you pleased and therein possibly lose your grip, so when the case worker telephoned and informed my mother that I had been slotted for a full-day group excursion up in the country, I was very glad.

At the time we didn't know that the trip was the featured activity in the special pilot program Mr. Ricks had briefly mentioned to us, a program, it would turn out, in which I should not have been participating. There must have been some clerical mistake, and/or something confused in the handoff between the professional therapy office and the case worker's office, and/or not fully comprehended by my mother when they called, but what happened was that my mother dropped me off at yet another barren-looking county municipal building for a half-day outing to some woodsy complex an hour away by bus.

The staff lady seemed taken aback on seeing me, asking my age, then checking a second time on her clipboard that my name was indeed listed. She had my mother sign a waiver and then directed us to wait inside. Her momentary disquiet didn't much register, as I was immediately focused on the large community room behind her, which featured both a pool and a Ping-Pong table and also a lit-up pinball machine.

There were some tough-looking teenage boys sporting wispy mustaches playing dice and smoking cigarettes around one of several card tables, and then a couple girls with their hair feathered and faces all made up sitting on the sofa affecting a posture of eternal boredom. They were smoking, too, and I took the ritualistic actions of butt-tapping and flipping the tops of their lighters and blowing smoke rings to be the signs that they were bad seeds or were aiming to be.

My mother clearly saw them as trouble and instinctively drew me to her side as we traversed the large room and sat by ourselves in a forlorn corner "reading" section set up with a couple rotating lawyers' shelves of books. We didn't know that this was a place where underage youths who had committed offenses like shoplifting or gang fighting or low-level drug dealing could hang out and also have their court-ordered counseling sessions, but my mother stayed with me right up to the moment the announcement was made to go out and board a full-sized yellow school bus, making sure I sat up front near one of the two burly male monitors who were chaperoning us, the other one sitting in the rearmost seat, presumably to keep the teens in line. The door accordioned shut and as we began rolling away everyone lit up a fresh one, the monitors and driver included. Through the scratched, dusty glass panels my mother waved at me with a pained face, but at the time I no longer had much sensitivity to her state of mind, this just yet another necessary appointment that she would put her faith in and relinquish me to, but now

I think of the caustic feelings she must have harbored, that she and my father had already failed me, my degenerate turn fouling any chance at a prosperous future. Right or wrong, it was all on me, and while Ella would turn out to be the winning child in every important regard, this didn't much figure to them then. I was our first boat, our last boat, the one designed to crest any wave, to weather any storm. They had never considered the possibility of a ruinous tempest within.

Early in the bus ride the two girls decided that I would be their mascot and had me sit with them and shared their bubble gum with me. They were named Krista and Maggie, both surnamed Murphy but unrelated, and even through the acrid billows of their mentholated cigarettes I could breathe deep the candied gush of their Love's Baby Soft perfume, the scent of which I knew from a friend's older sister, and often saw ads for in magazines, its slogan, **BECAUSE INNOCENCE IS SEXIER THAN YOU THINK**, mostly inscrutable to me but still unleashing a curious ripple down my lower spine. I had looked up *innocence* and *sexy* (no entries for *sexier*) in both my dictionary and children's encyclopedia, but I couldn't reconcile them, the *Because* only further confusing matters. Krista and Maggie, maybe fourteen or fifteen at the time, were likely a lot more innocent and less sexy than they presented, though to me they seemed to be grown women with their jutting busts (Krista) and cello hips (Maggie) and the rakish way they held their cigarettes perilously close to their sprayed feathered hair while they snapped the gum they were chewing, gossiping about mutual friends while cracking back at the boys' crude come-ons with insults about their greaser looks or limp manhood that were somehow also flirtatious, all while they peppered me with questions about my background and family and what I could possibly have done to get myself on this "perp bus" that they nonetheless blithely chuckled about like it was a pleasure boat.

"We're gonna get *real scared*," Krista crooned in a part–Noo Yawk, part-vampiric accent. I didn't know what she was talking about. I just liked the way she looked. She had freckles all over her naturally pale face, so many that she appeared midsummer tanned, and like Maggie she had those pixie features a lot of Irish girls seemed to have, pert noses and sparkly, gleeful eyes and pinchy mouths that in their case could spew the nastiest curses but also doofily giggle, too, like during our bubble-gum-blowing contest when my bubble popped and covered half my face.

"You have such cutesy little eyes, J.-G.," Maggie said, picking a pink string of gum from my cheek. She squinted, making hers into slits. "But how do you see anything?"

"He just has to get up real close," Krista answered, corralling me into the crook of her warm, damp armpit. The hard underwire of her bra pinched my ear, my temple pressed against her full soft breast that was maybe even fuller and softer than my mother's, and if the smell right there wasn't great, I closed my eyes and let myself drift off and bounce along on the jousty suspension of the bus.

"Hey, should we have him try?" Maggie was holding her cigarette out to me across the aisle.

"He's like ten years old!" Krista cried, clutching me even more tightly.

"C'mon, when'd you pop your cherry?"

"I started late, not 'til I was eleven or twelve."

"I'm talkin' about the first time you smoked, you dumb slut."

"Eat me, you fugly lesbo."

They flicked their tongues obscenely at each other and decided that it was indeed my time. Before that I'd only tried one puff of my father's pipe, coughing uncontrollably for a full minute, so I was uneasy when Maggie showed me how to hold the smoldering butt between my index and middle fingers, then inhale slow and steady before breathing it out. I coughed in a ferocious spasm again, though not long, and the next inhales went more smoothly, deeply, until I got a good rhythm. One of the chaperones noticed what I was doing and I reflexively crouched but he just shook his head, puffing on his own cigarette. For the rest of the trip upstate the three of us had a genuine social, and to me we could be having a plate of shortbread cookies and a pitcher of lemonade while sitting on wicker chairs on a breezy porch instead of being trapped inside a grimy smoke-hazed bus, the girls going on about certain boy teen idols they considered sexy or dreamy and the girl idols who were reputedly stuck-up or whorish, and then compared notes on the countless social service programs they'd been shuffled through, basically all a waste of time except for the ones that provided snacks or some spending money. I got gabby, too, no doubt from a nicotine overload that was like a brace of baby squirrels wrestling for space in my brain, and I ended up chattering away about things I didn't know I cared so much about, such as why all car bumpers weren't made completely of rubber, and how street-cart hot dogs were better than the store kind because of their casings, which popped satisfyingly when you bit them. The girls found me quite amusing, and even though I had no clue of what they were talking about, my inborn governor for caution got switched off and I blithely chimed in on their many opinions about boys and dating and clothes and cool cars et cetera et cetera, and at one point I was doing the hip bump with Krista in the aisle after Maggie tuned in "You'll Never Find Another Love Like Mine" by Lou Rawls on her portable radio. Up to that moment in my life I'd registered only fleeting tremors on sighting certain angles of the female form, these patches of an achy, moonlit hollowness pinging in my chest, but now I couldn't help but gape at the shock of pale belly skin when Krista raised her arms while dancing, or at the way her jutting butt collapsed drastically into the taut planes of her skinny designer-jeaned thighs, the shadowed crevice they made between them magnetizing a store of loose filings I had no clue were in me, such that I was pressing against her even after the radio song ended.

"Oh my god, J.-G.!"

By my shoulders she held me at arm's length, her hazel eyes widened with a roguish glee. "Are you serious?"

Maggie was covering her mouth, and pointing down at my shorts, where, it was clear, there was a nascent prominence. An almost bump. She reached out from her bench seat and poked it, warily, like her finger was the stick you used to prod a roadkill. Krista gave it a nudge, too.

"Boner Baby!" she proclaimed, and they both made faces like they were terrorized, shrieking madly. "How's it feel, you sick little wiener?"

I didn't know what to say, having no idea what she was talking about. I just shrugged. In fact, for a moment, I didn't even realize what *it* was; I knew I had a thing that I peed with, that it sometimes smelled bad, that I was supposed to wash thoroughly when I showered, but somehow, I didn't connect the vaguely numb tightness in my shorts with an actual part of me. If anything, I thought it was my own way of simply being happy, which I was, happy to be with these gregarious, assertive older girls, happy for the generous and indulgent attention, happy to be treated like a fast and genuine friend.

I could have ridden that bus forever.

Unfortunately, though they told us it would be a full hour's journey, it felt like mere minutes had elapsed when we pulled up to the security gate of the property, a massive complex of various large brick structures spanning the banks of a wide, blackish river. Somehow my mother and I had the impression that the day's program was to be held at a woodsy conference center, but this looked like a manufacturing facility with the towers and smokestacks and cyclone fencing ringing the property. The bus grew quieter as we rolled through a security gate and through the parking lot, the boys in the rear pausing in their rounds of boasts and invectives, and even Krista and Maggie grew slack in their gum chewing as they took in the ramparts of the severe, dismal architecture.

"Welcome to the Magic Kingdom, skidmarks," the chaperone named Gene barked as he turned in the aisle to address us. "Now shut up and follow me, single file."

One of the boys in the back started singing "It's a Small World" in a chipmunk voice and the other chaperone slapped the back of his head, which made everyone snicker. Krista and Maggie and I were in the front, so we followed Gene into the building, where we were funneled through a metal detector and quickly patted down by armed guards who were surprisingly jocular and friendly. It was as if they were ushering us into a children's museum or an aquarium, but my sweaty hand (that Krista now sloughed off) understood before I did where we were. This was a prison. Or it had been a prison once, and a gigantic one. After we all got checked they led us down a series of cold, echoey corridors and then out through a very long and narrow courtyard overgrown with weeds before we went back inside one of the tenement-like buildings that had been mothballed decades before. There some older, out-of-shape guards who looked like they were part-timing pensioners showed us a cellblock that looked like it was from olden times, with each cell having a solid metal door with a window of checkerboard iron bars that let in hardly any light, the stone-tiled floor that spanned the length of the cellblock designed with a trough down the middle, presumably to hose down any overflow from the old tin buckets that the prisoners had to piss and shit in. Two boys who volunteered got to be locked in, the guard pretending for a long minute that none of the huge antique keys from his set was working before finally releasing them. They showed us the spartan mess hall, which looked a lot like the cafeteria in my school except with much higher ceilings, and then the barber shop with its massive throne-like chairs, and the laundry room where they washed the linens and prisoner outfits in huge metal vats, and the large shelf-lined former warden's office that was empty of furniture and books and now stored old paperwork but that you could imagine was once creepily sumptuous with its majestic vista looking out to the river and hills past the main watchtower, a lair of almost unlimited discretionary power.

The room everyone got really excited about was the execution chamber, which in fact looked like a regular operating room with greenish tiles on the walls and floor except for the actual electric chair in which the death-row prisoners once got zapped. The same guard who taunted the boys with his "wrong" cell keys let a white kid named Spencer with long unruly hair take a test run in the chair. Spencer got his wrists and ankles strapped to the wooden arms and legs, with his heels set in metal stirrups and his head pulled back tight against the high-backed chair with a tattered leather belt. The guard took the liberty of explaining to us that the doomed man would normally have his face covered because it was easier to kill when you couldn't see the human face, and I think all of us stared at Spencer's dulled, lamblike expression at that moment and wondered if we could flip the switch. Once Spencer was ready, the guard signaled his colleague through the thick glass window in the adjoining chamber, who did the honors without flourish, opening a fuse box on the wall and pulling down a large breaker, all of which they may have installed for tours like this. Spencer, though, immediately thrust himself into the role by bucking violently in the chair, then jolted taut with a deadly surge of current, his eyeballs rolling up into his head while his jaw clenched in a tortured palsy. For a second I was terrified and was sure that we had been tricked, that this field trip was some sick joke to force us to witness a real electrocution. One of the other boys, a toughie named Geraldo with a fresh buzz cut, flinched enough to lose his balance and fell back onto Gene the chaperone before gathering himself and hissing, "You're a fucking retard, Spence." Everybody—including the chaperones and guards—laughed as Spencer then hammed it up with an especially intense case of the shakes.

I thought it was all pretty cool. As we were led out of the death chamber by the grandpa guard you could feel the rebounding energy, the fresh volleys of jokes and cackles echoing keenly and reassuringly about that dank concrete and stone as if in a cave we had long fully charted. And if a good part of me considered these kids to be genuine delinquents—I didn't think Gene's "skidmarks" comment applied to me—I felt a warm flush of something toward all of them. It wasn't that furious, bloody attraction one can have, when the iron in your veins can get clumped up simply by proximity to a like spirit, but a fascination with what they all had in common, which was the capacity, or the curse, of being able to step outside of a moment in order to commit some transgressive act, to not feel what they ought to feel, and thus fully, purely, keep separate, if usually for the worse. I realized that I admired this capacity, because I knew that it was a capacity I had, too, whether I could admit it or not.

The guard—I remember how his eyebrows curled up at the ends, the same ash-colored threads poking out of his ears—took us back the way we came in, past the library and laundry rooms, the antique cellblock, across the overgrown weeds of the inner courtyard, and because he was a soft-spoken older man with a doughy pink face I couldn't help but imagine we were going to get a tour-ending treat of an ice cream sandwich. Maybe even a hot dog—it was nearing lunchtime, after all. At the head of the corridor that would have led back to the parking lot he turned us in the opposite direction, then turned again down another long corridor, and we ended up in a very large, plain triangular-shaped room furnished exclusively with metal folding chairs, a single window covered with a metal grate cut high enough in the corner that you couldn't see anything but daylight. The walls that met in the corner were stepped with two big risers, making for a kind of amphitheater. Why anyone would put a window high in the corner or plan a triangular room struck me as odd even then, for despite its size the room felt pinched and oppressive, literally maligned by its acute angles. The guard gestured to a single row of chairs that had been set up parallel to the hypotenuse of the space, and as we each took a seat, I noted that there was exactly the right number of chairs.

"Okay, kids . . ."

For a longish pause we waited for what the man was going to say to us, maybe offer some pithy advice drawn from years of encountering troubled youth or tell a tallish tale about a daring prison escape, or even better a bloodbath of a riot, but he didn't speak again. He simply took in our motley array with a cast to his eyes that was faraway and sanguine, as if he were seeing us as already having grown to adulthood and endured and finally squared up with the bitter tumult of this life. Then a new group of three uniformed guards entered, this set younger and bulked up and not gentle-faced at all. Maybe it was that they didn't wear caps, but they looked more like career thugs than guards or cops, twitchy-cheeked and liable to break some heads. The lead thug-guard wore protective glasses like a lab technician or woodworker might, a clinical look that in this context read as menacing. He nodded to the old hairy-eared guard, who left the room without any hesitation, not glancing back at us even as most of us followed him out with our gazes.

I didn't know what the others were thinking, but I had a feeling that after the friendly, entertaining tour we were all expecting a live demonstration of sorts. How to handcuff a person. How to subdue someone who was resisting arrest. How to use a baton. I was beginning to understand what we were doing here. Get us closer to the action, closer to the idea of being a real perpetrator, a real criminal, and not just some random antisocial kid. A few men started walking in, behind them others, then more still, until the triangular room was pretty much jammed. They weren't guards, though more guards came in after them. I began to realize that something was up from the fact that they wore identical trousers, trousers that were an odd, bulky cross between janitor pants and pajama bottoms, their color an unnatural, industrial green, like the green of engine coolant. They all had the same sneakers, too, these cheap-looking beige canvas jobs that nobody would ever wear on the playground unless they wanted to get mocked. They wore different tops, though, T-shirts and muscle shirts and plaid button-ups and spangly disco shirts and everything else, which confused me even more. The most obvious thing was that most of them were Black, with the rest Puerto Rican or Dominican, a couple white guys trailing in last, if not as a pair.

Spencer, the joker of our bunch, seemed to track one of

them and the man noticed and came back and stood right above him.

"You digging me, punk?"

The man was white but his talk sounded Black, and older and harsh, like Cleon's adult brothers who were always riding him.

"You got a hard-on for me? Stand up and let me see. Cuz I gotta check your junk if I'm gonna be your bitch, right?"

Now everyone was staring at them. Spencer was still in his chair, his head craned upward but not quite meeting eyes with the man. There was no escape now. There wasn't even cover from the guards, all of whom seemed eager to see this encounter play out. I didn't know if I wanted to see it, for I didn't understand what the man was talking about, or why all the adults seemed deeply amused. The kids weren't amused. They were as still as they'd been all morning, stuck to their seats, not even chewing the bubble gum they'd popped and snapped through the entirety of the bus ride, their gazes averted in the hope that a veil of camouflage would somehow manifest.

"I said stand *UP*, bitch!"

I never experienced a person yell so loudly at somebody that close to them. I thought I was beginning to cry but something in me was turning sharper, brighter; my heart was pistoning so fast I thought I could hear its high whine. Spencer rose up slowly from his chair, his head wilted to a funny angle. You could tell how scared he was from his faint half grin, his disbelief, matched by the rest of ours, at how utterly real this was.

"Look me in the eye when I'm talkin' to you!" Our group gave full attention to him now. The man had mussy brown hair and a curly mustache and had a moon surface rime of acne scarring on his cheeks that seemed to turn redder with his growing rage. Spencer finally peered up at him.

"You a slice of pocket pie, boy," the man said, poking his nose near Spencer's ear, his neck. Grunts of assent from the other men echoed off the concrete block walls of the room. "Full of sweet filling I bet. Am I right?"

Spencer couldn't know whether it was better to nod or shake his head.

"After this is done you and me gonna get acquainted. Right here." He looked back at the goggled guard. "You cool, boss?"

The guard gave a sneering nod.

"See? Everybody loves a love story. And you know what you gonna find out?" He was close enough to Spencer that you could almost feel the space between them crackling with voltage. "You gonna learn what a dirty white dick tastes like. But you and blondie over there already know, right? Compared notes?"

Maggie tucked her chin in her chest, trying to hide behind her feathered bangs.

"C'mon, boy, talk!"

Spencer shriveled into himself, his arm shaking.

"You not gonna say?" the man suddenly hollered, the spit

flying. His teeth were large and yellowed, and I was sure he was going to bite off Spencer's nose. Then he snarled, "Fucking little bitch."

The man spat on the floor and walked away, leaving Spencer there as if alone onstage, standing before the risers filled with this audience of bristling, seething men. It seems impossible now, but up to that moment my childish mind was still trying to believe this was all a play, that they were actors in a story that they'd made up for us, instead of real prisoners who had committed real crimes and had been sentenced to rot here for years, or for the rest of their lives. Had our group of young troublemakers been sentenced, too, if in secret? Had my mother known this would happen when she signed the waiver? She was so often confused! An instant bitterness welled up in me toward my father, who was better at English and should have been there, but he was always too busy, too preoccupied with his work. . . .

Another man now stood before us, a leanly built Black man of average height. He had an attentive cast to his gaze. The other inmates, most all of them muscly and scowling, gave him their silence as he took his time surveying our lineup, examining each of us for a sustained moment before training his eye on the next. He took an extra beat with me, no doubt because I was obviously much younger than the others, and then an Oriental. He seemed amused by me, scratching at his tightly groomed mustache and beard. He was strangely dressed for being in prison, wearing a brown felt beret-style cap and a black suede vest over his black T-shirt, though these clashed with his rough-hewn prison-issue pants. There were ragged scars on his forearms. Like the rest of them he seemed to me to be a grown, middle-aged man, but he might well have been all of twenty-five years old.

"My name is Verrell but in here I'm Sir Marbles."

Sir M.! Sir M.!, some men hollered, like he was their team captain. Sir Marbles acknowledged them with a nod. He turned back to us.

"I don't know what you all did to have to come to this place, but I'm going to tell you why I'm here." He had a satisfying resonance to his voice, with the clarity of a TV news presenter, but street in intonation. "I was afraid of ending up here, because most every brother I grew up with did time. I swore to myself I'd never be like that. I swore I'd never get in trouble. Never do nothing like rob somebody. I kept to my promise. I never robbed nobody, never lifted a damn thing. Not even a piece of shit candy from a bodega. I bet every one of you is swiping goods all the time, am I right?"

He was beckoning us with his lively eyes and mouthful of stunningly clean, straight, bright white teeth.

"Come on, you sneaky-ass punks, don't get too shy now to cap. I want some *tales*, y'all. I want *deeds* and *exploits*."

There was silence from our group, but you could tell kids were itching to give it up to Sir Marbles, who was obviously chill and smart, a very different kind of cat.

"Don't disappoint!"

"I boosted some Pioneer 405s from Crazy Eddie's last week."

It was Jaime, a mixed white and Puerto Rican kid with a slight cleft lip. "Put 'em on my head and just walked out the store."

"Right on!" Sir Marbles stepped over to him and raised his hand and Jaime happily offered his palm and the man slapped him five.

"I wore two pairs of Jordaches out of Macy's," Maggie piped up.

"That's what I'm talking about, princess!"

Now others got to bragging, lobbing instances of their savvy thievery at the man, a clock radio and a box of cassettes from Korvette's, a catcher's mask and chest protector from busting a field locker, Clyde Pumas, boxes of old *Playboy* and *Hustler* magazines, a friend's mom's gold jewelry, the listing a running catalog of bright, if petty, victories.

"I got me a whole pastrami!"

"*Come again?*" Sir Marbles couldn't help but step over to the kid, a Black boy the others called Twinks, I assumed for his sparkly gray-green irises, which made him seem super approachable, but from how much space they gave him he was clearly intimidating. "What the *hell*, son?"

"When the deli guy went to the back I reached around the case and grabbed it like a football and booked. He come running after me with a baseball bat. No way he catches me."

"What'd you do with that?" Sir Marbles asked.

"Gave it to my gramma for a birthday present. She sure digs her some pastrami."

Everybody broke up, including the guards and the chaperones, too. Sir Marbles was chuckling with big huffs, nodding back at his fellow inmates, who were in turn nodding approvingly at us. We were getting acquainted now, transgressors all, and although compared to the others I'd committed far worse against Joshua Messing and in my mind against Tommy Reilly, I stayed quiet, though feeling a surge of solidarity that made me sit higher in my seat.

Sir Marbles must have noticed me light up and winked, and I winked back, and I was suddenly taken by the absurd notion that he would be a cool father (if he weren't in prison), someone who knew about the world and how strange things can happen when you don't want them to.

"Like I said, I wasn't like you brash punks." He laughed to himself. "I never was a thief. I didn't run with no gang. I didn't get into fights. I was a strange kid. All I did was read old newspapers and magazines left at the bus stop and hang with my moms. My teachers told me all the time how I was gifted. That I had a big future. 'No limits whatsoever,' one of them always said. And she wasn't wrong, you know? They saw I liked science and let me stay in the school lab for extra time. All by myself. I did experiments on osmosis and titration. Dissected frogs and a baby pig. Now that's some deeply fascinating shit."

He shook his head in wonder. "I bet some of you are secret

Poindexters like I was but don't wanna show it, right? Maybe you like reading about dinosaurs, or the ancient Romans, or you love drawing. Damn, maybe you dig *algebra*. But I know what y'all do instead. Sit around and smoke butts and front like all-world badasses. Pretty quick you get bored. I get it, I do. All of a sudden, you itching to do a deed. You wanna rumble. Stomp some heads. And the sorry-ass place you live, and your probably sorry-ass peeps, none of that says you can't. Matter of fact, it all's saying the exact opposite. So why not, right? Go the fuck ahead."

"Yeah, nigga!" one of our group bellowed, drawing the entire room's attention. The kid, named Marvin, blubber-cheeked and husky with a nappy Afro, was Black, but still. Sir Marbles stared at the kid for a long second, his face betraying nothing.

He continued. "Funny how things *transpire*, you know? I never wanted to be a badass, and I don't consider myself to be one now. Even in here. Right, y'all?"

"No way no how, Marbs!" a con shouted gruffly.

"My moms knew it, too. She was always trying to protect me, keep me away from trouble. Thing is, she had a thing for smack. She loved that China White." Sir Marbles glanced at me, though not with any enmity. "She had a rough life, so I couldn't blame her. It was her boyfriend I blamed, a light-skinned, smooth-talking motherfucker who brought her the drugs. He'd shoot her up first, then do himself. But not always. Sometimes he'd just watch her in her daze for a while before pushing up her dress. I hated him, but I knew she didn't care. It was part of the deal. Whenever he showed up, I made sure to split. Take my magazines and sack of marbles to the playground, maybe show the kiddies how to play. You can't help but love marbles. Every single one is its own pretty little planet."

He reached into the pockets of his vest and took out some marbles and handed out a few. I got one, clear glass with butterfly winglike wisps of red and blue in its middle.

"One day I come back from school and the motherfucker is there. Just watching TV on the couch and drinking beer. I ask where my moms is and he nods to the bedroom. I told him to get on then. He didn't scare me none. I was sixteen but the same size. Then the door to the bedroom opens and another nigger comes out with no pants on. He can hardly stand, high on dope. I start yelling for them to get the fuck out. They start laughing their asses off. I didn't care if it was at me. Folks been laughing at me every minute of my life. But they won't be laughing at my moms, even if she's *catatonic*. Situation's gonna be one way or another but she's not going to suffer that, too.

"So you know what I did? I kicked that shithead in the balls. He went down, fast. I was stomping on his ass when the other dude cracked me with his beer bottle on the back of my head. Somehow it didn't hurt me, and I swung around with my sack of marbles and caught him square in the temple. It stunned him, and he had to take a knee. I hit him again. He goes down, too, eyeballs rolling. TKO. But I didn't stop. I smashed his face until it was pretty much Sloppy Joe. The door's open to the hallway and our neighbor freaks because of all the blood, but I just go in to check on my moms. She's half awake and crying, crying like a junkie cries, high-pitched and whiny but no tears. It's a truly pitiable thing. I didn't care right then, though. I just covered her up and told her to go back to sleeping, that everything was okay.

"Soon enough a bunch of cops show up, guns drawn. No Pants already run off. They're yelling for me to drop what I'm holding and I realize my pouch of marbles is dripping blood. And now this hateful motherfucker, the one whose face I pounded, he's choking on his own blood. Cops yelling like mad at me, and he's going all gurgly and shit, and I'm just listening to him. The pigs don't give a fuck about him any more than I do, they're still shouting at me, ready to blow my head off. I drop my pouch and they pounce, dropping me to the floor. They beat my ass for a while before they cuffed me. Then they beat me some more. Meanwhile the motherfucker isn't breathing too good, so they radio the ambulance. Turns out they already know the nigger. But they don't do CPR or nothing. They don't want to touch him. Just waiting for the paramedics, while one of 'em has his knee on my back. We're watching him die."

Sir Marbles—it was clear now why he was called that—kind of winced, or maybe smiled, the creases around his nose and upper lip furrowing like a much older man's, and he stepped closer to us, facing Krista and Maggie, who were sitting beside each other in the center of our lineup of chairs.

He gazed at us with what you could only take to be a deep and sorrowful wonder.

"So you see, y'all, the situation I found myself in? For sure my doing, and also not. Maybe you can relate."

We nodded with fervor but it wasn't quite the response Sir Marbles was looking for.

"Next week I'm twenty-nine years old, and I already been in here for thirteen of them. Was supposed to be in for twenty-five total but I got fifteen added because I offed the motherfucker who raped me every day and night the first month I was in. That shock you? You punks probably think nothing can be worse than that, right? But you don't know yet what it's like when all you can hope for is your asshole to start bleeding quick and heavy, so it don't hurt so much. That's some fucked-up kind of hope. But that's the only kind in here. The only kind you're ever gonna have if you keep perpetrating. You dig being a badass? Well, badass is right."

His fellow inmates tittered and shouted, catcalling at particular boys and saying they wanted to do things to them that I couldn't understand but sensed were very bad. Others had risen and drifted a few steps forward, hooting and cursing. The room was suddenly surging with energy; I looked to the guards, but they hadn't flinched. In fact, they seemed almost pleased with how this visit was proceeding, as did our chaperones, including the head chaperone Gene, positioned by the door, who was openly chuckling.

Sir Marbles, however, just sighed. I don't know if something happened with the tube lights in that room, or whether it was my vision from sitting so motionless, but the coloring in his cheeks seemed to diffuse and mostly drop away and leave only this ashen veneer.

Then, in a voice depleted of any feeling, he said: "You two girls, please stand up."

Everybody now fixed on Krista and Maggie.

"Come on, now."

The girls slowly got to their feet while turning desperately to Gene the chaperone, but he just looked to the grim-cheeked head guard, who in turn tipped his head toward Sir Marbles, the real master of ceremonies. On the bus Krista and Maggie had seemed so mature and filled out but now they looked as wispy as the shoots of fine hair at their temples. Their sudden vulnerability was startling enough to me, but then Gene and the other chaperone started to leave, as well as the guards, the cohort filing out with an almost monkish silence. Only the head guard remained, but he had drifted to the periphery of the risers to sit chummily beside one of the inmates.

The men started cawing again and Krista began to cry, then Maggie, too, the girls huddling together miserably, as if caught out in a rain. I felt awful for them, scared of what might happen, and yet I couldn't help but see them like baby prey on a nature show, the wild dogs circling, a certain part of me inviting the next scene, when one of the dogs is scampering away with a hindquarter in its jaws.

When the metal door clanged shut behind our guardians, the air went foul. Maybe it was there all along and I hadn't noticed, maybe the air-conditioning had cycled off, but the sharp, musky reek of a dozen or so embittered men now filled the room. I didn't realize I was holding my breath until I had to let out a gasping exhale.

Sir Marbles noticed this and gestured for me. I went to him.

"Don't be fretting now, young blood," he said low in my ear, curling his arm around my shoulders. "Nothing's happening to you today. Promise."

That *Promise* was as steely as a sword. With both hands I clung to his wrist.

"Let's see some vanilla titty," somebody said from the risers.

"Cherries on top!" said another.

Shouting followed, a few men popping to their feet and pressing forward to stand with Sir Marbles and me. The girls crossed their arms over their flimsy blouses, but their skin-tight jeans made the shapes of their behinds immodestly apparent, and even I couldn't help but picture what they might look like bare.

"Why don't you unbutton that top, little lady?" someone said to Krista, though from his tone it was no suggestion. He was a very light-skinned Black guy with a rash of freckles on his cheeks, which stood out to me because I always thought freckled people seemed happier and kinder than most.

"Go ahead, both yous," the man beside him commanded. He was bulked up; all neck and shoulders.

Sir Marbles simply looked on. The head guard the same, though he did so with a smirk.

Maggie began to shiver, and though Krista was hugging her, her gaze, for some reason, locked on me, her eyes desperately pleading for an amnesty I could not grant.

"Don't be shy," the freckled man said. "We all pretty much intimates here." He reached out and with his finger lightly ticked the shirt sleeve of Krista's cotton blouse. She and Maggie collapsed even deeper into each other. He took a half step back, regarding them.

"You don't know nothing about us yet, right? Isn't that so?"

Neither girl did anything, not even look up.

"I get it. I'm not as smart as brother Marbs, but I know some things. I do. I know how to get folks comfortable. So let's get comfortable."

He nodded to the bulky man, who casually undid the knotted ends of the drawstring of his prison-issue bottoms. He stretched the waist and let them drop to his ankles. A homely guffaw broke out behind us. Although I was transfixed with bewilderment, I couldn't utter a sound. The man just stood there, his broad ass gleaming and palish in the room's cold tube light. The unkempt massing of his privates was a twisty jumble of hair and fleshiness that looked like some crouching, half-burrowed creature. It hardly seemed to belong to him.

"Now one of your turns," the freckled man said to the girls.

They couldn't move.

"C'mon, now. Who's gonna show and tell?"

"Blondie!" came a shout.

"Blue shirt! White belt!"

The room grew so clamorous that Sir Marbles had to wave his arms to restore a measure of order. The bulky fellow still stood there, bottomless. He was scratching at his groin, breathing audibly with his mouth cracked wide as he stared at the girls.

The freckled man, meanwhile, was all frowns.

"What we gonna do, Marbs? We all gathered here. The show must go on. Somebody has to decide."

"Make Chinky choose." It was the head guard, on his feet now with his chest all fluffed out. He was smiling for the first time, and I could see all his crowded, jaundiced teeth.

At first, I scanned around, wondering who he was talking about. Kids and even some grown-ups had called me *Chink* plenty of times, but only Joshua Messing had used the word *Chinky*, which now didn't sound so harsh coming from the guard. In fact, it felt almost endearing, and I realized I was grinning, though I felt no glee.

Sir Marbles took firm hold of my shoulder. Did he regard me with pity? A glint of shame? I can't be sure. To picture the young man now—and he was a very young man, regardless of circumstances—I have to say he projected a perfect equanimity. Because to him this whole convention, this place, himself, little me, the girls, the guards, this heated audience, comprised but another nil moment in another nil life. This is not to say it was meaningless. Just that none of us is exempt. We are subjects, all.

There were hoots and exhortations, but I could hardly hear them. I was rooted in, steady on my feet despite the floor rumbling from the cons stomping on the wooden risers. I looked at Maggie and Krista. Weren't we fast friends on the bus? Couldn't they be my sisters in a different family? Wasn't I already enamored of them both?

And yet the truth is this: I was not stricken with anguish. Instead, gazing at their cowering, I felt the freight of the power this young man was giving to me. A secretly vast, brimming reservoir. It was breathtaking.

"Fucking choose, Chinky boy!" one of the kids shouted.

It was Marvin, the husky kid who'd interrupted Sir Marbles earlier. He was bouncing and bobbing like a boxer.

Sir Marbles nudged me aside.

"You really some ravenous horny brother, huh?" he said, gently poking one of Marvin's fleshy boobs. "Munching loads of pussy, I bet."

Marvin mulled for a second, then said, "Uh-huh."

"Show us your skills, young blood," Sir Marbles said, glancing at the girls.

Marvin flared his tongue at them. Sir Marbles tipped his head and two dudes with enormous chests and arms came forward from the risers. I thought they were going to manhandle the girls, but they grabbed Marvin instead and dragged him before the trouserless man.

"I can't be here for this," the goggled head guard crooned, though he didn't move or look away.

They shoved Marvin to his knees and held him there, holding his face within a breath of the man's exposed groin. Then the man aimed the tip of his limp member at the kid's nose, his eyes, the crown of his head. I kept wondering if the man was going to piss on him and for a second it seemed he had, but it was just the boy's profusion of tears that had wet his face. After another minute they let him go, the naked man kicking Marvin in the ass to get him moving. He stumbled badly and almost fell face-first onto his chair. The inmates and guard were laughing. None of the kids was laughing, though, and neither was Sir Marbles, who'd been looking on dispassionately. He was patting my shoulder with a rhythmic tenderness, as if I'd been the one injured, as if I'd been the one wronged.

A couple weeks later, another warm and glaring midsummer's afternoon, my mother came into my bedroom with a plate of freshly made gimbap. I was surprised, as her gimbap typically appeared at the weekend picnics we'd periodically have with other Korean families at the local state park, or else on a long car trip, when she'd pass a Tupperware full of the sliced rounds to us in the back seat. Even though it was one of Ella's and my favorites, a treat we'd often lobby for her to make us, she rarely, if ever, served gimbap at home. Aside from her view that it was "traveling" food, it was something of a hassle for her to prepare the various fillings of the spinach namool, the omelet egg, the pickled daikon, the minced bulgogi, then neatly roll it all up with steamed rice in sheets of gim.

But that day she suddenly appeared with a mini pyramid of cut gimbap on a small plate. I was assembling the tiny gray plastic pieces of a scale-model P-51 Mustang fighter plane and would have sensed her approach had I not been using cement glue; the mingled scent of warm rice and roasted seaweed and the sweetened, salty fillings makes my eyes widen still. But what did I do but grunt at her and keep working at my project like any spoiled, churlish boy, despite the glee blooming in my throat?

Jeon-Gi-ya, you've been working on that all day. You hardly ate anything at lunch, so I made a snack for you. Ella already had some.

"Okay," I said, giving the plate a cursory glance. I knew how to best please her, and I knew, too, where she was softest.

She put the plate on the corner of my desk and stood fanning herself before the opened window. She peered out at the playground and fields. Except for the stormy days there was a constant clamor during the summer of children shouting and wailing. It was how I ascertained whether certain kids were out there while I sat on the floor pulling on my socks.

It's smelly in here.

I simply grunted.

I see your friends are playing baseball. Don't you like sports anymore?

"Of course I do."

Seems like you haven't been playing with your friends much lately.

I didn't respond, because I knew she wouldn't quite understand what I would say, and also because I didn't know the necessary Korean words. Though mostly I didn't want to try to explain how I was getting tired of my friends, who seemed to be growing more babyish each time we gathered. They bickered over the most insipid things, like whose sneaker tread pattern was "tougher looking," or else they cried too easily if they skinned a knee or were called a fairy. I found myself getting especially irritated by Gregory Fluss, whom I could always count on to be an eager play partner but whose very malleability now struck me as a signal, damning weakness. One rainy day when he came over, he asked me what we should play and I responded with the options I knew he enjoyed least, the card games 21 or Spit. Of course he assented. Gregory was heavyset and effective in sports like football or basketball, when he could employ his bulk to his advantage, but he wasn't terribly dexterous and so a fast-moving card game like Spit made him fumble. Nor was he great at math, which made playing 21 a chore for him, made worse by how I'd press him to either hit or stick. He had a hard time quickly adding middle numbers like 6 or 7, you could hear the tiny whispering as he counted in his head, and then any ace, with its value of either 1 or 11, would further complicate matters for him; this made me huff with irritation, which only stalled him more, which in turn was an accelerant to my umbrage. The next time I saw him, out near the basketball court, his greeting was the usual effusive calling of my initials. I turned, not even trying to pretend that I hadn't heard him. He waved me over. It would have been the easiest thing to wave back, to indicate whether I would play with him or not. Instead, I walked away.

Gregory hadn't knocked on our apartment door in a while, which my mother had certainly noticed. He always stuffed his face with the snacks she'd put out whenever he or other friends came over; Gregory especially loved the gimbap, which he called the "Rice Log."

Eat now or you'll have no appetite for dinner.

I took one of the rounds and popped it in my mouth, though staying trained on my hobby work. It took everything I had to quell myself.

But nothing of me got past her. She started to take away the plate and I picked and ate another of the rounds, and then another, until finally she ordered me to slow down. I didn't care whether I might choke myself; at that moment I half wished for it.

She peered at the top of my short bookshelf jammed with its armada of scale-model warplanes, tanks, gunboats.

You know there's most of the summer still left? You complain every day in the winter about not being able to play outside. Now look at you. You're like a crazy old man. Something is wrong with you. Tell me. Is something wrong with you?

"Nothing's wrong with me!"

I was nauseated with the thrill of my sudden vehemence. A fleck of rice had stuck to the gray plastic fuselage of my P-51, the sight of which made me feel ridiculous. I let it stay there, hating it. And I hated how it was often too sunlit in this room, I hated my still ugly airplane and its beads of excess dried glue, I hated how my mother somehow appeared whenever I felt even a fraction off or distanced from things.

She sat on my bed, right next to my desk, and reached to pick off the rice, palming it away as she did with all the detritus my sister and I constantly generated.

Your father and I met with the social worker yesterday.

This surprised me, both because my father was always too busy and because they usually needed me to help interpret.

He said that you might like having a new grouping.

I said, *Grouping?*

Other kinds of kids. He said it might make you feel better. Kids more like you.

"I was with those kids already." I pictured Krista and Maggie, terrified. Big Marvin.

You know, there is a church camp coming up. Some from our church will be going. You can go to that, too. You sleep there.

"In a tent?" In Cub Scouts we hadn't camped out yet, but of course all of us in our Pack had been gung ho for it. But maybe they had camped without me; I hadn't been to a meeting since my school suspension.

She didn't know the word for "tent," and I didn't know how to say it in Korean, so I quickly sketched one on a palm-sized notepad that I used exclusively for the purpose. I was decent at drawing, and in those early years in the country she and I found my notepad to be an efficient and helpful tool, this collection of random gaps in our language: a hammer, a sea lion, a chimney emitting smoke. My tent was in three-quarter perspective, with a flap door and a pronounced sag in the roofline, cribbed, no doubt, from a photo I'd seen in a Civil War picture book.

Could be you'd sleep in a tent. I don't know.

"Is it far away?"

I think so. They've had it for a couple years already. This year, it will be run by Reverend Hahm and his wife from our church. They'll look after you. There will be other kids, from other Korean churches. It'll be fun.

I pictured another long bus ride, on a winding parkway through heavily wooded hills, with a bunch of kids I hardly knew. I didn't care if they were Korean or not.

"I don't want to go."

Normally she would have made that raspy sound from her throat, spiked with annoyance and exasperation, and simply left the room muttering about me in the third person to Ella or to my father or to no one in particular. But this time she stayed quiet, regarding me, as she often did, with the solemnity of someone measuring out a last, slim hope.

Your father and I have decided that you will.

"What? I don't even have a sleeping bag! I can't go."

We'll go to the Army Navy store on Saturday with your father. They gave us a list of the things you need. We can't afford to buy everything, but we'll get you the most important things.

I was cross about being overruled but I could tell they were resolved. However, I could already picture the array of new stuff laid out on my bed. "Besides a sleeping bag, I want a Swiss Army knife. And a canteen!"

What's a "can-teen"?

"Don't you know?" I cried, overexcited with the prospect of a footlocker's worth of new gear. I quickly drew a round water tin, with a chained screw-top enclosure. It looked like a landmine about to blow but she got the idea.

I don't know about that. You're not going on some refugee march.

"Please, *Um-mah*!" I whined, though with a fawning ending lilt.

Okay, okay, we'll see.

By the time the weekend arrived, I'd already rearranged our bedroom into a camplike setup, using my desk chair and two others from the dining table to be the supports for a thin summer blanket that was the primary tenting, and then requisitioning Ella's smaller chair and Barbie house to prop the lower, protruding igloo-esque entrance. For some reason it seemed essential that we should have to crawl into the lair and have our lunch inside the hot, stuffy confines. Ella didn't mind, for despite how generally indifferent and brusque I was to her, whenever I paid her any genuine attention, she became my happy partner and assistant. She didn't even care that we had to eat our lunch of PB&J sandwiches—I had deemed that no Korean food was allowed because the tent was somehow an American space—crouched almost yoga-style over our feet. Later, before bedtime, we had our "campfire" of torn-up red- and orange-colored construction paper and ate actual marshmallows that our mother roasted over the stove burner using old wooden chopsticks as skewers. When my father came home late in the evening he got on his hands and knees and poked his head into the tent to bid us goodnight, both Ella and I flashing our penlights in his eyes. He retracted himself before suddenly thrusting forward with a ghoulish, twisted expression that made us scream before he let his face revert to its own rounded, gentle self. We laughed hard at that. It was too airless to remain there all night so at some point I nudged Ella, and we slid out on our bellies and climbed into our respective beds. The second night, after we'd finally exited and tucked ourselves in, Ella said in the dark, "I love playing camp. I wish we could do it forever."

Perhaps it was my experience in the pilot program that made me literally want to cave alongside my baby sibling, for my typical retort would have been to tell her to shut up and go to sleep, or else pedantically list all the reasons that camping forever would be impossible, but I just grunted gently; I knew what she meant, for it was pure, plain fun to pretend we were out in the wild, rationing bites of our sandwiches between the fanciful tales we exchanged about toiling and surviving in the elements. I also knew that she was subconsciously worried for me in her astute Ella way, grasping my hand as we lay in the tent though completely unaware of the details of my troubles. In any other time, I would have shaken her off, but now I took comfort in her tiny clutch. She was taking cues from our parents, who had been monitoring me from a safe distance, taking care themselves not to provoke or disrupt me. No one could have reported to them what had transpired during the field trip, nor had I mentioned anything except that it was "a waste of time," but I could sense their growing apprehension about my much-diminished socializing. Along with spending more idle time with Ella, I was reading even more than usual, borrowing a double stack of books from the R. I. F. van, the titles heavily tilted to story and picture books about war, which I had become obsessed with. I'd spend hours reading about the bloodbath at Antietam or the pitched naval and aerial battles of Midway. Back then the librarians in the van or at the public library in town didn't curate as much for age, they encouraged you to take out whatever you came across and took interest in, and when I saw my poor mother paging wide-eyed through the grim photographs of bloated rotting corpses and emaciated prisoners of war and the charred Giacometti-like remains of a tank commander as he writhed to escape the burning turret, I felt no shame and even a prickle of pride. I didn't blame my mother or my father for anything that had happened in the last couple months, none of it was remotely their fault, and yet I also didn't mind their having to feel a shiver in their marrow for what I might have turned out to be.

I knew that shiver, too, and couldn't bear being alone with it.

Between the few weeks we first went shopping at the Army Navy store and the camp drop-off day, my mother and father mentioned a couple times that they realized that my birthday—my eleventh—would happen during the camp session. They seemed quite concerned about it, and I began to wonder if I should worry, too. They asked me whether I thought they should drive up with a birthday cake to celebrate, or maybe even take me to a restaurant for dinner. This itself was a stunning offer, as we ate out rarely, usually on Lunar New Year when we went to a nicer Chinese place nearby, or if my parents had a special visitor from Korea, we'd go to the city and have kalbi and naengmyeon at Woo Lae Oak, in those days the only Korean restaurant in the entire metropolitan area.

I told them not to bother coming, saying I wasn't some little kid anymore. I was fine on my own. Instead of cake, I asked for Snickers bars that I could pack in my camping gear, one for each day I was there. My mother thought a stash of fourteen bars was too many, so we settled on ten, which seemed a less unreasonable and numerically satisfying compromise. After she bought them, however, she didn't allow me to keep them in my room. As noted, I had something of an addiction to them, and so she placed them upright in one of the wide, lidded glass jars she used for fermenting her kimchi. She put the jar on the kitchen counter, making me promise not to touch them before camp, and I'd sometimes sit there and stare at them and feel madly ravenous. My mother was savvy in most things but was especially so about me, understanding that without a ready incentive I might refuse last second to attend the camp. They never forced me to do anything, but they knew my nature and their goadings and persuasions were constant.

I didn't take even one, although when I knew she wouldn't be around for a stretch I'd unscrew the metal lid, the faint, garbagey odor of kimchi taint on the lining of the lid making me hold my breath while I took the bars out one by one. As I did with my Matchbox cars, I arrayed them in a reviewing line, perfectly paralleled and squared, then I connected them end to end and ran them the length of the galley kitchen counter. I stacked them as high as I could before they toppled. I'd then build a log-style cabin with them, manning the space with a squad of my green plastic infantrymen, the bayonet-wielding grunts poking out from the gaps in the walls, the prone snipers positioned on top. I'd stick my nose in as far as I could without toppling the structure, taking in deep sharp breaths to extract any hint of that oily, nutty chocolate through the wrapping. When I heard my mother's approaching shuffle, I'd stuff the bars into the jar and shove it back into the darkened corner of the counter.

By the time I started packing for camp, all the ends of the

candy bars were dented, the wrappings scratched and worn, a condition that would normally have activated certain OCD-like urges of mine to press them flat, to renew them with my keen attentions. Yet I regarded these slovenly frayings with a new placidity, one not unlike, I allowed myself to think, that of Sir Marbles. I took this as further evidence of my not being a child anymore, someone not easily besieged by emotions. I was a boy, yes, but a boy who had traveled in secret with breathtaking speed through an unimaginable scale of space and time and ended up back in his familiar rooms a totally different creature. Everyone and everything was behind a curved wall of glass, or maybe the glass was around me, the awareness of that partition making me quiet. I felt less lonesome whenever I laid out my new camp gear: a variable-beam, foot-long flashlight that required four D-sized batteries; a heavy-duty sleeping bag, wadded with dense cotton batting; a combination pocket compass and hand mirror; my trusted magnifying glass, not just for examining bugs and plants but to kindle an emergency fire; a large, somewhat rusted canteen (a new one was too expensive); and lastly, a Swiss Army knife, one of its tools a short but vicious-looking awl. My mother wasn't sure if I should have anything like a Swiss Army knife, but I convinced her that I would need it, for the hikes and the crafts.

She had borrowed most of the items from Mrs. Fredericks, a grandmotherly neighbor down the hall whose children were grown up, and who gave my mother valuable tips on doing business at the DMV and the post office, and about where to shop economically for food and clothing, and also how to prepare some classic recipes like macaroni salad and fried chicken that would eventually take their place on the rota of our family favorites. Whenever she could Mrs. Fredericks tried to help my mother learn English, gently correcting her phrasings and teaching her new vocabulary, and you could sometimes catch the mildest West Indian lilt in my mother's speech. Mrs. Fredericks was her first non-Korean friend. She was a devout Christian and had at hand innumerable sayings about child-rearing such as "Do not embitter your children, or they will become discouraged" and "All your children will be taught by the Lord, and great will be their peace." I wouldn't be surprised if Mrs. Fredericks had offered my mother—and by the transitive property, my father—counsel on how to handle me given the recent changes in my behavior. It's the only way I can figure why despite their constant worrying and haranguing neither of them probed me too deeply on what might have happened at the penitentiary, and then also decided to hand me over to the supervision of Reverend and Mrs. Hahm and their church camp.

The camp blocked out our session at a Christian retreat and fellowship center in the upper reaches of Dutchess County, New York, about ninety miles north of Manhattan. As noted, Reverend Hahm and his counterparts coordinated the participation of other Korean churches in the tristate area, and by that summer of 1976 there would be nearly a hundred of us campers from ages seven to twelve, the range intentionally set to preclude anyone in the throes of pubescence.

Twice a day in the week before we drove up to Charminster (the name of the fellowship center), I unpacked and repacked my things from the small footlocker we got from Mrs. Fredericks. I imagined myself as the quartermaster of my troop, and that I would have to make snap decisions in various pressing moments, testing various nesting arrangements for order of priority and swiftness of pulling. The night before camp, however, I flipped the footlocker over and tossed the gear and clothing back in as I found them, everything jumbled enough to make my nerves flare with the self-torture. If I were honest with myself, I didn't want to go to camp—I had no desire for befriending a bunch of new kids, plus I was nervous about the mysterious affliction of homesickness, which Gregory Fluss had suffered the summer before at his first camp, forcing him to return home after only two days. I was afraid of missing out, too, on the camp games and water sports and sleeping in the woods, et cetera, and most of all that I wouldn't be able to say I'd experienced such things, whether any of it turned out to be fun or not.

That morning of our departure for camp my mother made a huge breakfast of a cheese omelet and hash browns and pancakes and fried Spam, which my father and Ella dug into with fervor. *Let's make this a Saturday tradition, huh?* he even suggested to my mother, who flitted her hand at him as she served me another slice of Spam. I wasn't hungry and picked at the food. She was going on in her typically exasperated rhetorical jag, concerned that I wouldn't eat sufficiently while away and fall ill because of it. What kinds of food would they serve? Would there be enough fruits and vegetables? She wondered aloud if she should quickly make some gimbap or japchae that would supplement my diet the first few days, but my father shot her down with a sharp *Are you kidding?* He rarely objected to anything she said or did, she was the clear master of our realm and the longtime object of his affections that he had somehow with great luck attained, but even he'd get milled down by her ceaseless worrying and snap at her, which could send the rest of the day into a discomfiting spiral. She gave him a cold look as he chewed his mouthful of heavy American food, and while she didn't prepare those proposed dishes for me, she slipped a few sleeves of Korean honey-dipped cookies into my rucksack as we loaded the station wagon, making me promise not to give them all away on the first day.

The drive to camp took only an hour at most, though to me it seemed we were trekking to Canada. Aside from conferrals about the mimeographed sheet of driving directions and the hand-drawn map the church had distributed during the most recent Sunday service, my parents weren't talking. I realized then how much quieter they'd been around each other the last couple months, and less physically affectionate, too. Typically, my father was always coming up and embracing her from behind, nuzzling her ear and making her laugh, but they seemed to be sitting more in the living room on the weekends and reading their own books. In my self-centeredness I assumed it was because of their overriding focus on my run of troubles, my suspect character, my ever-clouding future. From my seat behind my mother, I could lean out the window and spy her face in the sideview mirror, and then angle on my father's high cheekbone and ear in one-quarter profile, their respective sunglasses hiding their eyes. Then it rushed back to me: a muggy, overcast recent Saturday, after they returned from a doctor's appointment in the city, when for a brief volcanic moment they had shouted at each other at the top of their voices. Like any pair they could argue, they could bicker and be short with each other, but that fight was unlike any other.

They had left Ella and me at home to be watched by Mrs. Fredericks, and after my father politely thanked her, my mother headed slowly to the bathroom, hands at her midsection. My father went to her, but the door was locked, and he whispered something, but she must have rebuffed him because he slapped the panel with his open palm and came back to the living room and began preparing his pipe for a smoke. Usually, he let me bang out the old ash and then pack the burnished cherrywood bowl with tobacco for him, but I kept my distance as he rapped it against the thick rim of the stone ashtray. Then he rooted out the shank a bit too vigorously with a couple pipe cleaners he'd braided together, the cobbler-like posture of his crouching and his pinched expression the first time I realized there could be something potentially risible about him. Of course, the pose was exactly what my mother saw of me when I bent over my scale models, none of which, despite my hours of trying, turned out anything like the illustrations on the boxes and were chronically misaligned and rickety despite my efforts. He started working on his other pipes, seeming to have forgotten that his children were standing there. I gestured to Ella for us to go to our room when my mother appeared in the living room in a thin cotton robe, her eyes and nose red and puffy, and her hair still wet from a shower. It was an odd time to take a shower; she usually took one in the evenings, before bed. Her robe was splotched with dampness, and you could see her skin where the fabric clung and her shape where it didn't and the light backlit her, and in another moment I might have been either awed or embarrassed by her carnality, but she looked so wounded and mortal that I grew afraid.

Stop with the crying, okay? my father said, not looking up.

She cried, *What would you have me do?*

Do what you want. What's done is done.

I know that! she exploded, clutching at her chest. *I'm the one who knows!*

I KNOW, TOO! he shouted even louder, a blast that made Ella fall back against me. It was so loud I thought he had physically hurt himself. He'd jumped to his feet.

Don't you realize that? he shrieked, his voice splintering into an unnaturally high register. And then it happened. He broke down. That was the very first time I witnessed him cry. He stood stiffly with his head hung, bobbing on his quaking chest.

By now Ella was crying, too, terrified by what had become of her parents. She went to my mother, who winced when she took Ella gingerly into her belly. I was terrified, too. But I didn't move. I didn't go to my mother. I let my father stand alone. I loved them and Ella, they were the entirety of what I could love, and yet at that moment our spacing seemed inviolable, almost geological, like we were any chain of islands. And it wouldn't be confirmed to me until many years later what had brought them to such grief: a certain elective procedure.

But some part of me already knew it from the snippets I had caught of my parents' heated whisperings in the prior weeks. Through the thin bedroom wall, I could hear their talk, half listening and accreting but not quite to the point of understanding. My mother was always complaining about the handful Ella and I were, but this last stretch was too much. I was too much. Plus, other issues: there was too large a gap in years; they hadn't saved a single dollar for buying a first home, for college tuition; another child would only be a complication, when things were already so complicated. I don't know who wanted it initially, who ultimately ceded, or if they'd simply headed into the city, with an appointment if not fully resolved.

Sometimes I'll find myself drawn back to that day; it's as if

I'm floating down a slow, wide river and an unlikely whirlpool near a bank catches me up in its sway, and I can't help but see again the grave woundings that were my parents' faces, still so young and beautiful then. How little you can fathom the consequence of a time. Inside the moment, you do what you can, you do what you must, persisting in your own unsung way, and whether you've lived a single decade or handfuls more you can practically believe that no other grave ordeals will ever come to pass.

So it was with such faith that I gazed out on our drive to camp, calmed by the dense woods of the parkway rushing by the window of our station wagon. The summer was barely halfway done but it already felt too long. My parents were ground down and weary, mostly because of me, and I had noticed that even Ella, ever resourceful and game, seemed less active than usual, almost, dare I say, inclining to indolence, the most telling indication being that her tea set wasn't always neatly arrayed, the tiny cups and saucers, though still paired, sometimes set at the doll-sized table at odd hours of the clock rather than at exact quarter intervals, the dolls themselves slumped on one another like someone had spiked their tea. Ella was hanging around our mother more often, too, taking over my role in the kitchen to observe her dinner preparations, while I parked myself in front of the window air conditioner and watched old black-and-white movies on the television. I was preferring these to cartoons, gripped by the war movies for sure but also the tony society comedies sparked by chatty, smart-alecky ladies, and the seafaring adventures that often ended with a valiant death, and the murder mysteries set in darkened cities where everyone was edgy and hard-worn, whatever intriguing lives that could remove me from the recent stretch of my own. Escape was necessary because I knew in my bones that there would be no absolution.

My going to camp, though originally suggested as something remedial, was in fact a liberation for my family, a welcome recess for us all. I was eager for all the attendant camp activities and rituals, but the happiness I felt was for my mother and father and Ella, who I hoped could forget me for a while, or else pretend that I was a very different kind of boy, or that I didn't even exist and maybe never had, the family just them in a sturdy and flourishing triangulation. This was a scenario that played in my mind with a surprisingly warm gleam. But we can't easily forget one another or who we are. You can't cede yourself to perfect oblivion. Little could we know, nothing at all, as we began unloading my gear in the dusty, unpaved parking area of the retreat center, that my days at Camp Charminster would be a time that we couldn't help but keep recalling.

The sight of all those heads of shiny blue-black hair in one place did impress me. At our church in Flushing, Queens, children played hopscotch or tag in the parking lot after the service, but it wasn't a large congregation. Here in the camp registration lines were dozens of boys and girls, each with a set of parents and a sibling or two or three, the sheer mass of us a buzzing new colony. When we got to her folding table Mrs. Hahm informed my parents that her husband was meeting with the camp staff and would try to greet us at the cabins. Then to me she pronounced, *You and your sister have grown so much!* her voice as gravelly as a lifelong smoker's, though I'm certain she was an ascetic. She was the sharp stick in the marriage, and her comment about me was in fact directed at my parents, and at my mother particularly, to say that our attendance record at church had been disappointing of late. This was an ongoing quandary with my folks, who as noted weren't devout and went mostly for the cha and dduk social hour after the service and preferred on good-weather Sundays to take us to a park or beach but did so with enough religious guilt to put more cash in the collection basket than they could afford.

I wouldn't be surprised if this was part of Mrs. Hahm's fiscal strategy for the church. Reverend Hahm was of course the leader of the congregation, the dewy-eyed sermonizer and double-handshaker and mournful blesser of the newborn and the dead, but Mrs. Hahm was everyone else, the treasurer and CFO, the dean of the deacons, the Sunday school principal, the foreman of the volunteer maintenance crews for the buildings and grounds, the altar flower arranger, the organist, the choir conductor, the kitchen and banquet food-safety inspector, and even the parking lot controller, the job she perhaps relished most of all because it let her wield a bullhorn and a bright yellow baton. On the busiest Sundays like Easter, she directed the church lot overflow to double-park in tight formation out on narrow Bowne Street, broadcasting step-by-step instructions for my harried father as he tried to parallel park in a spot barely adequate for our long station wagon, this while a blocked local motorist leaned on his horn.

Cut it now! Cut it! Now straight back! STRAIGHT, I said! STOP!!!

I remember my father fuming in the pew, his hands testing the spine of the hymnal book.

Mrs. Hahm checked me off on her campers list and told us

the name of my cabin: "Antler." From her strained English pronunciation, we wouldn't have understood her but I read it on the sheet while she explained to my parents about there being no visiting day, but that we campers would write daily letters that would be collected and distributed to our parents at the respective churches on mid-session Sunday.

We want our children to be both God-loving and independent, yes? she said, half eyeing me with her characteristically bent smirk, an expression that made her seem more like a salty wet-market stall monger than a reverend's wife. This plus her harsh voice would have been daunting enough, but she also suffered from deeply pockmarked cheeks, scarring from what was probably a childhood bout of measles. I always wondered if the scars might still physically hurt, but even then, I thought she must have an unhealed wound in her heart, having been so visibly marked by life.

After receiving a dark blue Camp Charminster T-shirt in the next line from the youth pastor of another church, a slightly built man younger than my parents who cheerlessly introduced himself as Pastor Yi, we made our way to the row of cabins, my father and mother each holding a handle of my mini-footlocker with a duffel of my clothes on top. Ella carried a canvas laundry bag of my footwear, sneakers and sandals, and included a pair of new hiking boots—an early birthday gift from my parents—while I shouldered my rucksack. I suddenly enjoyed the feeling of my family marching with me, it was the embodiment of the idea my mother was forever drumming into me, that our campaign was in fact my campaign, and that I—and not my father—was at the head of the column as we pushed our way into all the unfamiliar territories, and I made a vow to myself that I would try to be the best camper I could be, whatever that was.

I was also struck, no doubt, with the reality that they would soon be leaving me in this remote place. The retreat center was set in an area of hills dotted with numerous lakes and ponds, a web of streams and brooks running between the bodies of water, but you couldn't make out much of the topography because of the dense stands of trees and bushy undergrowth. I was accustomed to public parks with mostly wide-open spaces and a few massive, anchoring oaks or maples, and while it was all perfectly natural and beautiful here there was something about the spectral illumination within the thickets of foliage that made me think of long-held secrets, and knowing creatures, and even death. I was afraid I might start crying.

Somehow the sight of the cabins girded me. They were certainly decrepit, looking like something out of a TV cartoon set in the West, but hoary and quaint in their modest, welcoming huddle. There were three in this cluster, other clusters down the gravel road that eventually led to the lake, all built many decades earlier in a low-slung bungalow style. The structures hadn't aged well, their rooflines swaybacked and the covered sitting porches sagging at the corners, but they had a freshness from what was likely the preferred mode of upkeep, yet another preseason coat of brick red paint slathered over the previous coats, by what was likely a crew of high school kids, the surfaces of the trim and clapboards clotted up and lardy. Freshly spray-stenciled in white on the solid porch railing of each cabin was a name. Bear Paw. Coyote Den. And now here, mine: Antler.

Ella, an early reader, saw it and hopped the three steps onto the porch, nearly colliding with a young man.

"And who might you be, darling?"

"I'm Ella!"

"What's in the bag, Ella?"

"All his shoes!" She pointed down at me like I was some callous taskmaster, or a notorious criminal.

The young man smiled, and warmly greeted me and my parents, shaking our hands as he introduced himself. My first impression, in the whirl of the moment, was that he was pale and calm. And tall; he was a full head taller than my father. His name was Benjamin Frost, going by Ben, and he was the Antler cabin counselor. This was his second summer at Charminster. He was from Vermont and was a rising junior at a nearby Bible college, where he was studying theology. After college he hoped to join the Peace Corps. When my father interpreted this information for her my mother nodded, impressed, but she also looked relieved; I wasn't conscious of her feelings then, but this would be our first extended period being apart.

Ben Frost, which is what we all naturally called him,

ushered us into the sole, large room, where several other families were settling in their sons. It smelled like old wood, and dust, and more dust, and the floor creaked whenever anyone moved. He said I should choose a bed and set up my things before we went as a group to the all-camp gathering with Reverend Hahm. Another camper and his family arrived, and he went to greet them. There were eight single beds in the room, thin mattresses with striped ticking on narrow black metal frames set four-by-four on each longer wall. I was disappointed at first, as I'd imagined we'd be camping out in tents, or at least sleeping on canvas cots like soldiers did, but there was a military-style severity and order to the room that pleased me. I placed my rucksack beside the bed farthest from the door, in the corner, where there was no window at its head, which my mother didn't like as it seemed too dark, but to me it was clearly the most secure position, in the event of what exactly I didn't know. She didn't fight me and started unpacking, arranging my clothes onto the top of the small side table we each had, as there was no cabinet or bureau. As she folded tight little stacks of my T-shirts and socks and underwear my father wondered aloud if everything might be a bit too exposed, but she snapped at him that the duffel would become an unwieldy mess with me searching for the things I'd need most often.

He muttered something and busied himself with covering the mattress with a sheet, folding under the corners like he once taught me but that I could never do. Then on top he and

Ella rolled out the heavy, lumpy sleeping bag we got from Mrs. Fredericks. I didn't care one way or the other about any of it; I was angled on the other boys, assessing them in that manner all beasts instantly and instinctively size one another up for strength, vitality, confidence, power. Only one did I know from our church, a kid named Mickey who was a year older. I'd played stickball with him and the others after services and cha and dduk time in the basement and he'd impressed me with his easy, natural athleticism and sense of fair play. There were often arguments about balls and strikes and what constituted fair or foul balls—our field was an L-shaped parking lot full of cars—and he was always quick to adjudicate with what seemed perfectly reasoned decisions. Our parents were merely acquaintances, but Mickey came right over to me and my folks and told them what a good stickball hitter I was, which was true when I made contact but I also struck out a lot, which he didn't say, and I decided that I liked him even more. My mother exclaimed how lucky it was for me to have such a nice hyung in the cabin and without prompting Mickey said he would be sure to look after me. My parents were heartened that this clearly mature and kind boy seemed willing to be my friend.

Once the rest of the other beds were claimed, Ben Frost ushered the whole group of us campers and families out to gather in front of the cabin, as it had become too hot and stuffy inside. Just then another counselor and his cabin of younger boys marched by, tossing a mini-sized football back and forth, and once the counselor had it, he flipped it to Ben Frost. “Go out,” he said to one of his campers, clearly a sportier one. “Go out and Ben will hit you.”

The kid started backing up, and Ben Frost waved him to keep going, then waved him some more, until he was really running a pass route far down the gravel road, which is when Ben Frost stepped off the front stoop and with a quick pivot chucked it, the football flying high as a cannon shot as it missiled in a tight spiral, arcing down right into the kid’s raised hands. It would have nailed him right between the eyes.

He stepped back onto the first riser and turned to us. This was when we were first able to take in the full picture of him. Standing there, he looked even taller, though he was probably not even six feet. His pale complexion was slightly sunburnt, the ruddiness just deep enough to reflect the primed vigor of an athletic twenty- or twenty-one-year-old man. You could see the musculature of his limbs and torso and shoulders from his cutoff blue-jean shorts and his somewhat worn Charminster T-shirt, this one white but with a sunburst pattern tie-dyed in blues and greens, probably the first tie-dyeing most of us immigrants had ever seen. His light brown hair was, for lack of a better description, Jesus-like, parted in the middle with the flowing locks not quite reaching his shoulders, and tied by a headband from a rolled red-and-white bandanna. Unlike Jesus, though, Ben Frost was clean-shaven, his jawline and cheekbones angular against the willowy draping of his hair, the carve of his features so different from the fleshy faces of us campers. What I liked especially were his eyeglasses, very thin silver wire frames with small round lenses that made me think of the studious-looking WWI soldiers I'd seen in photographs, and which seemed to make even more vibrant his light blue eyes. And while I'd encountered plenty of white people up to that point, most of them were kids, or middle-aged and elderly, or if youthful they were the women who were my grade-school teachers; Ben Frost was really the first young white man—not really counting the ones at the penitentiary—I was going to get to know, and who was going to get to know me, and who seemed genuinely keen to do so. It was a thrilling prospect.

"I'd like to welcome you good folks to Camp Charminster," Ben Frost said, his voice pleasingly calm but resonant and full. He didn't rush a word. You already knew he wasn't the type to ever shout. "Reverend Hahm will be giving the welcome benediction at the Forum, so I don't have much to say except that I know from my last summer as a counselor how much fun your sons will have. Two whole weeks might sound like a long time, but I promise they will pass by very quickly. We will be experiencing and learning lots of things about nature and being outdoors. We'll get acquainted with a host of skills, including how to orienteer, how to start a fire with a flint, even how to identify poisonous and edible plants. We'll be helping on a habitat conservation project here on Lake Charminster, focusing on invasive species management. Naturally, we'll also be running and climbing and swimming, plus playing every kind of sport. Your sons, I promise, will sleep soundly. They will be well fed. And please know that while you leave them here, I promise to take good care of them. We're all going to become great friends. Well, that's it. If there are any questions?"

He raised his pale hand, a rainbow-colored lanyard encircling his wrist.

The eight sets of parents were silent, some checking around, others nodding. Regardless of how much of his greeting any of them understood, or the many worries they might have had about their kids being at the camp, they seemed assured by this gentle, confident young man who was the very picture of health and sanity. I noticed he looked everybody in the eye, not missing anyone, including me and my family, who were standing off to the side. Nobody asked anything, but the silence wasn't awkward.

"Well, thanks again." Ben Frost stepped down and gathered us campers in a circle. "Now, guys, let's have our first cabin cheer."

He hovered his hand in the middle, and we piled ours on his. Mine was almost at the top, as I wasn't quick enough.

"Okay, now. Let's do 'Antlers' on three. And loud. I mean *loud*. Got it?" We were wide-eyed, already game.

"One . . . two . . . three . . ."

"ANTLERS!"

I had not uttered the word before and yet it burst off my tongue as though I were sounding a last clarion for my life. It must have been like that for the others, too, from the roar we made. The shudder in my chest from our instant chorus nearly made me tear up—nothing can stir me more than an impromptu solidarity—and I had the urge to hug these boy strangers, and not because they looked like me. In fact, I wanted to hug Ben Frost just as much, if not more, for somehow it seemed that it was he (and not Reverend Hahm or the church association or my parents) who had delivered me to this place, it was he who would close this new circle and make it special and real.

Groups from the neighboring cabins were heading to the spot where Reverend Hahm would be addressing everyone and we followed them, Antlers in close formation around our leader, the families trailing behind us. A boost of gratuitous confidence lifted me. I kept glancing back to see my parents walking hand in hand, Ella to the side skipping in time with another little girl. During the car ride and while unpacking and setting up I had been trying hard not to picture bidding them goodbye; mostly I was frightened of how fearful or sad I might feel, it nauseated me to know I might not be able to master my emotions, but now I could look upon my mother's face and think only of how beautiful she was, so much prettier than the other mothers, who were coarse in their features, or else too made up, and then of how lucky my father was to be married to her, something I had heard his friends joke about more than once, and that he would sometimes utter, himself in a way that suggested he was undeserving of her.

Did I think this, too? Of course I did. We were all undeserving of her, I foremost because of how deeply I convinced myself into believing the opposite. My deserving her was a fate long determined, and now with the advent of this impressive Ben Frost and surrounded by cabinmates, I didn't feel any desperation about being separated from her, I wasn't scared or sad in the least. When we reached the place that seasoned Charminsters called the Forum, a semicircular open theater with three rows of wooden bench sections set into a wide, grassy embankment, I stuck with the quorum of us Antlers that hadn't drifted back to be with their folks as Reverend Hahm took his spot at center stage with the ragged Bible he always carried around while awaiting the last few stragglers. Beside me was a slightly bucktoothed kid who offered his hand and introduced himself as Min-Young but said that I should call him Recipe. I told him that's a funny nickname and right away he started to explain that he didn't cook or even love eating but loved collecting recipes that he'd cut out of the newspaper or magazines. Then Reverend Hahm began to speak in those especially sonorous tones he used from the pulpit. My Korean wasn't good enough to understand much of his sermons, and I couldn't decipher any more now save his regular entreaties to "Our Lord in Heaven" and "Jesus Christ" to guide us in what was righteous and good, and that we be safe and thrive in their everlasting love. My family sat near the other end of the semicircle, my mother trying to catch my attention, but I averted my gaze, focusing on the stainless-steel lighter that Recipe was furtively showing me. "Our campfires are gonna blaze," he whispered, the devil dancing in his eyes.

As my parents often noted, Reverend Hahm wasn't a natural orator, you could even say he was a consummately awful speaker, tentative and halting, even stuttering sometimes, but he was also humble and kind and never overbearing or dictatorial like other Korean pastors could be about their parishioners' levels of devotion. Unlike Mrs. Hahm, who relished keeping her people in line, the reverend was most comfortable in his own head, happy to study and contemplate Scripture for its own sake, something I saw him do in the rectory even after the service while the rest of the congregation mingled at the social hour.

By the time Reverend Hahm offered a *second* closing prayer, the primed July sun had vaulted to its zenith, the brutal combination leaving us wilted on the benches like pulled weeds. Even Recipe, who had been entertaining me through much of the droning benediction and endless blessings with his self-deprecating asides ("I don't know what stinks more, my feet or my breath," "When I squint my slitty eyes see even better. Same with you?"), had dipped his head between his knees, while kneading at his face with such vigor that I thought he might disfigure himself. Down a row a mother was propping up a listless young girl whose mouth hung open, likely from heatstroke. I checked on my family and my father, who for some reason had brought a Sunday blazer, was tenting it over the three of them. Reverend Hahm was bedraggled himself, his thinning hair dewy with perspiration, his soaked white dress shirt clinging to his chest with the somewhat lewd effect of revealing his brown nipples. Only Mrs. Hahm was seemingly unaffected, her tightly permed curls still crisp and springy as she pierced our collective haze after her husband had uttered his final *Ha-na-nims* with an announcement of the goodbye picnic lunch that was now ready outside the dining hall. I never saw a crowd of that size move with such concerted haste.

On long folding tables the dining staff had set out boiled hot dogs and buns and condiments along with huge bowls of macaroni salad and potato chips and aluminum pitchers of bloodred "bug juice," a powdered generic food-service punch that they would mix up by the vat. At the dessert table a silver-haired Black man in an apron—we'd soon learn he was the longtime camp cook, Mr. Hammonds—was cutting up large sheet pans of brownies, his white teenage helpers placing the squares on paper plates and spooning dollops of whipped cream on them. You could see Ella and the other noncamper siblings realizing just how much they would be missing out on, all this exemplary American food served in quantities that made you feel almost royal. I was eating with the other Antlers while Ben Frost told us about the traditional cabin relay race we'd have after our parents left, which only made me want them to depart sooner. *Leave us alone already! Let us have our fun!* But when Mrs. Hahm blared over the bullhorn that the luncheon was over and it was time for families to say goodbye, the bottom of my stomach dropped away, the two hot dogs and mound of macaroni salad I'd barely chewed threatening to flee me in a torrent. It was a habit/problem/reaction I could have to the suddenly stressful. Luckily my father waved with a gesture of "So long" that also bid me to stay put with my new group, and before I could wave back or start for them, he'd ushered my mother and Ella toward the parking field. I turned back to my cabinmates but snuck a last glance at them to notice that my mother, despite the heat, had tipped her head into my father's neck as they walked away, from the heat or heartache I could not know. Ella, though, caught me looking. I didn't wave to her, and she didn't wave to me, just keeping me in her gaze until they reached a bend in the gravel road, and they disappeared.

Recipe didn't like his brownie, and I ate the rest immediately after he offered it; I was suddenly craving fuel, or succor, or both. And looking out at the heads of all these similarly black-haired, pale-skinned campers, I had the strangest urge to pick a fight with one of them, to bruise and to be bruised, it was like tasting the iron of your own bloodied lip and sucking some more. Ben Frost had us introduce ourselves: name, where we were from, our favorite food and sport. It was difficult to register all the information, the overriding notion from the answers being that we were not as alike as we might have thought and came from many different places in and around New York City, along with one kid from Philadelphia, another all the way from Virginia. Then he had us count out. I wanted number five because it was my mother's lucky number, but a kid with a big kinky head of hair already beat me to it and so I waited for number eight, the last, which happened to be my Little League uniform number. "This will be your racing number," Ben Frost informed us, which made us all stand a bit taller. Before I could think too much of what this meant for me, we Antlers marched to the main playfield, a wide stretch of weedy, poky grass that was neither particularly rectangular nor flat, a gently wavy meadow that had been cleared of stumps and mown. The other cabin groups were there now, too, the huddled squadrons of us standing about the pitch while our counselors set up cones for the relay races.

The competition was divided between girls and boys, then contested by age, though because there weren't even numbers of groups the counselors arranged some kind of double elimination round-robin that was hard to make sense of, but it didn't matter, none of us cared, we were silently hyped up and tense as we scanned the two other cabins in our elevens and twelves boys' group, looking for clues to their athleticism as we unconsciously limbered up. I was technically still ten, and a few of them looked a lot older, filled out in the chest and arms. We watched the younger kids first, some of them agile little sprinters, others having big trouble with the uneven ground and falling. Everyone was quiet at the start but then we all started screaming, shouting. Though they didn't go head-to-head, the younger girls were clearly faster than the younger boys, which gave us the resolve not to let ourselves get shown up. When it was our turn, Ben Frost surprised us by saying that we'd go in reverse order, which meant I was leading off, and as I crouched at the start cone awaiting the whistle I could hardly breathe for the clotting in my throat. The sprint to the cone was probably no more than thirty yards there and back but I was so nervy I lost feeling in my thighs halfway there and stumbled badly and the kid I was up against scooted around the cone well ahead of me. He grinned archly as he passed by, his fat tongue glistening. Something in me fired then, a gapped circuit reattached, and had I been gripping the Knife I would have slashed his Achilles; I could feel the ground under my feet again, the pressing angle of a new gravity. I veered tightly around the cone. There was an uptick of shouting, and I was sure I could hear Ben Frost's voice calling my name above the din. And though I had no chance of catching my taunting opponent I tagged Mickey, who was just a few strides behind him.

Mickey made up most of the deficit in his turn and within the next two legs our cabinmates had us ahead. We won by nearly a whole length. As the next race was being set up, we slapped low and high fives all around, butting shoulders and shoving one another, euphoric with the idea that our group might be special, maybe even elite, which a returning camper, a wide-faced, owlish boy named David, confirmed with the pronouncement, "This is one truckin' gang."

I loved the sound of that, plus was relieved that my miserable stumble hadn't mattered. The next race was going strong and my near failing seemed long past, if not forgotten. This scandalously rutted field wasn't going to trip me up again, I would jet down the line and slingshot myself around the cone and spot my team an insurmountable lead. My ears were filling with the hollers, the huzzahs, my vain and prideful heart ready to spill open with haughty song, yet mute would I remain. Antlers are divine. . . .

But it was *this race* that was making everyone crazy. I finally woke up to the fact that it was the remaining cabin of boys our age against the lone older girls' cabin of twelve- and thirteen-year-olds. There was no correspondingly aged boys' cabin, something we didn't quite register or think about then, but it was clearly a purposeful exclusion on the part of the church association. These girls seemed older than that, some of them curvy and chesty, some tall and rangy, all of them looking keen, maybe a little dangerous. They certainly didn't want to lose to a bunch of immature boys. The ones awaiting their turn sprinted in place, they stretched their tanned calves, they waved their superb hair back and forth like silken lassos.

Yet it was a girl with somewhat shorter hair who caught my eye, she reminded me of one of the characters in a manga that a friend back at the apartments once showed me, the chin-length cut of it angled to fall over one eye and cheek. It was like a swaying curtain, hiding her and not hiding her.

Was she looking at me? I didn't know but I couldn't help but keep checking. Then it was her turn to run, and she very casually stepped to the line, standing upright with her hands on her hips instead of getting low and ready. When her cabinmate tagged her hand, she started off, though not bolting, more like loping, these initially languid trots that grew longer and longer with each stride until she was eating up the ground in these wondrous, quickening gallops. We couldn't know it, we had no conception of such a thing, but she had real coaching; it would turn out her parents had run track for the Korean national team. The patchy field was no matter, her opponent no matter, it seemed she was hardly exerting herself for how still her torso stayed while her arms and legs worked, her acceleration steadily building until she was moving at her top speed. At the cone she didn't so much turn as jump-stop, pivoting 180 degrees to gear up again and jet back at us, her rakish bob flaring like a careering sparrow.

"Holy schmuck-oly," Recipe moaned.

Another half length and she would have lapped the poor boy running against her. There was only one girl to run after her, and she could have skipped their cabin to a win, which seemed to the legion of us dim, chauvinistic boys an outcome both miraculous and tragic, when in fact it was totally predictable. But then it happened; after rounding the cone, the girl after the manga girl fell. I thought she had simply stumbled as I did, but when she tried to get up, she immediately collapsed, crying out. The last boy slowed for a moment as he approached her before realizing his lucky break, and he ran with a frantic, gleeful crimp to his face as he passed her on his return. At the finish line his cabin mobbed him like he was a rock star. Counselors were attending to the girl, who had clearly turned her ankle. For the rest of the session, she would slightly hobble about but didn't appear in the least unhappy about it.

I was focused on the manga girl's reaction to it all, but like her cabinmates she was solely concerned about the injured one, already past caring about some inane competition. After the girl was helped to the infirmary the manga girl stood a bit away from the rest, surveying the scene, the crowd. She pushed the hair from her face and her sweat-dampened temple. She let it fall but then ran the fat of her palm against her lips, I was almost certain, to try the saltiness. I'd do that, too, sometimes, taste test my various secretions, leakings, sloughings, no matter how vile. I decided I liked everything about her, her hair, yes, and her veiled eyes, her truly miraculous speed, but most of all the fine, clean angles of her elbows and knees, which seemed to me immaculate.

Meanwhile my fellow Antlers were going over strategy about the final race against these undeserving winners, who were the Coyotes, though it was obvious to us that they were no less athletic than we were. A big, swaggering kid named Jimmy Choi who had made clear to us that he was a returning camper at Charminster was arguing that Mickey should start instead of me in order to get us a solid lead, and that another fast runner, Sang from Queens (we had another Sang, whom we'd call Sang II, from Philly), should run either fourth or fifth, to close any deficit. He himself would run the anchor leg, because he hated nothing more than losing. Recipe laughed loudly and said somebody was dreaming about being a camp counselor someday. Jimmy Choi told Recipe that he ran like a duck and to shut up, which prompted Recipe to waddle up to him with his chest puffed out and his white buckers gleaming from flared duck lips and started hugging him with stiff, winging arms. Jimmy Choi was about to swing at him, but Mickey stepped between them just as Ben Frost reappeared after helping the girl with the other counselors.

"Good you guys are getting psyched up for the last race," he said all around, eyeing Jimmy. "But we'll stick with our numbers again. Got to have faith, right?" He extended his expansive, pale hand and we already knew to stack our small damp paws on top.

"One, two, three . . ."

"Antlers!"

As we broke Ben Frost thumbs-upped a kid named Peter, who had unpacked a lot of fancy-looking clothes and was from Connecticut: "Get ready, number one."

A little whoop of a cheer went up, but my breath had snagged, and I couldn't make a sound: we would go in normal order. Jimmy Choi was now stealing glances at me, as were the Sangs, along with even Recipe, who smiled tightly, trying but failing to gird me. In a way I was measuring me, too, as I had stepped out of myself and was replaying my fall and desperate, awkward scramble to get back on my feet. I began to see the wisdom of the egoistic Jimmy Choi. Mickey nudged me in the chest.

"You'll be fine, J.-G. Just run like a mean dog is chasing you."

This final race would cap the opening day, and the whole camp population was spectating, even the dining-hall staff. The Coyotes were being exhorted with lots of waving and hand gestures by their counselor, Herman, who was nothing like the fit and scrubbed Ben Frost, and instead the sort of unshaven young man I sometimes saw around the community college back home, often carrying a bunch of books or a guitar. Herman was competitive, however, and had successfully pumped up his campers, who looked primed and ruddy from the race against the older girls and were now bent on recovering their man/boyhood by utterly destroying us. To the casual onlooker they surely looked very much like us Antlers, but we already knew the truth: they were our antitheses, lurking and angling and thirsting to exploit, whereas we were sociable, comrade-loving, keen on doing things right.

There was one of them, though, who stood out. I don't know if he was the tallest boy in the camp, or the most muscular, but there was a manly broadness to his frame that made you think he was filled with an ever-powering breath and could hike up a steep hill or push against something tirelessly. He seemed older, too, but maybe it was the way his hair had a softly wavy comb-over rather than the basic, straight-down bowl cut the rest of us sported, reminding me of a picture of a young Winston Churchill in one of the many military history picture books I would borrow and serially renew. I noticed one older girl staring right at him and she somehow sensed my attention and our eyes met and she looked away, blushing. He drew other gazes, too, in the way especially impressive-looking people do, creating a sudden vortex wherever they were, like Cleon back home. Strangely, he had a similar look to the manga girl, and I realized that they could be the live boy and girl versions of Go Mifune in the *Speed Racer* cartoon, a character who (though I couldn't have articulated it then) struck me as androgynous. Watching the show, I imagined looking like him, handsome in that smoothly honed way when in fact I was the opposite, being doughy and roundish of face. This boy was now crouched at the starting line in a ready stance, his mouth pursed like he was drawing off a slightly bitter candy that he was nonetheless going to finish.

Two female counselors, Dahlia and Brenda, chanted in unison, "Ready, set, GO!" and the race started: the boy running leadoff against our (literal) fancy-pants Peter charged immediately to a huge lead and sprinted back a full half length ahead, poor Peter looking like he was running through thick, tall grass. But our next guys, Jimmy Choi and Mickey, ran with athletic, controlled fury, and by the middle of the race it had become a tight contest, with the Sangs getting even and Recipe, surprisingly, breaking into a lead. But then David, who frankly didn't seem terribly interested in the games, was loafing his turn, craning around like he was taking in a memory, and it grew clear this now neck and neck race would come down to the anchors. I felt Coyotes' gazes filtering out my mates and squaring on me, the Stumbler. Their anchor runner was already hopping up and down with glee, like I was a $5 bill left on the sidewalk. He was on the smaller side, with a pointy, otterish face, not physically impressive but looking lithe and speedy, and just before we got (nearly simultaneously) tagged, the kid made a pistol of his fingers, aimed right between my eyes, and pulled the trigger.

His nonchalance made me hesitate, and I watched him bolt away. I must have stood there for a full second. In the background I could hear Jimmy Choi, shrieking like I was sawing him in half. Recipe was jumping up and down, tugging at his own hair. It seemed that the whole crowd was raining down urgings, epithets, howls of disbelief; among them, I was sure I heard, a minor-keyed murmur from Ben Frost, a pained *J.-G.?* that made me lose the feeling in my legs. And I might have collapsed on my butt right there were it not for the manga girl, whose fluttering, uplifted hands somehow cut through the fog of my panic, her expression of bewilderment an uncanny combination of my mother's face of long-suffering disappointment and the arch curiosity of Katie Croker.

Like Mickey advised, I ran for my life. I was blind to everything but the ground barreling under me. I had drunk too much lemonade and had to pee and maybe this boosted me. I would have liked to think that I vanquished a worthy foe, but it turned out the kid was a thoroughly average runner, and I beat him with room to spare. The Antlers went wild, knocking me about in a giddy scrum. As the defeated will do, the Coyotes couldn't help but linger, heads hanging as they observed our flagrant celebration. My opponent was squatting a little off by himself at an awkward distance, giving a tiny miserable shake of his tiny miserable head. Did I love seeing that? I must have, because I was about to aim my finger at him and pull the trigger, too, but held back, though not from any sporting ethos. More, I was mentally preparing to be the focus of a jubilant if modest medal or ribbon presentation where I would be gracious and humble, but it happened that there weren't even any closing remarks, all the counselors and campers dispersing in various directions.

Some were heading back to their cabins, others going off to see the lake or do a short nearby hike, while our cabin decided to toss around the mini-sized football that Ben had thrown earlier. We were still surging with adrenaline plus wanting subconsciously to make a public display of our wide-ranging athleticism. We split up and stood at opposite ends of the field and took turns seeing who could throw and kick the ball the farthest, with Mickey proving to be the longest passer and Jimmy Choi the longest punter. Jimmy Choi, being Jimmy Choi, had to keep highlighting the fact, and he boomed one after another over our heads. One of them went long but awry and bounced hard toward the main gravel road of the camp, ending up beside a rusty old-fashioned well pump that was penned in by an unkempt hedge on two sides. I retrieved it and flipped it to David, who was trailing me, but I stayed back, suddenly craving water. I pumped the lever a few times, then bent down to catch the sudden gush with both hands, when I felt a tap on my shoulder.

It was the kid with the wavy hair, the impressive boy. Peering up like that, I thought he was as tall as a counselor, and I raised my hands full of water to him. I still remember my thinking: *It's so nice and cold, it'll taste good, you'll see.* I was ready for his acknowledgment, if not acceptance, when he surprised me by turning slightly away.

It was then he reared back and kicked me hard in the chest.

What exactly happened after that is something I still go over now and then. It's like any signal moment in the past; there's the flash of sensation, whatever it was that made your body thump, and then there are the details that are warped by that very pulsing and then by the strange gravity of time, all according to what you needed then or wish for now.

The first thing I needed to understand was why. I had merely offered him some water. Was it insulting that I was using a cup of my own hands? Was it too intimate, even gross? He could have simply declined or even shoved my hands away. Instead, the rubber toe of his sneaker caught me in the sternum, the blow so perfectly centered that it knocked me flat. I swear I heard a crack. Despite this there was no immediate pain, more a cloudburst of astonishment that what was happening was happening, and that it was happening to me. What followed was a subtle spatial-temporal aberration; eyes still closed, I could almost believe this whole scenario was a hoax, a perpetration of some malign higher power. Yet here was the boy, looming in blurred silhouette as the sun glared behind him. That's when a knifing ache pierced me as if my lung had also been punctured, that's when I started to whimper, wheezing fast, and started to cry.

"Take it easy," he said, kneeling to curl his arm around my neck and shoulder, to sit me up. Was this the same person, or had that other person kicked me and run off?

"Just breathe."

I did what he said, trying to slow down and calm my huffing. Meanwhile I was searching his face, which was serenely empty and betraying nothing except a completely humane concern for me, as if I'd accidentally tripped while he was ambling by.

"You're a good runner," he stated. He nodded with not a little deliberation. "Really fast and good."

I didn't like what he was saying, or how he was saying it, and I was going to protest, tell him that nothing about this was good or right, when in one swift snatch he pulled me up to my feet. He was at most a half-head taller than me but much, much stronger. Then, as if with the cheery vigor of having just made a new friend, he shook my hand. I found I was somehow shaking happily back.

"You should run more. You know what I mean?"

We stood there for a moment. I thought he would leave but instead his half-agape stare made it clear that he was waiting for me, and so I walked back to my still-playing cabinmates, turning to see him on the other side of the hedge, pumping the lever.

I rejoined my side and even caught a ball and then punted it back, when Recipe started staring at me.

"What the heck happened, J.-G.?" He was tapping fast below the corner of his eye. I touched my own cheek and something stung.

"I think I tripped."

"But you got cut!"

My index finger was smudged with blood, and I had the reaction I always had when I was a child at the sight of my blood, my thoughts racing from panic to shame to bracing for the alarm of my appalled mother, who would inevitably lament herself and the world for my carelessness, her seething tone an oddly cooling salve.

"Is it bad?"

Recipe peered gravely into the wound.

"We need to go to the infirmary!"

Somebody found out where it was and it ended up that Recipe and Mickey hustled me over to what looked like just another cabin, where an older white lady with long, straight salt-and-pepper hair was replenishing a glass-paneled cupboard from a box of first aid supplies. She made Recipe and Mickey wait outside as she blotted my cheek with iodine, having ground out her cigarette in a big plastic ashtray littered with butts. She'd shown my wound to me with a hand mirror; it was a small, rough-edged gash high on my cheekbone that was no longer bleeding.

"This is going to bruise up for sure," she said, gently probing around it. Her hand smelled sharply of ash and so did her breath, but she didn't have that smoker's rasp, her voice more a buttery, low bell. Her face reminded me of certain actresses in the old movies I'd been watching a lot of, wholesomely lovely like Virginia Mayo, or clever-faced but still pretty like Maureen O'Hara, but a version much harder used by time and whatever else.

"So, champ, should I be worried about what the other kid looks like?"

No, he's fine, I was about to say, when I realized she was joking. I stayed quiet then and her expression softened. She dabbed me once more with the antiseptic-soaked cotton ball and took out a bandage, but the little gauze pad wasn't quite big enough. She retrieved a larger, winged one from the cupboard, but when she held it against my cheek, we simultaneously realized that it would look funny, if not totally ridiculous.

"It's not deep and already coming together, so I think we can leave it bare. Just don't touch it, okay?"

"But can I swim tomorrow? They're going to give us the swim test."

"You sure can." She raked my hair back, her fingertips

soft against my temple. "If you want to tell me about something, hon, I'm good at keeping a secret."

While she gazed at me, I pieced together that I had probably struck the end of the well pump lever as I was falling back—it had been that close to poking out my eye. The thought made me shiver and I told myself not to cry when she leaned closer and wrapped her fleshy, freckly arm around me. As I was leaving, she gave me a coffee-flavored hard candy, which tasted just like how my mother took her coffee in the morning, two teaspoons of Sanka with lots of sugar and Coffeemate.

She gave me another wrapped candy and extra pieces for Mickey and Recipe and we sucked on them as we walked back to our cabin, Recipe going on about how I could be in one of the street gangs in his bad neighborhood in Queens, with my copper-stained wound and the dark purplish bruising that was now developing around it.

"You must have landed right on your face!" he cried. "What a badass!"

Mickey chimed, "Right on," though I could tell he wasn't totally convinced by Recipe's characterization of my mishap. I wanted to tell them about how the hard rubber toe of the kid's sneaker left what felt like a permanent dent in my breastbone, about how he was so calm and strange after that and that I wasn't sure what had happened. Most of all I wanted to tell an adult, or better, Ben Frost, who could be my righteous angel of vengeance, but then I realized my mother and father would end up having to know, too, and I could already picture the defeat in their eyes: *Really, Jeon-Gi-ya? Even here, among Korean kids? Why is trouble your twin?* They'd argue not with me but with each other, the heat in their voices having only grown more acute after that day they had come home from "the doctor." Who could endure another me?

As we made our way back, passing by the older girls' cabin of the Snow Leopards, two of the girls came straight out to us; neither of them was the manga girl. They were Julie and Peggy, both kind of brash, and they acted like they were our older sisters, which was why they were so comfortable telling us who they were and asking our names and what happened to my face. I told them what I told the infirmary lady, which they didn't think twice about.

"At first I didn't think you were gonna win, tough guy," Julie said to me. Her big moon face and thick Brooklyn accent were a surprisingly winning combination. "But boy, did ya. You came on strong! That kid you beat wasn't too happy about it."

"And neither was his brother!" Peggy said.

"You mean the hunky one?" Julie asked.

"I guess so," Peggy mumbled, cagey. But we all knew whom Julie was talking about, nobody questioning Recipe when he declared, "That kid is built."

Julie asked her how she knew them and Peggy, who was impressive in a grown-up way, maybe because she had naturally double eyelids and an upright, regal posture, said, "Their family goes to our church. The Rhos. You were running against the younger one, Hardy. His older brother is Dickens."

"*Hardy* and *Dickens*?" Recipe squealed. "What kind of names are those?"

"Famous authors," Peggy confidently answered. You could tell she was sharp, but also the kind who liked explaining things. "My dad said their dad loved books, so he named them after his favorite authors. *British*."

"Super weird!" Recipe proclaimed.

"But how old is Dickens?" Mickey asked.

Peggy had already caught his drift and said, "He's twelve but got left back a year and so he and Hardy are in the same grade."

"What's he dumb or something?" Julie said.

Peggy shook her head. "When he came it was first grade and he didn't know any English so they kept him back." She paused. "He's adopted."

"Really," Julie said, even more intrigued. "I guess that's why they don't look like brothers. I mean, the little one looks like a mean squirrel. Dickens is more like a friendly lion."

Mickey ventured, "Maybe he's not Korean."

This was a possibility that even Peggy had not yet entertained, and I'm sure we were all picturing his face and parsing each feature and wondering if he fit our conception of what a Korean boy should be like, not to mention wondering why he'd been adopted. Had his parents been too poor to raise him? Were they dead? I was thinking that this was the reason his demeanor could be so null, even after kicking me: Maybe the world was dead to him.

"I bet he is," Julie said. "But even if he's Chinese or something, what's it matter?"

"It matters if you want to marry and have babies with him!" Recipe blurted. All of us cackled—even me—and Julie play-slapped at Recipe's head and I know Mickey and I were both jealous when she and Peggy surrounded him and started giving him gentle noogies, which Recipe pretended hurt. Then another Snow Leopard appeared on the porch to say their counselor was starting their cabin meeting and we simply muttered goodbye and went on our way, saying nothing about meeting them again, the fact that the three of us didn't confer about how cool Julie and Peggy were a glaring confirmation of our immaturity. I glanced back as they ascended the short stairs and that's when I saw her, the manga girl, now standing there with her hands on top of the railing. Mickey said something about how great this camp was going to be and we concurred, and when I looked back again I thought the girl was giving me the smallest wave of one hand. But I was too shy to wave back.

When we entered the bunk room of our cabin Ben Frost declared, "The secret weapon of Antlers '76 has returned!" and the rest of the boys crowded around me, offering high fives for closing out our victory, bumping me on the shoulder, and mussing the crown of my head, the heady tangle of them unlike anything I'd experienced back at the playfields of Cove Gardens. Even haughty Jimmy Choi was plying me with feinting rabbit jabs to my gut, then cuffed me in a brief headlock before Mickey warned him to be careful of my wound. But I didn't mind; I was immersed enough in all the happy jousting that I'd forgotten the reason I'd gone to the infirmary, at least until somebody nudged my chest with a stray elbow and the tenderness made me catch my breath.

Once the hoopla subsided, Ben Frost announced that before going to dinner we would go over some rules and procedures and then do a practice cabin cleanup. Everyone groaned, but he was firm: "We have to do a run-through, because this place will become a horse stable otherwise. Ready, gentlemen? Let's go!"

Eager to please and impress Ben Frost, we threw ourselves into the work, taking shifts with the mops and brooms. It was obviously the first time most of us ever did anything of the sort; this was certainly my case, as my mother did all the house chores herself. Peter, the kid with the nice clothes, had to be shown how to use the broom, as he was violently jabbing at the wooden planks of the flooring, as if to scour them. Some boys got the window duty, wiping the mullions and panes and clearing dried-up insects from the sills. Others swept the porch. I was going full throttle with the toilet brush when Ben Frost appeared in the opened stall door and informed me that the yellow staining was from rust and not pee, and that I could stop now. Apparently, everyone else had finished up. I helped him put away the rest of the bathroom cleaning supplies in an old gray steel locker, then we washed our hands in the same basin, taking turns to rinse the soap.

He took a closer look at my cut and bruise.

"Maybe we should call you J. F. instead," he said, mussing my hair. I shrugged and he said, "Joe Frazier." We both laughed. He couldn't know that I'd watched replays of all three of his fights with Ali, and multiple times, and always rooted for Frazier because he was smaller and more serious, not so cocky. He was tenacious and purposeful. I hated that he lost those last two fights, and the picture of Joe Frazier's swollen, defeated face almost made me say aloud what this Dickens Rho had done to me. But the words wouldn't come out. I was silenced by the thought of how captivated Julie and Peggy had been simply talking about him, how intrigued Recipe and Mickey were by his funny name and murky background, and now I was mad at myself for not assuring him that I wouldn't tell anyone, so that he might easily forget the whole thing, too.

"You're going to have a wonderful time here at camp, J.-G.," he said, shaking the water off his hands. "It might seem like bad luck to have to go to the infirmary on the first day, but things will only be better. It'll be fun times. I promise."

I didn't say anything, nodding like I believed him. I certainly wanted to believe him. And yet soon after, while the garrulous troop of us Antlers marched to the mess hall for dinner, I straggled at the rear, preoccupied with the idea that

I might be the kind of person certain bad things happened to. Was there some quality I possessed that inspired kids like Katie Croker and Joshua Messing and Tommy Reilly and an otherwise impressive Korean camper to become my tormentors, my mistreaters? Did I have a certain look? In college, acquaintances and even some of my good friends would say I had a smugness to my expression that bordered on being irritating, which I'm sure is true, but I don't think I featured such a thing when I was younger, if anything I was too earnest and ready for whatever was on offer and perhaps this was the problem: Aren't there those who despise such keenness and want to knock it dull? Or did I look like I deserved trouble because I couldn't help but keep wondering when my fortune would turn? Perhaps it doesn't matter. The truth is that whether I was destined from birth to be like this or warped by my recent commissions and trials, by the time I got to Camp Charminster I was nothing like an innocent.

It was easy to keep a low profile those first couple days, which were a blur of introductions to camp activities and practices. While certain things had been instituted only for our group of Korean kids, such as the bilingual Bible study every day after breakfast, countless church groups and religious organizations had camped at Charminster, each cohort slotting their charges into the template of the daily and weekly schedule that over the years had become firm tradition. For example, swim time would commence at 1:00 p.m., to allow for an hour plus of rest after lunch at 11:30 a.m. (this is how quickly we ate), and arts and crafts would follow Bible study every other day, cabins and grounds cleanup on the others, with sports of all kinds allotted afternoons right up until dinner. The session would feature certain special events: a bonfire, an Olympic-style athletics context, and finally an arduous hike and double overnight in tents to commemorate how accomplished we had become as outdoorspeople.

Naturally kids had their preferred activities and events, most of the girls enjoying the crafting more than the sports, the reverse for us boys, everyone equally loving the swim time. I would say that without exception the Bible study was the most loathed hour on the schedule, even for the kids who seemed to pray hard, their eyes closed extra tight during the premeal benedictions. These days there must be kid-oriented Bible study syllabi employing lots of pictures and videos and games, but back then it was old-fashioned lessons about Faith and Salvation, Sacrifice and Suffering, told through the stories of people like Abraham and Jonah and Job, plus readings from Scripture that Reverend Hahm would recite and then speak about at length in his thick Korean-accented English, little of which got through to us. The young Pastor Yi was more fiery, almost aggressive in how he'd pick one of us to interrogate with questions such as what we'd done recently to demonstrate our devotion to Jesus Christ and show obvious frustration when the poor kid couldn't muster an answer. If I had to choose, my preferred instructor was Mrs. Hahm, who'd go over in vivid detail the excruciating trials of biblical figures with a relish that bordered on the sadistic, though you could sense her eyes were lighting up extra bright with visions of us feckless, spoiled kids in their stead.

What was universally beloved was having the meals in the dining hall. We'd drop everything and sprint over whenever they clanged the bell, a one-half-scale replica of the Liberty Bell, right down to the crack. I'm sure the food was passable at best, much of it coming from the emptied food-service-sized cans that you could see piled up in the garbage bins outside the back kitchen door, green beans and beets and cut corn and spinach, but we were always seemingly half starved from the constant activity and didn't hesitate to shovel our share onto our plates, especially the from-scratch dishes like fried chicken and chili and meatloaf and baked pork chops that could have been served in an old-time diner. In fact, we were thrilled not to see any even remotely Asian-style dishes, thrilled not to taste flavorings of garlic or ginger or scallion, or sniff any kimchi gases. This was straight-up American food, wholesome, facile, and inert, and we adored it. I particularly appreciated that no matter what was served, a platter of white bread slices always came as accompaniment, along with ice cream scoops of margarine.

The building where we ate was by far the largest at Camp Charminster, a Queen Anne–style mansion that was surely the hub of some wealthy person's country property before it was sold or donated to the Christian organization. The mansion's main floor had been blown out to be the sprawling dining hall, with most of the former walls taken down—you could see the ghosts of them in the tracks of replaced flooring—and support posts trisecting the space, the one remnant of the former layout being a wide wooden staircase near the head of the room that led to the second floor, where there were bedrooms and camp offices. The house smelled like most everything did at Charminster, of ancient wood that was powdery with dry rot and then of an errant sweetness from the husks of a million insects, the place like some giant, neglected closet. There was also the heavy scent of cooking oil, both hotly fresh as it was frying and crudded and stale on the walls and ceiling, and the deep hums and rumblings of the walk-in refrigerators and massive exhaust hood radiating out from the large banquet kitchen that during the prayer you could almost feel through the legs of your chair.

Outside there would be crowding on the wide grand stair to the entrance and when one of the kitchen helpers opened the double doors everybody bull-rushed into the space furnished with round plywood-top tables, scrambling for seats like they were playing musical chairs even though there was a designated table for each cabin, a chair for each camper. Maybe it was that inaugurating relay race, or that they ran out of hot dogs at the first picnic lunch and some kids got only macaroni salad to eat, but there was a dual ethos of competition and scarcity at Charminster that seemed antithetical to what you'd think would be the tenets of unconditional generosity and shared sacrifice in a loving Christian community.

The first night, we only revved harder when the counselors described to us how dinner was served, which was that a kid from each cabin table would be the "waiter" to the mess line in the kitchen, each bearing one of the large oval trays already stacked on the table as they race-walked to the mess line. Anyone running would be flagged and sent to the end of the line. The little kids got staged first, as some needed adult help, and then the rest of us would be released with an olé wave from Mrs. Hahm. You could tell from the incited expressions that kids were thinking *This is some camp!*

There was a rectangular table in the center of the room that was for the reverends and Mrs. Hahm, plus any other pastors or Korean church association people who might visit during the session. One of their chairs was reserved for a camper who'd done something humble and loving and Jesus-like, like a girl from the Gazelles cabin who was the first occupant; Reverend Hahm recounted to all how instead of playing with her friends during the first swim session, Linda Im from Rego Park splashed around with a younger girl who was deathly afraid of the water while that girl's counselor supervised the rest of the cabin. By the middle of the camp session nobody but the biggest brownnosers wanted to be chosen because it was far less fun to sit there with the godly old people and get probed with boring questions as you tried to eat with decent manners than to joke around with your cabinmates and your cool hippieish counselor and shove greasy food in your mouth. But those first few days there was a cachet to being chosen, maybe we thought there'd be some other prize aside from not having to claw and scrape for enough of a helping of mashed potatoes or pot roast, maybe we were still too attached to our parents and craved adult assurance, or maybe, as I did, we wondered if it would feel extra special and wonderful to be the focus of attention here, among this grouping of kids, when normally it might not be so wonderful at all.

The next kid to be recognized was some extra-smiley boy who shared the entire container of the gimbap his mother had made for him with the camp landscaping crew while they were taking a water and cigarette break, men whom Mrs. Hahm referred to as "the nice Spanish"; he got a second slice of that evening's blackberry strudel. It wasn't clear how the reverends and Mrs. Hahm learned of these good deeds, whether the counselors had been tasked to nominate deserving kids or if they were always on the lookout for exemplary conduct, so the feeling among us—again mostly just that first week—was that we should be vigilant, too, for chances to shine. There were various small indications. Random refuse and litter, typically ignored, got picked up and placed in the trash bins. You noticed bigger kids allowing littler kids to cut in front of them in the lines. Even at Bible study, when it was all you could do to keep your eyes open, there'd be a bunch of kids kneeling at the front where Pastor Yi was writing on a paper easel pad, all of them propped erectly on their heels, their hands poised to shoot up at the next question.

I wasn't interested in such minor displays. Being helpful or generous was fine, but I was shooting for something grander, an act of such self-effacing charity and rectitude that Reverend Hahm would approach my mother and father on pickup day and present them with a framed certificate deeming me Charminster Camper of the Year. It would emblemize more than my being thoroughly good, surely an episode that had me saving some camper from grave injury while putting myself at certain mortal risk. A capsized canoe, a predawn fire in one of the cabins. Or this: a hungry wolf—there were rumors of an ancient, renegade pack roaming these hills—cornering one of the younger campers and only I there to fight it off with my bare fists. I would bear a scar like the mostly disappeared gash on my cheek, but this one would mark me forever.

These and other scenarios were playing in a loop in my head, and by the fourth evening of camp they featured enough insistent, vivid detail that I was wondering if one of my cabinmates had packed a box of matches, and how I might induce him into being careless, reckless. Or maybe I would be careless, reckless. In your figments it's nothing to be a sociopath.

We were just about to start eating dessert when Pastor Yi rose from his chair, clinking his water glass with a spoon. Everyone was bracing for what we assumed would be his fiery launch into an extra Bible lesson. Unlike Reverend Hahm, who was contemplative and self-conscious whenever he spoke to us or gave a sermon, his baggy, wistful eyes seemingly thronged by the weight of this life, young Pastor Yi was unapologetically aggressive in his practice, quick to dismantle any hint of doubt or skepticism from a camper with a sharp, belittling tone, as he had done to a girl in that very morning's study session about the Crucifixion. The girl, who looked earnest and studious with her oversized, round-framed spectacles, was genuinely curious and wondered if Jesus might have lost His faith at that moment when God was not answering him, having been betrayed by Judas and abandoned by most of his disciples and suffering unspeakable pain. Pastor Yi lashed out at her, saying God was not to be heard or seen by us sinners but only there for our belief, and that with her very thought *she* was abandoning Him again. The poor girl tried to disappear, shriveling between her friends on the bench.

But Pastor Yi wasn't glaring or scowling now, instead beaming as he looked around the dining hall as if we were his favorite nephews and nieces. I was noticing how when he was with Reverend and Mrs. Hahm, Pastor Yi could be much more personable.

I have just been informed that God has shone His love and goodness through another of our flock today, he announced in Korean. Most of us understood a lot of Korean even if we couldn't speak it perfectly.

Hyun-Gil, would you please come up here?

There was a rustling of chairs as everyone cast about to see who it was. Nobody had yet risen from their seat and as he scanned the room you could sense Pastor Yi's impatience, his brow shiny with perspiration.

Hyun-Gil, where are you? he said, his perplexed register betraying the slightest scolding tone. *Why aren't you here?*

"I am," a voice called. It came from the stair that led down from the second floor. I startled; it was the kid. Dickens. The one who had kicked me and acted so strangely afterward. It seemed wrong, that he had such a normal Korean name. He stepped down from the last tread and ambled over to the adults' table. The rest of us would have quickly trotted over, but his pace was his own. He had no care that he was the center of attention. We marked every unhurried stride of his longish, tanned legs. When he stood beside Pastor Yi, they were almost the same height—the pastor was quite short—and I had the weird idea that they were secretly brothers, even though they were vastly different in age and in looks, not to mention the fact that the kid was adopted, if what Peggy reported was true.

Pastor Yi put his arm around Dickens, cupping his shoulder.

"Every-body," the pastor said in his choppy English. "This is Hyun-Gil Rho. Hyun-Gil father and mother are very devoted members of our church. He is here with his brother, Sung-Gil. Hyun-Gil, please tell what happened today."

"I found some money," Dickens said in a flat voice. There was a murmur from the room.

"Where?"

"Outside, near the canteen." The canteen was a converted garage space in the lodge that was next to the lake, where you could buy snacks with the spending money your parents gave you.

"Okay, thank you. This is what Hyun-Gil found and gave to us." Pastor Yi reached into the chest pocket of his short-sleeve white dress shirt and unfolded two banknotes. He held them up, one in each hand.

"Twenty-dollar bills."

The room was buzzing. Forty dollars! It was a veritable fortune, given that any snack you could buy at the canteen, like a Yodel or Slim Jim, cost either 10 cents or 15 cents, a regular-sized chocolate bar like a Nestlé Crunch, 25 cents. Most of us came with just a few dollars, some had $5, and you heard rumors about some super lucky (and spoiled) kid with $10, though who exactly that was nobody knew. What stunned was the thought of someone carelessly dropping those bills in the grass, and then even more amazing, you realized, was that they didn't tell anyone. Though maybe you wouldn't, either. . . .

Pastor Yi kept the bills aloft. "Everybody! It is easy to keep this money for oneself, yes? It is easy to take home after camp and buy whatever you want. You never have to tell anybody. Nobody will know. Everybody can think like this, because we are all sinners. But what we study in the Scripture on Sunday is nothing if we do not follow His teachings other days. Hyun-Gil! You came to me during dinner and gave these to me. For this, you make me proud to be your youth minister. You make us all proud."

He handed the money to Mrs. Hahm and started clapping and everyone else did, too, and then Reverend Hahm got up and he and Pastor Yi had Dickens wedged between them as if he were their sole, beloved dongsaeng, when we all could see that he was not like them at all, and never would be, these men of differing ages who had receding, thinning hair and were uncomely in their distinctive ways, Yi with his nostrily snout and Hahm sleepy-eyed and with an overbite. I wondered how they'd react if I stood up and declared that he had kicked me. Would they believe my story, when they were this keen to embrace him? Would they have me stand with them, too, even if I'd not done anything special or good, and merely suffered? I could show them the lingering blotch on my face, which I'd poked at too often, not willing to let it go. People were drawn to the discoloration. I wasn't aware of it then, but the aggrieved harbor their own brand of vanity.

The three of them took their seats and while Mrs. Hahm was announcing that the camper whose money it was should come to her after cleanup, you could see kids murmuring to one another as they eyed a beaming Dickens taking his apple pie with the adults, regarding him with an enhanced veneration that a part of me couldn't help but abide. But now my own slice of pie tasted sour, the dollop of cream on top gone runny. I pushed my plate to Recipe, who shoveled the slice onto his portion and dug in. Like everyone else he was simply thrilled to gorge on yet another grand American dessert. It was then that the manga girl happened to be walking by the adult table, perhaps having dropped off platters at the dishwashing window. Her head was craning back as she passed them and my heart began to drain, her gaze fixed, like everyone else's had, on only Dickens. Shining, winning Dickens. But when she turned, I sat up in my chair, sparked. It was curious; her face was empty, almost cold.

She rejoined her table. I kept glancing over, using Recipe's big, blocky head as cover so she wouldn't catch me staring. I wanted to see if she was looking back at the adult table. But now she was just gabbing and giggling with her cabinmates between bites of dessert, periodically flipping the stylish curtain of her hair from her eyes, each little toss of her head a summons to my spirit. Barely registering the chatter of my cabinmates, who were going on about the plan for a camp-wide bonfire after dinner, I wondered what those coal-black strands would feel like against my own cheek, if they'd be a smooth or rough brush, if they'd be cool to the touch. A couple times the ends caught the corner of her mouth, and she held them there between her fingers until they were slicked to a point.

"I'm gonna do a night swim!" Recipe said, nudging me to get my full attention.

"Why would you want to do that?" I said.

"Because it would feel so nice to get wet and then warm up by the bonfire. They said it would be down by the lake."

"So what, you going in your bathing suit?"

"I'm gonna skinny-dip, man!" Recipe shimmied, his tongue wagging. He was a total dork, but he was always funny. He was the only one of us who didn't shower with his swim trunks fully on, not minding pulling them down to his knees and exposing himself to wash his privates. Every cabin had to shower together, this every third day, at a specially purposed cabin with an open, communal room fitted with two shower fixtures, and later he really let loose, aiming his penis and threatening to piss on one of us. I didn't admit to ever doing the same.

Soon the designated waiters bused the dessert plates and before you knew it the bell clanged and we were all heading to the doors, everyone keen to stop back at their cabins to change clothes and get flashlights even though it would stay warm and muggy and light out for hours. In the scrum someone whispered to me, the warm breath tickling my ear, "I need to talk to you later."

It was the manga girl. Before I could answer she got caught in the current of bodies near the door and I couldn't be sure that she had been talking to me.

Still, I was stunned by the declaration, if equally exhilarated, as were my fellow Antlers, first the Sangs, who told everyone back at the cabin that they saw her leaning very close to me by the doors. They all wanted to know what the girl had wanted, and I refused to tell but they ganged up and started tickling and rabbit-punching me and finally I related exactly what she'd said. Sang II's eyes went buggy, and he couldn't stop antically giggling, activated by the idea of such a forward girl. Sang I, who was normally soft-spoken and serious, strangely kept mooing like a cow. David tongued his lips lasciviously; there was something very advanced about him. Of course, the jerkish Jimmy Choi resolutely shook his head at the sheer impossibility of it.

"I wonder what she means by 'need'?" Mickey said, genuinely pondering.

"I got an idea!" Recipe cried, then crossed his eyes and made big duck lips and kept trying to hug and kiss me.

Though I was now otherwise certain, I insisted that she thought she was talking to someone else. They didn't quite believe me, but then we refocused on kitting up for the bonfire and they left me alone. I aimed to be prepared, so I put on jeans and my new hiking boots and let Peter spray me with his special bug repellent after I first shellacked him with it head to toe. Apparently, he got bad reactions from mosquito bites (as I sometimes did) and his doctor mother made him promise that he would put on this stuff (which the ROK soldiers purportedly used) whenever he went out at night. The problem, as we began to realize as we hiked through the camp property and down the gentle, grassy slope to the lake, was that it had a sharp, insistent odor, this weird combination of kerosene and then something funky and fermenting, like bad cheese, or doenjang. I actually didn't mind it at first, I kept breathing deep and filling my nose with its vapors because I always liked the smell of gasoline and paint thinner and other like solvents, but as we approached the lake I started to fret over the prospect of meeting this girl who needed to talk to me smelling so funny that the rest of our cabin was now forcing us to keep to the rear so they wouldn't have to trail through our volatile stink.

Two male counselors and Pastor Yi were just finishing building the pyre when we arrived at the designated spot very close to the water, a concrete pad that clearly used to have a structure on it and was charred along all four sides, though of course the whole camp crowded in on three. I didn't see the manga girl, though I had to assume she was among us. They had to keep pushing us back from the pile, saying how ferocious the flames would be. What was surprising was that they weren't using logs or pieces of split wood, especially given that we were standing in the heart of a dense hardwood forest, but instead random items of refuse like flattened cardboard boxes and whole fruit and vegetable crates, heavy commercial pallets and old railroad ties and even a broken antique ladder, plus boards with faded paint and sections of rotted plywood clearly torn out from some of the cabins. The pile was as tall as Pastor Yi and at least four times as wide, and the only thing that looked natural about it were the fresh green cuttings of thin leafy branches that they'd laid on top, which I didn't know enough to criticize. Basically, it was a garbage pile with a crown of laurel, though when Pastor Yi, the sleeves of his white dress shirt rolled up over his elbows and his broad forehead shiny with sweat, raised two squared cans of lighter fluid high above his head, the mob of us gave a shout so hearty it echoed back serially from the woods around the lake. Yi seemed to yell out, too, his face bent and feverish as he emptied both containers on the pyre, the streams of it arcing cleanly and then in sporadic bursts, all that lighter fluid smelling great.

Someone yelled for everyone to move back some more but before we could Pastor Yi tossed a burning rag on the pile and the mound *whoomped!* like in a barbecue kettle, if exponentially greater, the ignition thudding us a step backward. Very quickly the fire was roaring, crackling, and popping, the branches on top smoking at first but then burning brightly in the fast-encroaching dusk. We had to retreat a few yards back as the flames grew, the clingy humidity of the evening nullified by the blasting dry heat of the bonfire. Some kids drifted toward the swimming dock, a three-sided fiberglass enclosure for swimming in the shallows off the small, pebbled beach, but they were warned to stay clear of the water. I wasn't a pyromaniac like a lot of kids were and watched the others throw twigs and pine cones into the fire that popped like popcorn and shot out a few smoking embers, almost reaching us as we sat in the cool grass. It was getting dark now and with all the kids and adults in the dancing firelight it was difficult to tell who it was if they weren't right next to me, like Mickey and Recipe, who were totally into the fire and constantly leaving and returning with foraged things to chuck in and watch burn. At some point neither returned and I wandered in search of them but futilely, and when I got back to our spot my cabin had all gone elsewhere, and I sat among unfamiliar kids in this unfamiliar place that suddenly felt like it was totally cut off from the world. I thought then about my parents, and Ella, and how they were probably watching TV together and snacking on potato chips and cubed cheese, and I felt something drop away in me so fully that I thought I was going to pass out. Was this homesickness? I tried to right myself by looking for my new mates, and then the manga girl, and Peggy and Julie, and even, I had to admit, Dickens Rho. An antagonist at least roots you. But I was lucky, as right then two counselors stepped forward with guitars slung around their shoulders. It was Herman and Dahlia, and you could tell they were accustomed to playing together by the playful ease of their tuning. Herman then strummed a few chords, and Dahlia responded with some of hers, and before you knew it, they were singing a song.

They had strong voices, Herman kind of higher than you'd expect and Dahlia kind of lower, the combination pleasing and full as they harmonized on a song I didn't really know but had heard before on the radio: "Blowin' in the Wind." The counselors sang along, maybe a few of the older kids, though none of the Korean adults, and afterward the pair went right into a few other popular folk songs of the era, "Take Me Home, Country Roads," and "Bridge Over Troubled Water," and then "Diamonds and Rust," which Dahlia sang solo and, I noticed, sometimes meeting eyes with Ben Frost, who was now stationed near the fire to ward off anyone trying to add any more fuel. It was only when they began singing the opening words of "American Pie" together did most everyone join in, including the reverends and Mrs. Hahm, who appeared to know the lyrics by heart, but even if you didn't by the end you could sing the chorus with everyone else, *This will be the day that I die*, giving us a haunted, tingling ending.

"Super job, people!" Herman said. "Now that we're all

warmed up, Dahlia and I are going to introduce you to our favorite Charminster camp songs. The tradition is that we sing these after dinner each night, and on the campouts, so let's learn them together now, okay? We'll start with 'If I Had a Hammer.'" He started strumming an upbeat rhythm and Dahlia, her index fingers conducting us, sang: "If I had a hammer / I'd hammer in the mo-or-ning. . . ."

She repeated the simple opening stanza, which we now picked up, and our voices joined hers, and she stepped into the crowd opposite from where I was and took the hands of kids on either side of her, prompting them to do the same, and then again, until the chain came around and a girl and boy clasped my hands. I winced at how clammy and hot they were but Dahlia started swaying to the song, and soon had all of us swaying, too, and when she sang "If I had a bell" we already knew that the bell would ring instead of hammer, ringing out *The love between my brothers and my sisters, oh-oh*, words that we were suddenly belting from our guts, my own voice breaking with how loudly I was singing, practically hollering. The kids I was holding hands with had to shake me off.

Herman strummed the melody of another song, "Rise and Shine," and he started singing all about giving God your glory glory and Him telling Noah to build and fill up his ark, and that we were "Children of the Lord," an idea I'd heard plenty of times before at the church in Flushing but that only now made any sense to me, or maybe it was about having no sense at all, just a knowing ardor that got me singing with this urge to pour myself completely out.

I got tugged on my elbow and when I turned it was the manga girl. I almost jumped. Everyone around us was singing and she pulled me away from the gathering back into the shadows and said, "This is a bunch of BS, don't you think?"

I nodded even though I didn't know what "BS" meant. Then she commanded, "Let's get out of here."

"Are we allowed?"

"Who cares?" she gasped, offended by my meekness. "I just hate these songs!"

She walked ahead of me, and I followed her, switching on my flashlight. She was wearing a long-sleeve shirt with the sleeves rolled up, stitching ornamenting the shoulders. It was a Western-style shirt, which I thought only a boy could wear, but it looked great on her.

"Hey, cut that light," she ordered. I did and kept following her. A half-moon peeked through the clouds, and she moved confidently in the bluish dark. There was a trail through waist-high brush that went around most of the lake, which she somehow seemed to know, and after about forty or fifty yards she turned and we climbed a short rise and pushed through some prickly bushes onto a clearing, where a big sloping rock went all the way down into the water. We sat in a natural shelf of the granite right by the water's edge. Back at the swimming dock the bonfire had settled into itself and was burning less vigorously now, its firelight tracing the silhouettes of the singing people and shimmering on the surface of the water. She brushed away the hair that covered one eye and tucked it behind her ear, her whole face even prettier than the half, the firelight making it glow. I decided right then that if she were willing, I would marry her someday. This was my interpretation of the welling in my chest, this before I had ever touched a girl (aside from my mother and sister), much less kissed one. She leaned down and made a ladle of her hand and scooped up some lake water.

"I'm so thirsty!" she said, then took a sip. "Mmmm. I love *champagne*." She sounded just like Rosalind Russell. "Don't you? You must have some!"

I didn't know what champagne was, but she tossed the rest of hers and took a fresh handful and held it to my mouth. I knew that you shouldn't drink seawater, but this was the first time I'd been at a lake, and the water in her palm smelled almost sweet, if not fresh. She decanted a little onto my lips; it tasted like mud, though much more alive, or maybe it was bullfrogs, and I knew I didn't want to taste it anymore. But she wanted to give me another drink, so I took it, listening to her talk.

I would learn that her name was Susan Sun. She was from Staten Island, a place I'd not heard of at the time, partly because I was almost completely ignorant of the geography in and around New York City, but also because none of our family's friends or acquaintances resided there. Very few Koreans did back then, nor do many live there now, for whatever reasons. But Susan Sun was from there, her parents running a dry cleaner in a neighborhood called Old Town. I kept imagining a craggy harbor full of high-masted wooden ships and a sleepy quay of tidy, hoary shops, one of them theirs. Inside her mother did alterations at the sewing machine, while at the counter her father took in blazers and overcoats to be cleaned, both patient and amiable and speaking, to my ear, a fluent and almost unaccented English. Susan was never in the picture, instead she was off somewhere by herself, likely perched on a cliff reading some book she was always carrying, the city skyline in the far background. The reality was surely different; there was probably little calm in their strip mall store overflowing with hangered and bundled clothing, the traffic on the boulevard hectic and loud, her parents and customers too often barking indecipherably at one another unless their Susan, just back from the school day, could make sense between them.

"What's your name?" she asked. I was still swallowing and before I could answer she told me her full American and Korean names, where she was from, what her parents did past and present, plus a half dozen other facts and references to her school and favorite teachers and books that were already giving me a rich picture of her busy eleven-and-a-half-going-on-nineteen-year-old life. I told her mine.

"Really? Your name is Jeon-Gi?" she said, giggling. "Like, 전기?"

With her finger she wrote out the Hangul on my palm,

and I nodded. I wasn't much good at reading or writing Korean, but I knew my own name at least.

"I knew there was something different about you!"

"What's that?"

She stared at me for a long second, then raised her hands in that way she did.

I could only shake my head.

"You really don't know, do you, *Jeon-Gi*?"

Nothing registered, if only because I was focusing on my own name, the array of the English letters, then the Hangul, the sounds it made as this oddly wonderful girl spoke them, sounds I felt I could live inside of for a long, long time. But then I heard it in the form of my mother's voice, not calling for me but shouting it from our apartment's kitchen window to my father while he and I were throwing a football on the playfield:

Jeon-gi-ga nah-geos-oh! The electricity went out!

Ohhhh, was my backsliding thought. How dumb could I be, how vastly, and ironically, dim? It's unbelievable, I know, near ridiculous, but I never mentally placed that word and my name next to each other, never making the simplest link, never once entertaining the possibility that they could be the same. Nor did my parents ever mention it, only responding in the way most Korean parents would when asked (and when I inquired), which was that one of the grandfathers hired an astrologer who, given the hour of my birth, the day's weather, the wider celestial gyres, would come up with the most luminous, the most impressive, the most historical and consequential of names.

Electricity.

Was it all a joke?

I sat helpless on that ungiving rock. I wondered how I could least shamefully slink away. Lucky for me, Susan just softly punched me on the arm and shook her head, amused, if still curious. She was a whiz, as fleet of mind as she was of foot, but it would turn out that this life was something that kept tripping her up with its petty ruts, its trivial compulsory detours, when all she wanted to do—all she could do—was revel.

"So tell me, *E*," she said, instantly forging her private nickname for me, "why did you come to camp?"

I didn't have much of an answer to this, either, and I certainly didn't want to explain how it was probably my parents' last resort for my being rehabilitated into a reasonably normal kid, and I heard myself mumbling on about sleeping in a sleeping bag and having new hiking boots to wear.

"Okay . . ." she replied. "I guess that's *interesting* stuff. But what are you *hoping* for?"

"What do you mean?"

"You know . . . what do you really want?"

I still wasn't getting her.

"Like if you could make your dreams come true. What would it be?"

I thought about this for a moment, particularly the last dream I could remember having, which was yet another version of a recurring nightmare about being trapped in the mazed basement of a creaky Victorian house, this time my mother's muffled voice calling me for dinner.

"That people would like me," I blurted, startling myself with both the answer and my willingness to utter it.

Susan gravely mulled this.

"Is this because of what that kid Dickens did to you? Why you think people don't like you?"

I whispered, "You saw?"

She nodded. I thought I might start to cry from the shared knowledge of it, but her expression hardened and I realized she was on my side, even though she clearly hadn't told any adult what she saw. In fact, I was grateful that she hadn't.

"He was at camp last summer, too. He kept shoving kids off the deep-water float and the lifeguards wouldn't let him go out there for a whole day. Then he started untying the tops of some girls' bathing suits in the shallow section, but he didn't get in any trouble. He tried to pull mine, too. I know why you didn't fight back. He thinks he's so wonderful, and other people do, too, just because they think he's so nice-looking. Do you think he's nice-looking?"

I shrugged, not wanting to be like those other people in her eyes. I was going to ask how she felt but I guess I already knew and didn't need to hear her say that about him again.

"Anyway, he's a jerk. You know that, and I do, too. A real jerk."

She reached out and offered her hand and she had us shaking vigorously on what I took as a binding pact of belief, if not action. Her grip was warm and damp, and although it was just the kind of sensation that would normally make me squirm, I pushed through my obsessive-compulsive recoil and held on tight, then tighter, the little horror cresting until it flowed over into something approaching pleasure, our palms slick against each other's.

She pulled us up so that we were standing on the rock. At the bonfire they were singing a new song, "This Little Light of Mine." I'd heard it before at our church, but it sounded ten times more joyful here with all the kids clapping and belting out "Let it shine, Let it shine!" with an almost desperate thunder. Susan could see I was itching to clap along, too, and she coaxed me to do so even though she didn't like the songs, or even the bonfires, or, as I would soon grow aware of, much else about the camp. Something had certainly come over me, perching on the sloped rock like that with her. I didn't mind making myself look silly for her, clapping up above my head like a circus chimp might, and soon enough she was laughing and clapping, too, and we clapped harder and harder, if not singing ourselves, exulting in our little renegade fellowship.

My Antler mates, of course, were all over me the next morning for details of my time at "the Petting Stone." After getting back to the cabin it was lights-out with strict radio silence that Ben Frost monitored until we all fell dead asleep (surely within minutes), and as we were vying before the two rusted porcelain washbasins to brush our teeth, Jimmy Choi aimed his frothy toothbrush at me with a maniacal leer and insisted that I tell them exactly what happened. I'd not heard the term "petting" before he said it and pretended to know what it meant, though I think most of us there had no idea beyond the imagined careful stroking you might give to a fluffy bunny so it wouldn't bolt away. Did you pet each other's hands? Cheeks? Regardless I was elated to learn that where Susan had taken me was a notorious Charminster spot and I held my head high with my best gentlemanly airs and said, "None of your beeswax."

Jimmy Choi erupted with a hoot, white spittle flying. With

his forearm he shoved me, but it was the kind you got on the infield after executing a nifty double play.

"You got some attitude, J.-G.! You kinda burn!"

Still, the boys kept pressing me, and I had to offer them some basic scraps. I told them that we'd held hands the whole time, which was not that much more impressive than clapping in unison but enough for them to know that I had at least made actual contact. I could feel the new regard for me around our breakfast table, an acknowledgment that toggled between respect and envy and fully charged me up. I found myself pointing and gesticulating like some gym teacher or talk-show host, basically making a larger presence of myself than I needed to, sort of like Jimmy Choi naturally did. It was easier to fib to them because we had indeed held hands, if, in reality, it had been for no more than a few seconds. And I thought myself gallant, in that I didn't tell them how her hand was softer and smaller than I expected, and that when I sniffed my own hand after she let go it smelled funky and alive, of swamp punks and thistle, this aromatic, weedy tea.

One thing, though.

I stated that it was "easier to fib," but this suggests that it was expediency driving me. The truth is this: I had no trouble lying to them, these boys that I both immediately and generally and then particularly liked. Looking back on it, I know from the start I felt comfortable whenever we convened, completely accommodated and welcomed by our merely gathering, whether that was crowding in at the washbasins, or stamping our feet beneath the dining table during the singing, or lining up on the deep-water float to hurl ourselves into the murky lake water. Yes, it was being at camp with other kids who (mostly) were excited to be at camp, everyone game for whatever might happen, but it was also a matter of being seen differently and not as the kid who was something other than Irish or Italian or Jewish, Black or Puerto Rican or Dominican, or whose mother was indecipherable and always anxious-seeming, or who always took his place without a murmur. You'd think it would be easier to make up stories or play loose with details or outright cheat or lie to strangers and other people who didn't know you and you didn't care about, but measure by measure, day by day, I found the opposite happening.

It began in the most minor of ways. While there were certain designated activities in the weekly camp schedule—arts and crafts, Bible study, sports (softball, flag football, Newcomb), and swim hour—most of the days were devoted to what the counselors called "free time" (with some of them, though never Ben Frost, referring to it as "me time"), which meant that we were often left with big blocks of the day to amuse ourselves. This was a natural extension of the unsupervised way most of us grew up back then, which we didn't mind at all, maybe the only disappointment being that we couldn't hang out with Ben Frost more so we could marvel at his athletic gifts and expert knowledge of orienteering and try to impress him in any way we could. At some point he'd be absent, he would have simply slipped away, and if one of our unofficial cabin leaders like Mickey or Jimmy Choi didn't propose a game of hoops or soccer we'd sit on the peeling, splintery boards of the cabin porch or steps and jabber away about whatever while playing card games like 21 and Spit or a version of jacks called gohng-gi.

To me playing jacks was something girls did, along with skipping rope and making bracelets and rings out of wire or string, but gohng-gi had already become a Charminster (Korean) camp tradition that the returnees taught the rest of us right away. It struck me even then as a game peasant kids might play, as we used rocks as the jacks. There was no ball, just the five rocks you needed to find and select carefully for size and shape. Too large made it more difficult at the end, when you had to catch all five in midair, but if they were too small it was harder to swipe them up in the preceding rounds; likewise, if they were too smooth. But if sharp and angular, which made them easier to snatch, the stones could hurt, pinching or jabbing the flesh between the fingers. You figured out quickly what the ideal rock should be, and a critical part of the contests, which we'd do in a single elimination round-robin, was the pregame hunt for them around the cabin. The gravel road out front was of course our main quarry, but it had long been picked over for the best gohng-gi stones, and whenever it got decided that we'd play everyone would sprint outside to forage. I don't know why we didn't just keep our stones after the first time. We didn't, it seemed somehow antithetical to the game, or bad form.

After the first couple times searching, I found myself tossing any decent rocks where others wouldn't find them. Maybe others were doing this, too, though I never caught anyone doing so, nor did anyone catch me. I don't know why I did it. There I was, kneeling in the dirt, looking for a slightly better rock than those already in my hand, and if I found one, I'd peer around for a second and then flick the reject into the high weeds. I got no flush of pleasure from it, no glow of triumph warming my chest. There was no pang of remorse, either, nothing like guilt or a second, lingering thought. It was as if I were not conscious at that moment, more like a being inscribed with the simple instructions that I should do whatever I could to gain any advantage. Creaturely instinct, I guess, though I wasn't desperate to win. I was good at the game and won my fair share of matches, but more than that, I genuinely cherished playing with my mates, I gave hearty hurrahs to them when they won, they felt like cousins to me, if not outright brothers, fellows I could imagine bleeding for, and maybe shedding blood, too.

This didn't mean I wouldn't pretend that I'd snared the right number of rocks for that round, or glance at somebody's cards if they weren't aware they were showing, or try to confuse a kid new to a sport with a complicated rule interpretation; regardless I always seemed to get the benefit of the doubt, my new friends were quick to heed me, naturally and with ease, a state of harmony that was shocking compared to the constant noise of (the mostly) petty strife on the playground of Cove Gardens. Here, I was appreciated, like when I dove and caught the volleyball in a Newcomb game against another cabin, saving what would have been a match point. Afterward—we eventually won in overtime—Peter and the kid we nicknamed Fluffy tried to lift me up onto their shoulders. Fluffy was originally in another cabin but joined ours a few days into the session because we liked his game spirit and also because he was having some troubles with his group. They were the smallest boys in the cabin, Peter a bird-boned Poindexter and Fluffy rotund but very short, and they could only boost me high enough to topple me onto the crabgrass. We had a big laugh over it. I gently ruffled Fluffy's head like everyone did because of his strange Afro-like hair, the woolly kinks of it often netting filaments of cobwebs and tiny bits of leaves and crumbs. One time Recipe picked out a flake of a potato chip from Fluffy's hair and after a brief inspection ate it. I can't be certain of his real name—it was maybe Dwayne or Wayne, something atypical for a Korean American, but we loved that he embraced his role as our cabin's mascot/lucky charm, that wild head of hair our homey talisman.

Yet even with Fluffy I couldn't help once telling him during a head-to-head round of 21 that he had 16 instead of 17—like Gregory Fluss he was awful at math—and whisking away the cards to start another hand. There was no final victory because of it, not even a momentary advantage, just a gain that was measurable only in my welling realization of how implicitly I was trusted here. It was a fidelity I'd never known outside my family, a fidelity that made me feel like the Invisible Man in the old black-and-white movie I made sure to watch every time it was on TV. I marveled at the capacities of this person who could venture anywhere he wanted, unnoticed and undisturbed. What freedom, what license! And although I could understand why his condition could be a curse and might cause him to go insane and lead to his ruin, to me he was clearly flawed from the start, someone who was doomed no matter what.

I, on the other hand, was gliding steady. The first week passed in an instant, a constant whirl of sporting and social activity that like any orientation week at college set in motion the forging of shorthand profiles (whether fair or not) that everyone would casually deploy, at least for the most prominent kids. Thus, Mickey was the star athlete and Golden Boy, Jimmy Choi his somewhat sinister counterpart, Julie our Queen Bee who dispensed both snappy advice and criticism, Mi-hae the Sensitive Beauty, Recipe the camp Comedian/Clown, and so on. I was squarely in the next tier, which perfectly suited me, though I was thankful that I was not a rung lower in the ranks of the completely anonymous, my status confirmed when I was voted the Antler cabin vice president, a position that solely meant that I'd serve as Mickey's second for any coin flips and rules arguments. I was happy and content to be there beside him, the gang looking on. I had found a good position, a position that fit me better than any other I had known.

Yet on my own, hanging around with whomever, I began larding my life and times with small, insignificant lies, lies that didn't even make me seem more cool or impressive and sometimes did the opposite, like when I told the soft-spoken, long-haired David that I much preferred reading over playing sports. I did love reading but would without pause drop any book whenever someone shouted up to our apartment for me to play. At Charminster we were naturally all mad for sports (David included) and there were few books around camp, only one big plastic bin of mildew-smelling kid detective and paperback Westerns tucked in the corner of the main meeting hall. I certainly didn't bring any. There was no occasion for saying what I did, we were debating the pros and cons of our favorite dining-hall dishes—for me the spaghetti, for him the fish sticks—but something about David and his long hair and raggedy way of dressing and the fact that he lived only with his father (who was an art teacher!) made me say it. He didn't have much of a response, simply blinking hard a few times. We went on chatting until some others corralled us into going hunting for frogs and my comment was instantly gone, which was fine with me. All I thought I wanted was to inscribe the moment with something that might in the tiniest way make it more amenable for us, clinch our friendship, there was nothing more to it than that, but when I look back on it now, I know it wasn't generosity or warmth of heart driving me.

In truth, I was experimenting. I was testing the feel of airing some notion about myself, then watching how the information would fly for this kid or that or one of the adults, how they would take it in and digest it. David didn't react much, but I could tell he was snagging on why I wanted him to know such a thing. It's pathetic and gratuitous, no doubt a little cruel, but I was fascinated by how I could unsettle him, even if in the most trivial way. And I realized it was only because he naturally accepted me and took me at my word that he was my unwary captive.

I did this with all my cabinmates, telling a skyful of misleading and phony facts and anecdotes that individually were unremarkable but if seen all together comprised an obnoxious constellation. I bragged to Peter that I had two brand-new pairs of suede Clyde Pumas in Knicks blue and also orange; Peggy and Julie heard of my finding an abandoned kitten in the laurel bushes back home and how I carried it, on foot, to the ASPCA (whereas it hissed at me when I tried to pet it and I got scared); Jimmy Choi got an earful of my complaints about a bossy teacher I pranked by shoving chalk shards between the seams of her erasers (when I was in fact her dutiful eraser clapper); the Sangs learned of how my cucumber pickling experiment won first prize at the science fair (where it deserved to win nothing, being simply two jars of my mother's oiiee-kimchi, one freshly made, one old); or what I claimed to Mickey, my protector and big-brother figure, which was that my best friend back home was Cleon Washington, who was not only Black but had spent time in prison and had described to me exactly what a day there was like. Mickey asked how old he was, and I said seventeen, which wasn't that far off but which he still didn't seem to believe. Soon afterward Mickey got a terrible rash on a hike from some poison oak, but I still made sure I was the one to go to the infirmary to replenish his cotton ball and calamine lotion supply.

With the adults I could be more grandiose if they asked about my life, as they weren't likely to be able to test my sporting skills or intelligence; and so Mrs. Hahm was impressed to hear that I was voted to the all-star squads of both my Little League and Pop Warner teams, and Mr. Hammonds, the cook everybody called "Fryer," no longer had to wonder what I was up to staring so intently at his pantry wall of giant food-service cans, since he was now aware of my status as a silver medalist at my school's Math Olympics and knew I was calculating how many cans of peaches he likely used to make dessert for the whole camp.

"And here I was thinking you were a little slow!" he laughed, tweaking my nose. This was before the dinner bell was rung one day when I was doing my turn with a few others setting up the chairs and tables. "You know what? Maybe someday you'll go to the fancy university where I work the rest of the year. It's in the *Ivy League*."

I acted as if I knew what that meant, or what "I-V" even was. It would turn out that I did attend that very institution, my first year overlapping with Mr. Hammonds's thirty-fifth and final year as a cook for my residential college. He was known as Fryer only at camp. The last week of spring semester the residential college master threw him and a longtime maintenance man a retirement party happy hour where they ordered in boxes and boxes of the renowned local Neapolitan-style pizza. Sadly, there were only a handful of students amid the crowd of staff, and those of us who did show up each got to take away a full pie. I bid congratulations to Mr. Hammonds as I left, and he thanked me and shook my hand. He looked fatigued as always, but content. It was the last I saw of him. I hate to think about it, there are reasons that will become evident, but although we had had a few pleasant exchanges in the dining hall during the year, I never identified myself as having been a camper long before at Charminster.

Soon enough my field widened. I didn't discriminate. Whoever crossed my path could be subject to my mendaciousness, the style and scale of which had an ever-widening range. I could never anticipate what might emerge from my mouth, the words often a total surprise. One time I told a nice little girl whom I'd helped up after she tripped on a stair step that she looked a lot like my own little sister, who was a cripple. The girl weakly smiled and skipped away. Another time some younger boys were tormenting a poor bullfrog by the lake with a sharp stick, and I stopped and said that I'd been sickened once by a highly poisonous one and almost went blind and that they should just kill it. They wouldn't, so I was about to do so, lifting my foot to stomp it, when they cried for me to show mercy. So I did. Another instance was when I told a self-styled junior gangster in another cabin—he was from some rough neighborhood called Bed-Stuy, which is what we called him—that I went to juvenile court for having shot at cars with a BB rifle. It went on and on, so much so that it became a tic, a compulsion from deep within me that was bent on dark invention. The only people that I never stretched anything with were Ben Frost and Susan. Ben Frost for the obvious reason that he was our and my hero, excelling at everything we thought cool and worthwhile and being smart and kind and thoughtful besides. It would have been like lying to Jesus.

Susan was a different story. Aside from plain liking her, maybe loving her, thinking she was perfectly fantastic, she was nervy and vigilant, and the idea of telling her untruths was ludicrous; she'd see right through me before I could unfurl the first limp threads. But there was also a somber feeling I had that she was trying to stay ahead of something that was invisible but building, a vast force like a tsunami. I was too young to understand it, but I can see now that her quirky energy and wild charm were a form of running, her head start against that wave that would inevitably come for her. And you can't outrun that.

Susan and I would have liked to spend more time together

as we settled into the heart of the camp session, but the boys' and girls' cabins were often segregated for the various activities. This wasn't because it was a church camp, we were young enough so that there was nothing moralistic for the adults to worry about yet, just the generally sexist way things went back then on the assumption we wouldn't want to be mixed. And then we segregated ourselves during the many hours of free time, we Antlers in particular running in a herd, usually drafted by either Mickey or Jimmy Choi to go on some trek or to contest another boys' cabin in capture the flag or a tug-of-war. If it was raining, we'd bunk in and play gohng-gi or make a new lanyard while counting the lightning strikes. My assessment was that Charminster was like the army except without the cigarettes and guns and dying. Camaraderie was king. I'm sure the girls' cabins were just as tight, and nobody was into attracting the sort of attention that mixing boys and girls would beget. As such, the picture of Susan or myself simply walking across the property and calling on the other to hang out was far-fetched, if not downright ridiculous.

The only periods when there was always overlap were during meals and the time on the lake. Swim hour was by far the favorite activity for all, save for those who didn't know how to swim and were forced to take lessons. I knew how to swim, as did Susan, and although we had both passed the deep-water test, we chose to stay mostly in the shallow section even though it was kind of gross. This was the area marked by a three-sided polyurethane dock, the two parallel sides ending at the shoreline, and with garden-type wire fencing attached to the inside face of the dock and going all the way to the bottom, effectively enclosing us like farmed fish. The purpose of the fencing was to prevent you from trying to swim under the dock to the deep section, as there were numerous support struts in the way. The lake bottom was naturally soft and although the camp had created a small pebble-layered beach, once you went in your feet would get sucked in a little, making the water murky as you moved around. Plus, the younger kids always had their swim time before us and you knew they peed like crazy in there (although to be honest we contributed our share, too). But once in that cold swampy water we forgot about any foulness, plunging headfirst to retrieve weighted lanyards we'd throw, or, if we got frisky, to snatch at the ankles and calves of the opposite sex. Susan and I were part of these games. We mostly stuck to the retrieving, but when the warning whistle from the lifeguard signaling the imminent end of the swim hour both she and I would dive for each other. I didn't know which was more thrilling, to tug on a foot or to get your foot tugged. Yet it was thoroughly innocent, the exhilaration flashing bright through the veins, like the charge you'd get from a scary amusement-park ride. Only when her hand lingered on my ankle, or my hand more firmly held hers, did the feeling change, or maybe it wasn't the feeling that was so different but the idea that the feeling shouldn't be experienced in public, out in the open.

It was during this time that something disturbing happened. It was maybe the eighth day of the session and both swim areas were teeming, the older kids and strongest swimmers jumping and diving off the float in the deep section, the rest splashing about in the penned-in shallows. Susan and I were on shore looking for smooth, round stones for a terrarium she had started in a large glass honey jar we got from Mr. Hammonds, having already collected some tiny ferns and moss and bits of wood. The last thing we required was a living creature, a cricket or beetle or what I was hoping for, something special like a garter snake or praying mantis, something as special as Susan. Sure, my friends at camp and home and school were genuinely fun playmates (despite the intermittent frictions), I esteemed them to whatever respective extent, but with Susan I found a joy in simply being with her, whenever and wherever, happy and carefree. I told her I was going hunting and she indicated that she would stay on the pebble beach and rearrange the terrarium with the new foliage. I was keen on surprising her with some exciting quarry. The trouble is that it's not easy to locate interesting fauna when you need to, despite its constantly buzzing and slithering all around you otherwise. There were only black worker ants pursuing their ceaseless labors, so I had to trek farther from the lake into the woods, where I found a rash of baby caterpillars on the undersides of fern leaves, and then the molted husk of a very long snake that I was glad I didn't encounter alive. It was quite dark beneath the canopy, the shade tinged with the scent of cold earth and pine bark, and as I ventured deeper, slung low to the ground, I grew afraid, sensing the eyes of some predator scoping me, a fox or maybe even a wolf. But I couldn't turn back empty-handed. My pace quickened and I realized I could hardly hear the shouts of the swimmers, and that I had hiked much farther than I intended, cresting a gentle rocky rise and then descending where it was shadier and cooler still, the air fresh and leafy smelling. I saw the stream then, or more a trickling that was a long step wide and filtering down over mossy slabs of rock, and when I tracked its course down a slope it led to a pond no bigger than a volleyball court that likely appeared and disappeared seasonally, appearing and disappearing for long enough that there was a corresponding, if smaller, break in the canopy. The sky was bright, and it was amazing how sparkling the water was, I could see water bugs rowing the placid surface and a school of fat tadpoles darting about near the undisturbed bottom, and I thought of how Susan would still happily drink from it.

I had hoped for anything but a frog, their legions something of a plague around the camp, huge specimens like the one those kids were menacing and medium ones that fit in the cup of your palm squatting in any half-covered place, and then baby ones no bigger than your fingernail hopping madly about in a bid to survive, most of them unintentionally crushed underfoot to become tiny stamps of frog jerky, but I decided this pond would yield me a distinctive specimen that would show how much I thought of her. There were none about, however, after I hunted the perimeter twice, and I sat on a fallen tree trunk wondering if I should return with a few of the garish pink-and-cream-colored mushrooms that were sprouting in the mealy, rotted wood. I was wondering if I should collect some for the terrarium but started tossing twigs in the water instead, which was fortunate as those mushrooms were probably lethal. One of my throws overshot the water and the branch landed near a rock. Then the rock shifted. I threw another near it and it kept moving and I hustled over to see that it was a turtle, its dark shell flecked with dried mud. I picked it up and the turtle immediately retreated inside. He was heavier than I expected, meaty and dense, and to be honest dispiritingly ordinary, little about his shape or color to get excited about.

But he was alive, and big, and in my hand, and I'd let Susan decide if she wanted him. I started hiking back to the lake as quickly as I could, but it was awkward with the turtle in one hand while pushing away branches with my other, the footing not so easy, either, as I navigated the rolling, uneven terrain. I sped up when the trail was more open, anxious with the notion that the turtle needed to be in water soon, or at least dampened, and that Susan might dislike turtles, or maybe like them so much that she'd find it cruel to imprison one in the terrarium. The thought of her frowning made me stumble and the turtle slipped from my grasp. He skidded down a short slope and then dropped to a ledge below it, landing with an ugly *thwack* that I felt in the dead center of my almost stopped heart.

I scrambled down the embankment; the turtle had bounced hard twice and ended up a few feet away in a swath of ivy. I was sickened by what had happened, but he looked so peaceful nestled there in the dark green leaves that I couldn't help but kneel close. His shell was intact, despite a fresh scuff in the armor. With a branch I slowly flipped him over, half expecting to see his guts spilled out, but his underside was fine. I picked him up and he stirred, his front feet barely pushing out from the sockets. He craned his pokey head, this tiny old green man, then pulled back, though not all the way.

I went on with him then, steadily, tightly cradled in my elbow like a football, stiff-arming branches to clear the way. I would never drop him again. During this first week of camp, during premeal prayers and Bible study, I'd heard countless times from the reverends and some of the more religious counselors about the loving mercy of God, how vast and all-encompassing it was and how we were graced by it no matter what we had done, or would do in the future, which seemed to me too good a deal to believe, but in the denseness of the turtle's coldly alive body I thought I could finally feel what everybody meant by our living blessedly in His Glory.

As I approached the lake nothing seemed to have changed, everybody dashing about and shouting; maybe I hadn't been away for very long. The only difference was that Susan wasn't present; the terrarium was there, gleaming in the sun, abandoned on her towel on the far, quiet end of the pebbly beach. She said she liked "privacy," which I was grateful included me. I looked to the crowded float bobbing in the deep water, and to the kids scampering on the deck of the dock that penned the shallows, where everyone was splashing about, but none of them was Susan. I feared something awful was happening, that my friend was in distress, wherever she was. Without being aware of it, I had drifted into the water. Some kid was shouting at me—*Hey, whose turtle is that?*—but I couldn't respond, not because of the weirdness of the question but for the ball of worry clogging my throat. To picture myself now, calf-deep in the olive-colored water, it must have looked like I was stricken with remorse and finally returning the poor, limp creature to its safe and rightful place.

It was then that Susan, in the near corner, rose up from the water, her hair slicked flat against her head. I could only marvel at the sight of her, her dark blue one-piece darker still and glistening against her boyish figure that could have been the mirror of mine except for the first pearly buddings of her chest, which I imagined slightly hurt, or at least got easily chafed like my penis did when I pulled on my rough bathing trunks. How sensitive and unprotected we were then. I waved, lifting the turtle so she could see her prize, but she didn't see me, standing there in the almost chest-high water with a funny stiffness as if she were peeing. Then she flinched, one arm flailing, and appeared to wince. But, in fact, she was smiling, and I couldn't help but smile, too, seeing that, when right in front of her a swimmer popped out of the water with a huge, fountaining gasp. I started wading deeper to join their fun when I realized the kid was Dickens Rho, his sturdy back shimmering and dripping madly, shamelessly. The sight of his naked torso that close to her sucked all the breath from me. I had completely avoided him since that first encounter, in fact almost convinced myself that the incident never happened, or had happened to somebody else, this even as I was hypervigilant for his whereabouts, plus eager to hear any gossip that confirmed his reputation, as Susan herself had reported, of being a conceited, albeit handsome, jerk.

Dickens turned and swam, and I already knew what would happen next: he stood and waited for her to do the same, which she did, and without hesitance, submarining to find and then to pluck at his feet, his ankles. Hold them, if you dared, for as long as you could your breath. We called it Flipper, after the TV show dolphin. That's how the game was played, the way she and I always played it. My thoughts were storming with how things had been initiated, who had first signaled whom, or whether it was somehow prearranged, at least provisionally, for whenever I might depart the scene. Of course, this notion was ridiculous; Dickens wouldn't hide his intentions because of me, and Susan wasn't sneaky. She was forthright and poised and real. But she was also, evidently, subject to his vital, maleficent energy; when she breached the surface her expression wasn't any different, but her throat and cheeks were splotched pink with a flush, despite the chilly lake water. Before her Dickens stood impassively, his casual stance burning me.

I pivoted hard toward the shore, nearly losing my footing in the mucky bottom. I thought I smelled the turtle in my grip; he'd been in the sun for a while now and his shell was dull and dusty like the sheets of dried squid my mother would sometimes roast over a stove burner and tear into strips for my father to snack on with his bottle of Rheingold beer, the scent of soured malt and burnt shellfish clinging to me for days. I no longer wanted to hold or even touch the creature. I was sorry that I'd ever found him. His beaky mouth was cracked ajar in a weary grimace, and I felt just like I thought he looked, we were fellow prisoners in misery and helplessness, and yet I barely quelled my urge to spike him like a football or at least hurl him deep into the lake.

Instead, I would leave him inside the terrarium: a notice to her of my stung fidelity. Even then the position I most favored was of the wronged. But the opening of the jar was smaller than I expected; he didn't quite fit when I tried him headfirst. It seemed like he'd go in backward but I feared him biting me and so I angled him like he was doing a twisting back dive, and this time it worked . . . until not. He got caught just past his middle, where his soft hips would be, the sides of his shell wedged against the opening. I tried to move him, but he wouldn't budge. His legs were pulsing a little, these near-imperceptible shivers. He was stuck in his belly-up position halfway inside the glass, the underside of his neck bluishly pale and crepey, like a very old white grandma's.

"Wow, J.-G., he's so cute!"

It was Susan. She plopped down on her towel, dripping all over, and looking relieved to see me. There was no sign of Dickens. I was still holding the turtle and something in me commanded that I couldn't leave him this way and I shoved him as hard as I could. There was a *snap* that sounded just like when my father would crack the crab legs for us that we bought at the market sometimes in Chinatown. The turtle was inside the terrarium, and maybe for good.

"Where in the world did you find him?" Susan said brightly, though not meeting my eyes. I didn't want to meet her eyes, either, afraid of seeing the truth of her feeling. I gestured vaguely to the woods. She had lifted the jar and was examining the turtle from various angles. He wasn't moving much but at least he was on his feet.

"He's in his new home now," she said. "Or maybe *she's* in *her* new home. What do you think, J.-G.? She could be a girl!"

"I guess so," I said, even more horrified. I'd been barely tolerant of the needless suffering I'd put him through, but in my chauvinistic upbringing the idea that the turtle might be a female made me nauseated.

"Let's get water lilies for her," she said. "And some wildflowers, too. She should have a pretty place to live, don't you think?"

She picked up the terrarium and led us to forage in a small swath of meadow between the lake and the cabins. Recipe saw us leaving together and waved, then militarily saluted us with a daffy smile on his face. But I wasn't puffed up or pleased. As we began scavenging at the edge of the woods Susan was chatty and hyperverbal as always, yet there was something overpositive about her talk of bringing him home after camp, there wasn't the usual skeptical edge, and I knew she must have realized I'd seen her playing Flipper with Dickens.

I went along, ever-grateful to be in her vapor trail, though this time I got a different glimpse of the future than those I'd been conjuring, one in which she and I were no longer best friends, nor siblings from another mother, nor a loving-if-chaste husband and wife, but rather partners in a venture that was suddenly failing fast. The flowers we were picking might as well have been dried. We couldn't know it then, I don't know how it would have changed things if we had, but Susan and I would end up at the same university, along with Mr. Hammonds. We live in a tiny world. She was two class years ahead, having skipped a middle school grade, and we rarely came across each other on the expansively strewn urban campus. But one night my sophomore year she knocked hard on my dorm door and barged in mid-rave about some argument on a new feminist semiotics she was having with a famous Comparative Literature professor whom she was also seeing romantically, or at least sexually. She was dripping from a freakishly warm November rainstorm, but she wasn't shivering, and when I gave her a towel, she dried not herself but a tattered old volume of Shelley poems she'd "freed" from said professor's office. She didn't seem to notice how drenched she was, or how she was nearly tearing the cover from the fragile book with the towel as she paced my tiny room, or how I stood with my calves pressed against the edge of my single bed whenever she neared me because of her hot, bad-smelling breath. By the time she left I'd hardly said a sentence, the few words I did utter, "Not sure about that," my lame response to her request to stay the night with me. She shoved the Shelley in my hands and, almost grazing my lips with hers, blurted, "Read and learn!" Then she flew off, leaving my door wide open. In the spring I heard she'd taken a leave of absence. I don't know if she ever returned to finish her degree. That night was the last time I saw her.

I still have the book, and whenever I pull it from the shelf to look up one of the poems or sample a random verse—*Like a child from the womb, like a ghost from a tomb, / I arise and unbuild it again*—I remember the force of nature Susan was, or more accurately, had within her, how a wisp of cloud could become a dark sky could become a storm. Then instantly clear again, or not.

Carrying the terrarium, she started humming one of the only camp songs she had professed to liking, "Amazing Grace," though she did so with surplus ornamentation, trilling and warbling like a maudlin organist as we searched amid the knee-high grass. I disliked the hymn, its plaintive strains made my insides tremble, yet I was softly humming along with her, too, for she was Susan and I was J.-G. and I wished only to be close to her. It didn't matter about a Flipper game. I found a sprinkling of small, white, five-petaled flowers (a variety of foxglove, I'd later learn) and called her, waving her over. She waved back. I had a full bouquet when I reached her, its perfume sweet and vital. My forbearing tribute. Susan was holding the terrarium with both arms, not so much cradling it as wrapping it tight. I tried to peer through her clutch, and she turned away, but I knew. Finally, she handed me the jar—it was a jar now, nothing more—and I peered at the turtle. It was lying flat on its belly, its head crooked sideways, its baloney-colored tongue draped limply. I gently shook the glass and its head lolled free the other way.

Susan gave a weird, high howl. She turned and began walking away. Then she was skipping, almost as if she were giddy. But she started to run. I set the jar down deep in the grass and followed her, trailing her as best as I could until she veered off to her cabin. I kept going to mine.

During the next few days Susan and I kept to our own orbits. Seeing each other around camp was unavoidable, and we would smile and flash the peace sign (which I had learned from her), but we made sure not to get stuck sharing any private time together. For what was there to do or say about the turtle, or her Flipper game, that would make things happier for us? I could only guess what she was feeling, whether it was remorse and embarrassment for herself or pity and sorrow for me, but I knew what I was feeling, and I was afraid that I might say something mean to her, hurtful enough to push her away forever, and I certainly didn't want that. So, what I tried to do was what one of the numerous therapists I'd had sessions with suggested that I do, which was to realize that the searing ingot inside of me was not in fact mine, and that it was fueled by other people and situations she called *circumstance*, something that was always fickle and mysterious and often beyond my control. In the morning as I lay awake before anyone else was up I thought of the smug, magnetic grin of Dickens Rho, and of the too-small opening of the honey jar, and even of the ravenous heart of Susan Sun that motored her headlong into everything, and could thus cool myself. But I could never wholly blot out the idea that in me was a lode of a material too ready to burn.

I did let my cabinmates speak of me and Susan as still being special friends. I played along with their jokes about us "going steady," welcomed the benign jabs and taunts about the necking and French kissing that I was doing all wrong when we went off into the woods, even though it was obvious to everyone that absolutely nothing was happening or would happen. I was old enough to know some things from romantic scenes in movies I watched with my parents, plus the one Sunday morning I walked in on them hugging naked in the bed, but actual sexual activity was as distant from me as the idea of going to a job each day like my father did. I understood it was coming for me but had zero desire. With my cabin it was the chatter itself that was the point, our early rehearsals of the idiotic sparring and parrying that would take up an alarmingly large measure of our idleness in the coming years but that by primordial design served as the simplest mechanism for us becoming true friends, and in this case nearly blood brothers. I never felt comfortable being the center of attention, but it was a light mantle for me with our co-captains Mickey and Jimmy Choi, and wacky Recipe and groovy David and Peter the brain, and the good Sangs and Fluffy, these sweet, indefatigable, as yet unfettered boys.

The prevailing focus, though, wasn't on me and Susan. The real hype was on the two-night sleep-out scheduled for this last week of the session, when we would carry all the necessary clothing and gear and provisions while ascending the steep and apparently at points treacherous three-mile trail that traversed the stone spine of Greer's Ridge and then slip through the infamously narrow passageways of a massive rock outcropping called the Juicer before hiking down to the tent sites around Trench Lake, which was much rounder than long and narrow Charminster Lake and supposedly so deep and dark and cold that bizarre, nightmarish creatures dwelled at the bottom. There were numerous tales of kids getting concussions or breaking ankles on the "Trench trek" who had to be stretchered off the ridge and sent home in ignominy. Ben Frost had gone over what we needed to bring for ourselves and for the larger group, as each cabin was tasked with lugging some of the food supplies we'd need to prepare for three days of meals. So along with our compasses and bug spray and sleeping bags each of us would have to hump an extra load of canned vegetables or bottles of ketchup or a sack of buckwheat flour for the wild blueberry pancakes that were the traditional final breakfast. The reality was that the day before two members of the dining-hall staff drove a 4WD pickup truck on an old logging track to Trench Lake with a back bed full of perishables like milk and ground beef and eggs and cheese plus sliced white bread and sacks of potato chips and coolers of ice water for us to make bug juice, plus the pots and skillets and utensils to cook it all. We heard that the idea of us bearing some of the provisions ourselves came not from one of the reverends but Mrs. Hahm, which made total sense, as she was a natural taskmaster and had made three boys who'd skipped Bible study take turns cleaning the lone and always splattered toilet in the main meeting lodge for the rest of session. "That lady thinks she's the boss of the universe," Jimmy Choi complained while we were readying our backpacks. He was a chronic Bible study truant. "I hate her almost as much as I did my Little League coach. He was this old Chinese guy who never played baseball, and he didn't know most of the rules. All he knew about was volleyball, so he made us jump a lot. We never practiced enough hitting and fielding. He just had us run laps around the field, jumping. Not even on the bases. God, I hated him!"

"Don't hate, Jimmy," Ben Frost told him as he came around to check our packing. "It won't get you anywhere good. And you should know that it was one of the counselors whose idea it was last summer that we hike in some of the food."

"Really? Who?"

Ben Frost gave a prideful smile, something you never saw.

"No way!"

We were paying closer attention now. Ben Frost helped me stuff the last of the three cans of cut corn into my backpack, pulling hard on the zipper to close it tight. He tested it with one hand, lifting the backpack like a light barbell. When I hefted the shoulder strap I had to recenter my footing.

"You guys know I'm a reader of the Bible. I think it's a book full of wisdom, especially if you don't take it too literally. You'll know what I mean by that when you're older. Anyway, you're probably thinking that there's some lesson I read in there about self-reliance, about self-responsibility, which is why we're each carrying this extra weight. But this wasn't the reason I suggested it to Reverend Hahm. In Galatians it talks about bearing your brother's burden, and I thought that would be a good way of thinking about why our man J.-G. here, for example, is going to lug all this corn. He's going to enjoy having some of it himself, but really, it's for the rest of us."

"Can J.-G. carry my green beans?" Recipe asked, waving two cans. Everyone cracked up.

Ben Frost was laughing, too. "But you know what? I'm confident that if you truly needed him to, he and any of the rest of you would. Being with all of you these past ten days, seeing you work and play together, I can say I know that about all of you. We're brothers and sisters, both here in this camp and out in the world. It's what we do for the welfare and joy of others that means anything. We're nothing if not that."

We were nodding at his loving, groovy message, which was a message we rarely heard from our parents, who were necessarily focused on figuring out and getting ahead in this unfamiliar world in whatever way they could, accruing some measure of surplus and the security (mostly psychic) that comes with it, but our feeling was mostly for the messenger, who was golden even in his humility. That's the thing about meeting an exceptional person, especially when you're young, it doesn't matter who they are or where they're from or what they look like, you want to be with them, align with them so closely that you become them. A few of us, including me, had made bandannas from strips of the tie-dyed T-shirts we'd made during arts and crafts and wore them just like he did. We resolved that once back home we wouldn't be cutting our hair. We scrutinized Dahlia to catalog the many ways she was beautiful to him. One day, during swim time, I spotted his spectacles on a towel and quickly tried them on. Everything was blurry and warped, which shocked me, given his wide range of prowess, but it made me esteem him even more, knowing no deficit could ever hobble him.

We Antlers trooped with fresh purpose as we began our hike to the campout, keeping our shoulders unhunched and backs firm like Ben Frost at the head of our column, the increment of toil from the provisions like a shot of a vitamin that would only make us stronger. Still, the heavy morning air was sapping, warm and damp beneath a batting of lingering fog. It was the kind of light that is diffuse but almost blinding, and you had to squint as the sun got stronger and began burning away the mist. The heat grew stifling. Now it made sense why Ben Frost told us to wear our swim trunks instead of hiking shorts, as we'd want to jump in right away when we reached Trench Lake.

We had set off as the first of the five cabins on the campout—two girls' cabins and three boys'—and by the time we took a break at a man-made clearing halfway up Greer's Ridge our backs and shoulders were soaked through from the press of the backpacks. Ben Frost mopped his face with his bandanna and then wiped his wire-framed glasses as we sat on the cut logs and opened our canteens. He'd warned us to ration our water during the hike as there would be nothing potable until we got to the tent site by the lake, but here was David chugging from his canteen as if he'd just crossed the Sahara, and Sang II carefully decanting his water into the tiny opening of an anthill, and Jimmy Choi wildly fountaining his head and face, his tongue extending and twisting to catch the runoff. Recipe realized he'd left his filled canteen on his cot, so Mickey and then I gave him sips from ours after making him promise not to bogart the nozzle with his lips. Recipe being Recipe, he complied by pouring Mickey's into his mouth but then wickedly slobbered on mine. I chased him around the clearing and finally cuffed his neck and pried my canteen from his arms. I cussed him but he wrapped himself around me, theatrically panting like he was dying of thirst.

"Check out these two!"

I knew whose voice it was, and I grew cold. There was a decent gap between the cabins, but Dickens had caught up to us. Since that first day he'd steadily grown popular with his cabin and with the rest of camp. My cabinmates seemed uncertain how to react, unsettled by the exuberance of Dickens's tone. Up trail, Ben Frost was talking with the other cabin's counselor, Herman, who was gesturing to the top of the ridge while trying to light a cigarette. He was breathing heavily, the sweat soaking through his dark baseball cap.

"You guys are tight, huh?" Dickens was talking not to me but to Recipe. "Best buddies?"

Recipe didn't reply. He'd let go of me, but he stayed pressed to my shoulder. He always told me he loathed Dickens, but whenever he was close by Recipe got nervy, shrinking a little. I suppose I shrank, too, if in another way, more desiccating, hardening.

"All right, gentlemen," Ben Frost announced, coming back with Herman. "Because of how hot it's gotten we're going to take a bypass trail that stays more in the shade."

"We're not going to go to the top of the hill?" Jimmy Choi asked.

"We'll summit the ridge on the return. This other trail will be less steep, and this way we get to the Juicer sooner, and to Moss Falls. Herman's cabin will wait here for the Snow Leopards and let them know the new routing, and they'll pass on word to the next cabin, and so on. Okay, Antlers. Let's load it up now."

Our crew got ready. I hooked my canteen on my rucksack and put it on. Then I had to help Recipe with his, one of the shoulder straps having come loose at the bottom. Stuff like that was constantly happening to Recipe. His sneakers were always untied, his mattress was always skewed and half off the cot, he once stumbled and dropped our table's platter of spaghetti and meatballs all over the dining-hall floor. But he'd pop right up with a doofy face and do a crazy dance. He was always ready with a flourish, a finale.

"So long, dodo-birds," Dickens said, his voice rougher and parroty. Recipe and I were the last of our cabin to mount the trail. I tried to ignore him, but Recipe turned and gave him an odd squawk, flapping his chicken-winged elbows. That was when I heard Dickens hotly rasp: "Especially you, faggy boy."

We were walking for a bit, with Recipe trailing me, when he muttered, if not quite to anyone, "I'm not a faggot."

I didn't know what to say. I'd heard kids use that word before plenty and sometimes I had, too, but like a lot of the things we said I had only a murky sense of what it meant.

"I'm no sissy." He sounded as serious as I'd ever heard him.

So I said, "I know."

"Good."

I was pretty sure I understood what a sissy was; it was a boy who was weak or a crybaby or maybe was girly in the way he talked or used his hands, none of which you could ascribe to Recipe. Recipe *would* hang out with girls much more often than the rest of us, sit on the grass or the lodge steps with Peggy or Grace or even a random younger girl and play gohng-gi or cat's cradle while they chatted away about other kids or movies like it was the most natural thing. At first, I thought it was a little weird, but once I got to know him, I figured he was popular with girls for the same reasons we liked him, because he was antic and screwy and sometimes straight from Mars plus ever willing to make fun of himself or us, but gently and with warmth.

Soon Recipe had gathered himself and begun humming "Don't Go Breakin' My Heart," which had been on the radio constantly that summer, and I started humming along, too. But as we hiked onward, I got quiet thinking about the epithet, and how Dickens had clearly tarred Recipe with it and not me. Dickens was his own rank of jerk, he was my least favorite person on Earth, and yet I had to marvel at the gift he had for picking out some quality in a person to warp and make ugly and take advantage of. For example, I'd overheard him tell Peggy how she would be even prettier if her nose were less flat, and afterward I couldn't look at her without thinking that very thought. During a game of capture the flag, while on the periphery, I'd seen him briefly mimic the ducky way Sang I ran, waddling laboriously with his chest pushed way out. It was almost funny. Dickens had not said or done anything to me after that first day, but I couldn't help wondering what attribute of mine he would target, and whether I'd have recognized myself and darkly laughed and gone over to his side if given the chance.

We hiked in silence through the dense, charged heat. The more circuitous route to Trench Lake took almost two hours, in part due to the rest breaks and stops at those two special sites, the Juicer and Moss Falls. Halfway there the trail led to a giant, house-sized rock with a crack dividing it in two, which created a very narrow passageway that you had to squeeze yourself through, thus the name. Although we could have bypassed it everybody was keen to go through the cleaved rock, our one returning camper, Jimmy Choi, going on about how he'd heard about one tubby kid years before getting stuck and that it had taken a few hours for the emergency crew to pull him out using ropes and engine grease. He was lucky, because they were considering amputating one of his arms.

Ben Frost wouldn't confirm or deny the story—he had the scantest devilish streak—but did say that as the lead group, our job was "not to gunk up the works." This only served to make the space between the rocks appear even more impassable; it looked barely wide enough for your head, much less the rest of you, but once you stepped in there sideways, dragging your pack at your knee, you realized it was doable. The most important thing was to stay calm. The rock was at least fifteen feet high, and the passageway through it was shadowed and dank, and there were sections where you had to twist with some finesse to keep from getting jammed. We kept our trail order so I was last, before me Recipe scooting through the ten-yard-long crevasse so quickly that it seemed intentional on his part to disappear from my sight. He was tall but very skinny, skinnier than most of the typically scrawny Korean kids here and certainly skinnier than still-husky me.

I had stopped because my rucksack was bulging at the top and had snagged near the beginning of the passageway. I had to turn it over but then one of the cans of corn fell out, which I had to repack and then try to secure the prong of the belt-type buckle of the top flap, all with one hand. I could hear our guys cheering Recipe as he exited the other end, which only made me fumble and keep missing the eyelet. I was breathing hard and sweating, my mind starting to race through images of myself tearfully begging some fireman not to saw off my arm, and of my mother and father red-faced in shame, and of Dickens and his cabinmates sauntering up to me with delighted, leering grins, and instead of focusing on getting moving again I got floodlit with the idea that I could just as fiercely blame my fellow Antlers for the predicament I was in, perhaps blame Recipe most of all. I wrenched at my pack, causing more things to spill out, including my flashlight, which landed hard and sounded like its glass lens got cracked. I was going to pull the bag with all my might even if I had to dislocate my shoulder forcing myself through the crevice.

"Hey, J.-G., what's up?" It was Ben Frost, peering down at me from the top edge of the rock. He was too big to get through the Juicer the normal way so had done it by suspending himself high up between the walls of stone, where the space was much wider, this by the sheer strength of his arms and legs, and then spidering forward.

"Looks like you need to load up again, huh?"

"My pack came open! I have too much stuff!"

"You'll be fine."

"It's all a mess!" I shouted, the volume of the reverberation startling both of us.

Ben Frost paused a beat. He spoke like it was just the two of us and we had nowhere we needed to go. "Go slow. Pick up one thing at a time. Okay. Good. Just like that."

I followed his instruction until everything was back inside my pack. The flashlight wasn't working, and I saw that the little bulb was shattered. I ground my knuckles against the stone. Still, I threaded the eyelet and cinched the buckle. I dragged the pack along the ground where it was wider and I twisted and shimmied and eventually got through to the far side, where everyone was waiting at the continuation of the trail. Ben Frost had already hopped down from the rock. My cabinmates cheered, clapping my back. Recipe wrapped himself around me with his customary bear hug. This time, though, I stiffened, and I knew he could sense it. When we mounted the trail again Recipe skipped ahead to talk to David about a comic strip they liked. The others abided the gap. I wanted to stay at the rear and feel my blood ebb and flow and ebb, the wake of which left me in a raw and shaky state.

It was good, at least for me, that the hike was so difficult and slow. By the time we neared Moss Falls, I had run through my ire for my mates and the world and was too weary to drink in more. The rest were spent, too, drained by the stunning, vaporous heat and the weight of our packs, and when Ben Frost warned us to watch our footing in this next short but steeply descending section of trail, there was a collective, murmurous sigh. We had dropped well off the pace of the group in front of us, who were nowhere in sight, as had the cabin behind us; this was a march that was testing to all. We Antlers trudged the loose ground of the descending path. I almost slipped, my legs jittery. Then I heard Jimmy Choi, who despite being at camp before was here for the first time (now being old enough for the overnights), mutter: *This is it?*

Recipe said, "I guess it could be like Eden."

"Welcome to Moss Falls, gentlemen," Ben Frost sighed. "Or maybe just Moss."

It was a waterfall, yes, but now a waterfall without much water. Still, it was quite beautiful, the sort of "sylvan glade" you often read about in college literature classes. These falls weren't the typical kind that spouted from a hillside when the flow was strong but rather, Ben Frost informed us, came over the "capstone ledge," a broad, thick plate of jagged, striated limestone that extended out from the slope like a tabletop. The drop had to be twenty-five feet. We stood below in what was a natural quarry, its walls composed of a smoother, darker rock almost completely covered in moss, this amphitheater of a deep, earthy green that surrounded various pools of water. After a heavy rain or during the spring snow melt, Ben Frost told us, the flow of the falls could be many times more forceful than the drippy cascade it was now and filled the main pool to almost chest deep. It had been only a normally hot summer but one sorely lacking in rain.

But it didn't matter; we shed our boots and waded into the various rock-strewn pools; the ankle-deep water was clear and cold enough, the bottoms gravelly but not sharp. Where the falls had gouged the stone over the centuries it was nearly waist-deep, and we took turns in twos to squat in its well and splash our sweaty heads. The falls above were like a dwindling, last-chance shower. We opened our mouths to fill up with the water, though we didn't drink it, having been cautioned by Ben Frost about *Giardia*. When most everyone's turn was done the last two, Fluffy and Recipe, started flexing beneath the gentle trickle in a bodybuilder's pose-off.

Mickey was beside me and we were laughing at them, then we were doing the same.

"I was kinda worried back there," Mickey said, referring to, I realized, the Juicer. "I mean, not for you but for me."

"You got stuck, too?"

"No way." He raised each of his knees, to show the fresh raw scrapes. "I crawled through as fast as I could. I really hate tight spaces."

"Is that why you don't have a sleeping bag?" Mickey only used blankets on his cot, beneath him and for cover, and because he was clearly the finest of us in bearing and character, nobody questioned him about it, not even Jimmy Choi. He had them tightly rolled up and tied to his backpack.

"Yeah. I kind of freak out. It's like being a mummy, getting zipped up like that."

I nodded, though to me it was a comforting sensation,

how babies must feel getting swaddled. Most nights it had been too hot inside the cabin to encase myself fully, but sleeping outside in the cooler night air it would be perfect.

"I wonder if they'll let us sleep right next to the campfire," I said.

"I hope so. We can roast marshmallows while lying down. The night hiking will be fun, too."

"My flashlight's busted," I groaned, remembering. "What am I going to do?"

"Maybe one of the counselors has an extra one. If not, you can go with me."

"Those trails aren't wide enough for two."

"You can lead us," Mickey offered. "I'll go behind you. We can get Peter to go behind me. He's got that huge lantern thing."

Indeed, Peter's flashlight looked like an old-fashioned oil lamp, which you held from the top by a wire loop. He was embarrassed by it, and sore at his parents for making him bring it to camp. It was heavy, being metal and loaded with a single, huge, squared battery, and it shone like a lighthouse. After about twenty minutes of the hike, Ben Frost had to carry it for him.

"Okay," I said, and Mickey low-fived me.

"It's all gonna be good, J.-G."

I wanted to thank him, not just for the idea of how we'd night hike but for his talking about the Juicer, which I knew was his way of showing his concern for me. But I knew I didn't deserve any concern, given all the little false things I'd said and done to him and the rest. I kept quiet.

Once Ben Frost finally got Recipe and Fluffy to come out of the water, we began pulling on our socks and boots. Recipe was still horsing around and had Fluffy lean over Jimmy Choi, who was propped against a rock and placidly sunbathing, and squeezed out the water from Fluffy's spongy hair onto his face. Jimmy was livid and we were all cracking up and he chased them with a stick, but he was laughing, too. Jimmy then asked Ben Frost if he was going to show the rest of us "the special spot" and Ben Frost pretended to be deciding, but we demanded to see it and he led us to claw up the near side of the mossy face on a line well-hidden by brush. The stone was slick and the footing loose and it would have been difficult to clamber up without our boots on. Then we had to hop down onto some sharp rocks right next to the dripping water, crowding onto a platform of stone just big enough for us to stand shoulder to shoulder and back to chest in this cavey hollow. Everyone was hooting and howling at the sparkly light filtering through the feeble tumble of waters, but I could only see the illumination as murky and gray, like a grimy shower door, and it dawned on me that the hours of our brotherhood were draining away too fast, and luckily the scatter and splash got our faces wet enough to veil my own tears for having ever deceived any of them.

At the camping site there was much for us to do in setting up, and I resolved to be indispensable. It seemed only right: save for my family (and maybe not even them), I knew now that these boys, and by extension Charminster and (almost) everything in it, were the very best things in my life. The kitchen staff had trucked up not only food and drink and picnicware but also the tents, two for each cabin, which we were tasked with erecting, and without any guidance from the counselors. Reverend Hahm, who had ridden up in one of the pickup trucks to greet us and bless the overnight, quoted Hebrews 3:4: "For every house is builded by some man; but he that built all things is God." He spread his arms wide to have us take in the scenery of the petite lake and surrounding woods, which was indeed the picture of something an Almighty might have made.

Mrs. Hahm had tagged along, too, and she stepped in front of him in the middle of his exhortation about our accepting His Bounteous Love and lectured in her messy, strident English about how it could be "dangerous" for girls and boys "going to nature together" and having "funny lover feelings"; we'd heard a rumor that a boy and girl had been caught playing doctor in the woods during swim time, but no one knew who they were or if it was really true. I'd never played doctor, but David told me he had with his older cousin Kathy, who'd examined every part of him. David was advanced that way and had smuggled into camp one of his artist father's small, leatherbound diaries full of line drawings of nudes and charged us a dime to take a quick minute's look. After Mrs. Hahm's diatribe about fooling around he nudged me and hotly whispered: "Like your hanky-panky with Susan Sun!"

I chuckled, more anxiously than with pride, as I had been trying hard not to think about her anymore but was now miserably failing with her standing up at the front with her fellow Snow Leopards, the curt flip of her damp, black hair—every cabin had stopped for a frolic in Moss Falls—gleaming in the bright sun. I was half hoping and half fearing Susan would glance back to me, but she stood motionless, and a sliver of my heart died while Mrs. Hahm rasped on about us shaming our parents in ways she didn't specify. Whatever it might be she was warning against, my earlier shaming of my parents gave me no interest in doing so again. Reverend Hahm waited patiently for her to finish and then shut his eyes extra tight as he pressed a fist against his solar plexus and unwound a prayer for our well-being and goodness whose extra length was no doubt an acknowledgment (if not endorsement) of his wife's vehemence.

When it was over we got moving on our job of setting up the tents. We were dazed by sitting on our haunches under that searing sun, but to see the splayed tents-to-be in the plan of an enchanting little village overlooking the lake gave us a surge of delight. It was the kind of outpost I had read about in adventure novels where you could live with your mates in self-sufficient perpetuity, hunting small game, fishing and foraging, and chopping down trees for shelter and cooking fires. The tents, likely dating from the 1950s, were made of thick mustard-colored canvas panels that zipped together and had an entrance flap for one wall and a mesh window stitched into another, the structure requiring at least a dozen aluminum posts that came together in an unnecessarily complicated arrangement that somehow Fluffy and I were quickest to understand, maybe because we had both done extensive building of scale-model planes and ships and cars, so after we got our mates squared away and about to raise our first Antler tent, Ben Frost had the two of us go around to the other cabins to see if they needed a hand.

To various extents all of them did, the exploded havoc of canvas panels and metal struts and rope more evident for the boys' tents than the girls', but it was only the girls who gladly waved us over. We first helped the Gazelles, who unlike Peggy and Julie and Susan of the Snow Leopards were in the same school grade as us Antlers and thus our putative counterparts, though by some telepathic agreement our cabins had kept a comfortable distance from one another. Despite this, we knew all their names and they knew ours, and the two of them who'd flagged us, So-hyun and Alice, gave us a sour candy to suck on while we began threading the base supports of their first tent. Like most everyone else, they were sweet on Fluffy, who was a giggly doughnut ball of a kid, short enough not to intimidate even the youngest ones and never minding whenever any of us wanted to touch his hair. Once for some nervy tykes he craned down his steel-wool mop that tinged auburn when the sun backlit it and let them burrow their fingers deep in its tangle until they squirmed from the tickle.

So-hyun stood over Fluffy's shoulder as he knelt and worked, carefully observing his progress. Jimmy Choi contended she was the prettiest of their cabin because she had large, round "American" eyes, an aesthetic proposition that was new to me and seemed to make sense although picturing my mother and my sister, and Susan Sun and Peggy, and others with narrow eyes, I had thought they were plenty pretty, too. So-hyun and Alice were a clever pair and used words I'd never heard before like "sequence" and "perplexing" while pointing out that Fluffy and I might be connecting certain tent supports incorrectly, even when they were propping things up. They were correct; we switched the struts and the tent didn't sag on one end as before as I zipped up the front flap—later we would break the bad news to our fellow Antlers, who had to dismantle and rebuild ours—and they each pumped my hand once in thanks but pressed Fluffy between them in a big, joyful hug like he was some kind of cartoon character come to life.

Fluffy was flying high, strutting his stuff as we went around to check with the other cabins assembling their tents. You'd think he would have been accustomed to such treatment by this point in the session, but I knew from the many details he'd told me about his neighborhood in Jersey City, where he didn't venture out much because the kids were rough on him and called him "Nigga-Chink" because of his kinky hair and slanty eyes and swarthy complexion, that Charminster was a special place for him, too. I was only happy for him. He was our mascot and our friend and our cousin and our brother. He and I were not rivals for anything or anyone. And yet I couldn't stop screening in a mean dark garret of my mind the frames of his puffed, anguished face as some sneering boys poured a half-pint of chocolate milk over his head, or wedgied him by his underwear on a playground fence post, or booted him hard in the back and told him to get lost, ugly flickerings of his days that nauseated me but that I didn't try to quell. It was as if I thought my hard imaginings would keep him alert, keep him vigilant, for I knew he shouldn't dream of a place like this too much, he shouldn't forget how it was and would be again in the bloody throat of the world.

By the time all the tents got pitched, both with and without our help, a good number of the kids had ended up lying about the weedy grass with their arms flung over their eyes. The kitchen staffers had set out several folding tables laden with trays of ham salad sandwiches and corn on the cob and those tiny boxes of raisins for dessert. It didn't matter that Fluffy disliked both ham and raisins, or that it made me crazy whenever I ate fresh corn how the kernel fibers would get stuck in my teeth, the counselors decided that for our efforts we would be first to fill our paper plates and we did just that, piling on the triangular sandwich halves and the cobs and taking a few raisin boxes each. The others looked like POWs in their sun- and hunger-beaten silence as they watched us stuffing ourselves by the water's edge, even Dickens, whom I noticed in the corner of my vision, standing there looking, for once, thoroughly trounced, slack-jawed and dead in the eyes. I knew he was watching me, and for him alone I gnawed at that cob, raked it with disregard for my jammed teeth, cringing and reveling and raging all at once.

After some rest time, the counselors announced that we would have the inner-tube races in the lake. Everyone cheered, desperate for the cooling water. We already knew that only those of us who'd passed the deep-water test at Charminster Lake could participate, the others serving as judges; as reputed, Trench Lake dropped away dramatically after just a few steps in, as the counselors Herman and Brenda demonstrated while wading in hand in hand in their cutoff jeans. Brenda was wearing a tie-dyed bikini top that barely held in her breasts, Herman shirtless, his pale torso soft-looking and tufted with light brown hair at his sternum and below his navel, their collegiate fleshiness so much more ample and florid than that of my thirtysomething immigrant parents, whose slender frames hadn't yet been filled out by American life. Brenda and Herman took a couple halting, almost matrimonial strides and then fell as if stepping off a cliff, plunging beneath the surface. We waited. They didn't rise. We waited some more. One of Brenda's campers let out a high shriek. Then they both popped up at the white buoy in the middle of the small lake, still a decent stone's throw from shore. The two also served as lifeguards during swim time and were excellent swimmers. We cheered again, this time louder. They swam back to us like swans, hardly making ripples.

The inner tubes, from semitruck tires, were large enough for two of us to sit in. It wasn't a formal competition between cabins and the counselors paired us randomly with any camper, whether boy or girl. There was groaning at first, some sighs and hesitation, but quickly everyone got into the spirit of the game and climbed aboard the tubes and held on for when Ben Frost and Dahlia sent off teams with a shove toward the buoy, which you had to navigate around and return, like in the opening day's footrace. After that you paddled with your hands, employing your feet more like rudders after realizing they were useless for propulsion.

I was paired with a very tall girl from Susan's cabin named Esther, who seemed easygoing and had fetching, high-angling eyes and smiled a lot, but was so disinclined to speak as to be nearly mute. Even her cabinmates, who liked her, had little idea what she was truly like. At that age, and being female, her great height was a millstone, causing her to hunch down a few notches to the rest of us. In the coming years, one assumes, her stature and good looks would play out differently in the wider world. When our heat began it was a shock when Esther started hollering, screaming for me to paddle as furiously as she was with her mad, windmilling scoops. She had long and powerful arms, and as much as I tried, I couldn't keep pace. Unevenly powered, we kept turning too much to her side, losing to two scrawny younger boys by three full lengths. Esther wasn't sore, though, and neither was I, and to my surprise she wrapped me in a sweetly sweaty and slightly rank lake-water bear hug after we stepped ashore, momentarily lifting me off my feet like my mother sometimes did. The heats were continually launching so no one much noticed us amid the hoopla and commotion but somehow Susan and I caught each other's gaze. She was smiling wryly, likely more *for* me than *at* me, but I quickly mortared over any difference. That she might still be on my side was the only thing that mattered.

The races went on until everyone who was eligible got a run. The poor kids who'd failed the deep-water test were relegated to the shallows and served as finish-line judges; back then you took what you got and no one in charge much worried about it. By the end, though, there were no winners and therefore no losers, just all of us drenched and chirping about how fast or slow or wayward certain tubers were, like the team that Herman had to swim for and tug back after it had drifted weirdly to one end of the lake. It seemed funny to me that no one was talking about the near incident that had occurred, one that involved Dickens Rho.

In truth, it was brief enough to be hardly noticeable. To anyone else it probably looked like some extra splashes in the water, but I was always aware of his presence and doings. I saw what was happening from the first moment of contact between his tube and the other, which was in the heat before his and returning to shore. The racing had been designed like this, no doubt to multiply the mayhem, and a few of the teams naturally went out of their way to invite collisions. I was tracking Dickens's progress and when he and his partner, who were instead intent on defeating their opponent and moving quite fast, were about to be rammed by the onrushing tube, he tried to ward it off. But the combined speed of both, and Dickens's levering arm, caused the tubes to tip, and one of the other riders and Dickens both fell into the water. This had happened to several other tubers, and quickly enough those kids had climbed back aboard, as did Dickens's counterpart now. The racing continued wildly around them. Dickens, however, couldn't find his grip on the slick black rubber and flailed awkwardly before dipping momentarily beneath the surface. It should have been no trouble; he was deep-water certified. Perhaps he had inhaled some water, or suddenly gauged the vaunted depths of the lake, or been startled, as I had, by how frigid the water got if you let yourself descend even a couple feet, but when he resurfaced his arms poked out, all wooden. I saw his handsome face contorted in a grimace. He was panicking. I knew I should cry out. Raise the alarm. There should be an irrepressible human response.

I closed my eyes. I saw a lifeless body, a frantic scrum, people in tears. It was only for a breath, but it was smashing. Then I saw Dickens struggling to haul himself atop the tube, with Herman in the water pushing up his legs. Dickens got in the tube. He was fine now, half grinning the way the unscathed do after nearly being undone.

"You see that?" Esther said, her hand visoring her eyes as she looked out at the water.

"What?" I mumbled. I was drying off my face, peeking out from the drape of the towel.

I don't know what she could have known about me and Dickens or thought personally about him. Maybe, like everyone else, she found him impressive. She was about to say something but then her nature prevailed. She skipped away.

I was energized the rest of the afternoon. I was game even for the chores, which after an already fully active day of hiking and tubing there was some grousing about. We had to go draw water from the well pump by the old pavilion and carry it back, and gather kindling and start the cooking fires, and finally do all the necessary prep for the dish each cabin would contribute to dinner. Ours, Ben Frost told us, was the main dish of the dinner, something called Campers' Stew, which would require the cans of vegetables we backpacked in, plus some of the fresh ingredients that the kitchen staff had delivered. They'd already packed up the lunch tables and left on the rough road back.

"I volunteered the Antlers," Ben Frost said. "I'll show you how, but you guys are going to make it. It's one of my favorites."

Despite this endorsement most of us weren't keen to get involved, especially after Jimmy Choi said cooking was for girls. Ben Frost, forever unflappable, handed him a can opener. He opened the first can, the others taking turns with the rest, but once that was done most everyone drifted off to the lake or back into the tents. I was happy to stay. I wanted to try to cook, no matter what Jimmy Choi said. In fact, my mother would say something similar about cooking whenever I loitered in the kitchen, never letting me help because of her fear that I would cook too often when I was a husband and spoil my wife. I do cook regularly now, and if I spoil my wife in this way, I don't care. There's such scant time, in sum. With my mother, I enjoyed watching her wash and cut the vegetables and then butcher a hunk of meat or a chicken, which she did without any of the impatience or angst with which she went about her duties outside the house, like the grocery shopping or going to the post office. In our kitchen she was confident and methodical, she kept to her own pace and rhythms, and at the end of her many ministrations something good to eat would appear. Rarely was it bad. It was with her in mind that I raised my hand to chop the onions and carrots and potatoes and green peppers for the stew when no one else immediately volunteered. It was also, of course, to please Ben Frost. He set me up with a large cutting board placed on one of the picnic coolers and showed me the knife I would use. The steel blade was dark gray with faint mottles of rust, and the very tip was broken off. It had a smooth burled handle of a reddish wood, and it was heavier than I expected, like when you picked up a lead fishing weight.

"Have you ever done this before?" Ben Frost asked. "Because I can show you."

To anyone else I would have fibbed, equating watching my mother use a knife with my having done so, but to him I shook my head. He pulled a large yellow onion from the net sack and sliced off its root end and then peeled its paper with his fingers. Then he cut it in two and then chopped one half radially and then the other way, leaving a pile of die-sized chunks. He then showed me how to grip the other half with my fingers bent, and I marveled at how sharp the blade was, so unlike the serrated carving knife I'd flashed at Tommy Reilly, the menacing teeth of which you could tap with the pad of your thumb and not be cut. You had to saw at things with that one, use your whole angry arm. This edge dove right through the crisp flesh of the onion, and we started to tear up from its spicy gas, which I'd seen happen to my mother, and Ben Frost and I both started acting like we were seriously broken up and sad, which was the very opposite of how I felt. It's an odd picture of my happiness, knife in hand, but there it is.

Ben Frost deemed me ready to take command and left me to dice the potatoes and carrots while he supervised the others in propping two oversized cast-iron kettles on a metal grate at the edge of our campfire. The idea was to shovel hot coals beneath the pots with a camping shovel so it would simmer slowly. The pots were huge, looking more like bathtubs for small children than cooking equipment, and they were just as heavy. Stoking their own small cooking fires were the other cabins, who had their own designated dishes: skillet cornbread, and cheesy baked potatoes wrapped individually in foil, and Dutch oven mac 'n' cheese, and for dessert, s'mores. It would turn out to be a lot of food but as ever the charge was to keep us occupied and busy and too tired and sated to get into trouble, and maybe teach us a few useful things, too.

I still know how to make Campers' Stew, or at least the Charminster version of it, although I've not made it since. I was feeling carefree and confident that day. Wielding a long metal spoon of Mr. Hammonds's, I spearheaded the process, sous-chefed by Peter, who was gung ho, and David, who mostly wanted to watch. We browned the ground beef, the fleshy, greasy aroma of which drew the others toward the pots, followed by the fried stink of the onions, which drove most of them away. Next, we put in the rest of the fresh vegetables I'd chopped, and then all the canned ones, including baked beans and tomato paste. Ben Frost had me add some secret ingredients: dollops of bright yellow mustard and squirts of Worcestershire sauce and jars of pickled peppers that he specially requisitioned from Mr. Hammonds. As we stirred the now boiling stews, they reminded me of something that Gregory Fluss's mom would regularly have simmering on their stove, a sort of chili I loved the taste of but that gave me nasty gas. This stew was a lighter shade of red, flecked with corn kernels and greenish bits. At this point a few random kids were skeptically examining it and saying it looked like vomit and Recipe goaded them on, musing whether it was colorful and chunky like stuff that blasts out of you right after eating too much, or else the kind that you gag out in waves hours later. I was going to tell him to shut it but then got spooked with the prospect that everyone else would be too scared to try it or hate it if they did and blame me for ruining this long-anticipated first campout night.

"Hey," Peter said to me, pointing down at one of the kettles. "Is it supposed to be boiling like that?"

I pushed past the kids and saw that the kettle, maybe too full of stew to start, was starting to bubble over on the side where the flames were licking up high—people had been blithely feeding what Ben Frost said should be at most a steady heat of embers—and the liquid was hissing as it contacted the edge. Was this the way it was supposed to be cooked? Ben Frost had gone off with a group of campers and the other counselors to fetch more well water—you didn't have much supervision then, even around open fires—and my remaining cabinmates were even more clueless than I, in fact worse than clueless, given how they were cheering the burbling and splatters and sudden flare-ups. These fools only relished disaster! Ben Frost had placed the kettles on the grate himself, and it would be way too heavy for just one of us to lift. The bigger trouble was that he had put them in place while they were still cold, and now the handles were as hot as white coals.

Peter, his old-man baby face pinching up, said: "I think you better move your stew, J.-G."

"It's not *my* stew!"

It shook us both, how sharply I shouted at him. But he was right. The crud building up on the inside of the pot was starting to burn.

"How are we supposed to take it off?" I yelled. We didn't have any oven mitts or anything else to pick it up with, were we even able.

"How should I know?" Peter yelled louder back.

David idly murmured, "You should be dancing," the reprise of a disco song that was also popular on the radio that summer. He was annoying enough, but then the other kids took it up, chanting it while bopping side to side in the exact right tempo. They all knew piano or violin and I hated them. But when I stared at the fire ruining my stew it wasn't they who were torching. I was picturing myself stepping into the white-hot coals. I wanted to lift the kettle with only my forearms like Kwai Chang Caine in the credit sequence of *Kung Fu*. I wanted to be seared with punishment, right down to the bone. I wanted to be destroyed.

"Hey!"

Peter was clawing my shoulder. "What's the matter with you? Are you psycho?"

My hands were about to grasp the handles. "I have to do something," I gasped, choked with smoke. It was all being wasted, my painstaking chopping and frying, my initial sampling of the stew (as Ben Frost had advised me to do), which was meaty and sweet and rich, not fishy and funky like so much of the food we all ate at home. That food was good, but this was both delectable and undemanding, as easy as eating doughnuts. I was going to serve it in the styro coffee cups that David had built into a steep pyramid, to Peggy and Julie, and to the counselors, and then to Susan Sun, for whom I'd ladle a perfectly tasty cup, plus a special one for Dickens, whose cup I'd spit in and then fill to overflowing.

But it was all nearing disaster. The whole inside of the pot was scalded, the rim blistering. No counselors were in sight. There was no more time. And then it struck me. I plopped down in the dirt.

"What are you doing now?" Peter asked, his hands on his head.

I didn't answer, trying to unsnag a lace knotted around a cleat of my hiking boots. The laces were thick and red, and I thought they looked cool and tough against the dark, burnished leather of the uppers. I worked quickly and pulled off both sets. I handed one of the boots to Peter. The other I gripped by the sole, showing the opening.

"I'm gonna put it over a handle, and you do the same."

He looked at the massive pot, realizing what I was intending. "No way. It's too heavy for us!"

"We don't have to lift it. Just pull it away some."

"I don't know about this . . ."

"Just help me, okay?"

"The fire's really hot."

"Will you stop being such a Poindexter?"

Peter's mouth crimped; he'd surely been called that a lot back home, being a brain, and I knew it would sting extra, coming from me. I didn't flinch. I stepped toward the fire, watching my footing; all I had on was socks, and the base of stones on which the grate and Dutch oven sat looked like it might suddenly crumble to nothing, for how superheated everything was. But Peter was right; leaning this close to the flames, it felt like my eyelashes were singeing. But there was no choice. You could smell a different, sharper burning. I eyed him and he was wincing from the blast of furnace-like heat, but he nodded. I reached out and shoved my boot over the iron handle and Peter used the other for his and I barked *Now* and we pulled the Dutch oven forward a few inches clear of the flames. Peter was heartened and we scooched it a little more, which seemed to me enough, but then without warning he tugged on the pot before I could pull on my side and it tipped off the grate. I quickly shoved it back, but he was shrieking, shaking his hand wildly.

Some stew had splashed over and scalded him. He was wheezing between his teeth at an unnaturally high pitch and for a second I thought he was faking it, holding his hand stiffly at the wrist like it wasn't a part of him. But then we both saw it: a welt the color of unripe strawberry had bloomed on the back of his hand and two littlest fingers. Bits of stew clung to the angry, raw skin. His hand looked monstrous. This is when Peter dropped to his knees and started to cry. Really bawl. When you're a kid, there's nothing like the pain you feel when you realize you should be scared. I told him to shut up, and for a moment he did, but then he was only crying louder and drawing attention, and I stood over him like those men in the penitentiary had over the mouthy Marvin, my hands tensed in the air like I was already choking him.

Suddenly David nudged me aside, ordering Peter: "Stick out your hand!"

David doused it with two styro cups full of water, having instinctively run to the lake and filled the cups. Peter wailed, the sudden cold maybe worse. But at least he could breathe now, if low and fast. Dahlia, who'd been hanging out with her younger campers, had sprinted over and immediately had us throw dirt on the roaring fire to quell it. None of us had thought to do something as simple as that. While examining Peter she asked what happened and I said he spilled the stew and she gave me a funny look but didn't say anything, and neither did Peter. He wouldn't look at me. She walked him with his head tucked snugly under her tanned arm to one of the counselors' tents, where there was a first aid kit.

"Shoot!" David exclaimed, bemoaning the fact, I thought, that it wasn't him snuggling up close to Dahlia, whom he would always stare at without shame. He was constantly talking about girls and how he was going to "get with one" soon. But he was pointing to my hiking boots, one of which was still partly on the grate. I snatched it off. It was scorched on one side with random marks, like a badly grilled steak. The heel of the rubber sole was partially melted and was now uneven. The other boot, which Peter had used, lay in the dirt, its leather upper broadly stained with the greasy red-orange liquid of the stew. I wanted to chuck them into the lake.

"Look at it this way," David said, standing beside me. "At least you saved your dish."

I tried to keep thinking that when we gathered for dinner soon thereafter. The other dishes looked good, especially the mac 'n' cheese the Snow Leopards made, which was butter-colored and creamy with extra cheese melted on top. The baked potatoes were fat and bursting out of their foil wrappers, and I had to admit that the skillets of cornbread from Dickens's cabin had come out a fetching golden shade. Even the Campers' Stew, which had turned a lot darker and crusty on top around the edges, drew an eager queue. I was afraid to taste it despite Ben Frost saying that it was "definitely flavorful" after sampling some to check its seasoning.

Everyone filled up a paper plate of food along with half a styro cup portion of stew and congregated by the lake to eat. I hadn't taken any stew yet and was scanning around and watching kids eat and I couldn't help but remember one afternoon the summer before when my mother brought snacks and a cooler of lemonade for my Little League team. At the end of practice, she and I passed out little paper cups of lemonade and one kid made a face and complained that it was too sour, which prompted everyone else to say the same and spit it out. I was furious at her for making it wrong (when it was likely that kid just being picky) and sulked the whole drive home. I'm sure she thought I was rotten, spoiled, and disloyal, but as it was, she took it harder than I did.

Now everyone was munching away and chatting and laughing and I thought, *Okay*, and went to the folding tables to get some for myself. But passing by I heard a kid groan, "Ooh," after tasting a spoonful of stew, and I noticed another boy put his clearly unfinished cup down in the weedy grass, and then I saw a girl offer hers to her counselor Brenda, who immediately shook her head.

Your hearing is keenest when you fear the gossip is about you. By the time I got to the tables and ladled some into my own cup, word had spread: *Don't eat the stew! The stew is burnt!* I was certain that people were staring at me. I wondered how I could slip away and hike all the way back to our cabin, but then I realized all I had for footwear now were the sandals I was wearing. Or maybe this should be my plan: I would run away, get my feet badly scratched and my legs cut up and have to stay the rest of the session with the kind infirmary lady. I sneered at my father's perennial advice, that I give my fullest, best effort and hope for good results. It wasn't working for me, and never did, everything I laid my hands on getting messed up and ruined and ending in my disgrace. All I needed was to look over at poor Peter, trying and failing to use a plastic fork with his bulky, bandaged-up hand. Only Recipe had come for seconds of the stew, insisting that it tasted like the favorite part of the pork ribs his mother made, which were the crispy, blackened tips of the bones. He tried to get me to slap him five but I'd left him hanging.

I trudged away from the lake and wandered into the woods, alone. I needed to be alone, because now a terrible notion was seeping into me, something even more caustic than the rage and shame. It was the idea that I'd been let down, but let down by none other than Ben Frost. What had he said? *Definitely flavorful.* He was not a careless person, someone who spoke or acted idly. Although I didn't yet know the word, I understood what sarcasm was, but was this it? Had I misread his tone? Or was it his aim to deceive me, because he had come to realize what an awful person I was, the kind who takes sides against his own mother with other snot-nosed, ignorant boys? Hadn't he encouraged me to try cooking the Campers' Stew, saying how I always seemed to enjoy eating, and thus invited my humiliation? Maybe Ben Frost wasn't as special as I thought. Maybe he was imperfect, like the other people I loved, like my mother who always mangled her words at the store, or my father who was always too busy, or my sister who did everything right except for enduring grief and insults from the likes of me.

I wandered deeper into the woods, finding the old pavilion, nothing changed in the still strong light of the early evening garlanding the treetops save my own sight, which was stripping everything of any sparkle; this undercanopy might as well have been a dimmed cave, the fetching, fern-lined trail a jagged rut in the dirt. If I had some embers, I could set the creaky wood of this decrepit pavilion afire, and then crouch in the middle of it like that red-sashed Buddhist monk in a photograph I'd seen in *Life* magazine, the flames completely enveloping his body but not yet marring his smooth, young man's face. He wasn't even wincing. Could I repose in such beatitude? With that much forceful calm?

A switch can get flipped. Not for everyone, surely, but for me it has happened too often in my life. It's a dark capacity, to be able to check what was a broad, surging river of feeling right down to a trickle.

I protested this world so much I could disappear. I could die.

"Hey, man, up here all by yourself?" It was Mickey, with two styro cups in his hands. He would pile on, too? But the cups, I could see, were filled with purple bug juice. The low walls of the square pavilion had simple benches built into them and he sat beside me in the corner.

"I saw you heading off and then you didn't come back."

I was silent.

"What's going on?"

"My hiking boots are ruined."

Mickey grunted. He handed me a cup and tapped his to mine and we drank. I was thirsty enough that it tasted wonderful.

"Let's go back now," he said. "Everybody's going to have dessert."

"I don't care," I said, trying to sound defiant. "I don't like s'mores. Marshmallows are weird."

"I'm not so hot on them, either. But at least we can have some chocolate, right?"

"I'm not hungry." Though in uttering that I suddenly realized how hungry I was; I'd never made up a plate. And now I felt doubly self-pitying, my mother having conditioned in me an irrational fear of hunger, its pangs sure portents of illness. For some reason I suffered a lot of high fevers in my childhood, one extreme enough that my parents took me to the hospital. Growing up, my one responsibility was to make sure my belly was always full, to keep up my strength. To the day she died my mother worried aloud that those fevers had somehow altered my brain.

"Let's go back now," Mickey said, gently rapping my knee like a father might. "You really want to stay here all night? Plus, I really want some of that chocolate. Did you see those huge Hershey bars?"

I hadn't but I'd seen those bars before, when some rich kid at school brought in a bunch of them for the class, bars the size of a shoebox top and as thick as your hand. We got up and we finished our juices and headed back. There was still plenty of sunlight and I slowed down when through the trees I saw kids tossing their dinner plates and styro cups in garbage bags.

"You know, the stew really wasn't that bad," Mickey said. "I ate mine."

"It wasn't burnt?"

He shrugged. "Maybe a little. Recipe sure liked it."

"He likes everything."

"Yeah. But others did, too. Especially after Ben Frost said it was a little smoky but still good. He said it was like 'Kansas City barbecue.' I don't know what that is. Do you?"

I didn't know, either, but it didn't sound so wonderful to me. Still, the fact that Ben Frost had defended my half-burnt stew was heartening. Maybe he hadn't meant to trick or, heaven forbid, betray me. But where was he now? Everyone was lining up at the campfire where they were just now setting out the ingredients for making the s'mores. It was not an ideal dessert for them to prepare, given that each serving had to be put together individually, but nobody seemed to care that it would take forever. There was nothing else to do. I saw Dickens and his brother and friends near the front, beaming as always. As Mickey and I passed by, Dickens said, almost affably, "Thank God for this dessert."

"What'd you say?" Mickey snapped. Dickens just chuckled, completely ignoring us.

We ended up at the very back of the line, my fault for having fled. I should have felt bad for Mickey, yet I couldn't help but keep stepping to the side and stealing looks at Dickens. His self-assurance filled me with loathing and envy; I imagined myself saying the same thing to him about having ruined something with such straightforwardness, with such audacity. He somehow sensed my own feeling that I ought to be punished for my failings, his nose for someone's softer spots a capacity I realized I wished I had more keenly. This is what they mean by keeping your enemies close; you think you are learning how to deal with a foe, anticipating their tactics, their antagonisms, rehearsing all the ways of defending yourself, but what happens is that you begin to see certain concordances, reflections of the contours of who you might be.

I was looking for Susan, too, among the groupings of girls, but I couldn't locate her. Was she actively avoiding me? I wondered what she might say to me, whether she'd try to soothe me or distract me, or else expose me with the cold fact that I'd taken on the task of cooking not out of a sense of duty or Christian selflessness but for the chance of adulation from my cabinmates and other campers and yes, from even Dickens Rho. Was this place different, or was I? I would never have sought out such attention or veneration on the playgrounds or school grounds back home. But here, at Korean Camp

Charminster, I could imagine myself being propped at the center of the throng, celebrated by raw throats and hearts.

I half shut my eyes, imagining there to be a pause in time, this private gloaming I could conjure when I needed. I thought I saw candles then, or a crown of candles, this wide torch that was dancing before me, my chest humming with a pleasing melody. The secret to happiness is to be able to deceive yourself. You push on when there is no evidence that you should.

Yet every so often, the universe will oblige: for here before me now were Susan and Recipe, bearing a large sheet cake between them, its thick lard of white icing aglow from the light of many candles, and they were singing Happy Birthday, as were Ben Frost and Dahlia beside them, while Herman strummed his guitar. They set the cake on a folding picnic table. Everyone was joining in, and so I was, too, when Susan said, "Hey, dum dum, are you going to blow them out?"

I pretended to be the fool who didn't realize it was his own birthday, holding my head in shock as I gawked at the eleven fluted blue candles that my mother, I would soon learn, had slipped Ben Frost on drop-off day along with some money for a cake, or in this instance a tip for Mr. Hammonds, who had made it from scratch. There must have been other kids with a birthday during camp, but only my mother had thought to mark it, no doubt out of her manifold worries for me. I pivoted, raising my hands. I killed all the candles in one furious exhalation. A cheer went up. Recipe hugged me and I would have squirmed away except that his embrace corralled Susan, too, inadvertently pressing her face against mine, her parted lips mashed high on my cheek. I leaned into her; she didn't shrink away. It must have been for no more than an instant, but I thought I could taste the warmth of her mouth, as fecund as summer lake water.

I had trouble falling asleep that night in the tent. Despite how exhausted I was—how exhausted we all were, after the lengthy hike and full day—my thoughts kept turning, turning. Of course I was centered on Susan, and what I now took as our kiss. To my surprise no one had much registered our contact, not even Recipe, who before he dozed off in his tartan sleeping bag muttered only how he liked the smell of Susan's hair. I liked it, too, knowing exactly what he meant, a piney, smoky fragrance from the numerous campfires our group had set that afternoon using green wood and boughs, mixed in with the dense, waxen scent of her scalp. Like the rest of us she wasn't shampooing her hair much, if at all, dependent on the swim sessions and cursory shower time to hold off any stink. We were all still young, hairless except on our heads, and although my memory may be faulty, I never thought anyone smelled bad except some of the male counselors, and then even Dahlia and Brenda, who usually smelled more than fine but sometimes, maybe late in the day, could grow almost sharply spiced to my nose, overripe. Our odors derived from our always dank sneakers and then the farting, which David shamelessly led us in. His farts were more rank than the camp septic tank when it overflowed the first week and had to be pumped out. It seemed, in retrospect, he had trouble digesting the usually greasy, often creamed, camp food, and it was extra choking in the tent that night when he let loose.

Amazingly, the two others in our tent, Recipe and Peter, didn't wake up, though Peter moaned like he'd been gut-punched. David must have roused himself, and he snorted to clear his airways. "Man!" he hissed, realizing I was also awake. "Smell that? That's your damn cooking, J.-G." He'd had thirds because he was so hungry, which at the time had pleased me.

"I gotta get outta here," he said. He unzipped himself from his sleeping bag and pulled on his boots; we slept in regular clothes, shorts and socks and tees. I slipped out of my sleeping bag and found my sandals and followed him out, securing the tent flap. It was a little chillier outside, but the air was fresh and temperate, and the three-quarter moon lamped us. He had his flashlight but we both decided he shouldn't turn it on.

"What time is it?" David said.

I shushed him, as we were under strict orders from the counselors not to leave the tents after lights-out unless there was an emergency; the implication was that there could be wild animals lurking about, like wolves or bears.

"After midnight, I think," I whispered. He started walking, and I followed him. All the tents huddled in silence. I kept my voice as low as I could. "Everybody's asleep."

"You weren't."

"That's your fault."

"Yeah, right," he said, smirking. "I bet you were awake with a bad boner because of you-know-who."

"No way," I protested, surprised that he'd noticed us. I didn't like the word *boner.* Of course like all boys I'd experienced erections, at random times, over nothing, they could appear and disappear like desert clouds, though at that point I hadn't yet fully confronted the idea of what they were good for, being more uncomfortable than pleasurable. What I was certain of at that moment was that I wouldn't ever want anyone to see mine in that state, not even my mother.

"Well, I know I'd have a big one all night," he said, cupping his inner thigh. "They like them big."

"Why?"

"Gosh, you're such an idiot," David scolded. To hide my ignorance, I didn't pursue it. We followed the trailhead up away from the lakeside and the tents and he stopped, turning on his light.

He trained the beam on the narrow trunk of a white birch tree, briefly examining it. Then he gave the flashlight to me to hold. He took his own Swiss Army knife from his pocket and pulled out its awl. He started jabbing the bark of the tree, chipping at it like it was ice and then scraping and scoring, using his free hand to pick off flecks. He worked for what seemed like a long time, working and then standing back from it in the way his art professor father might pause and ponder a canvas. I considered David to be a slothful sort of kid, he liked to lie about and read or pick at weeds or do nothing, but now he was totally focused on what he was doing. When he was done, he blew at the trunk and wiped away more flecks and said okay. I turned and aimed the light. And there it was, his handiwork grooved into the soft flesh of the young tree, an outline of a hand-sized heart with **SS + JG** carved deep in the middle.

"Someone's gonna see this!" I gasped.

"So what! Be proud of your love!"

"What if *she* does?"

"Even better."

It was then that we heard a faint peal of laughter. David's face crinkled and we turned in its direction. Now there were voices, and more laughter, and David instinctively hunched and started heading toward the sounds. I hesitated and he waved furiously at me, appalled at my meekness. I followed him; I'm only brave when I think people can see my cowardice. We hiked with stealth, creeping like guerrilla fighters along their deadly trail. Soon enough we figured out that the voices were coming from the pavilion. We stopped twenty yards short, the swaybacked roof visible through the moonlit trees. You couldn't see their faces but from the voices it was our counselors, Herman and Brenda, Dahlia and Ben Frost. Then we could smell something burning, but it was sweeter than the cigarettes my father sometimes smoked with his friends when they played cards, more like the spiced punks people burned to keep away mosquitoes. In the dark a tiny glowing ember floated back and forth like a bumblebee.

"I'm good," we heard Ben Frost say.

"You're such a choirboy," Brenda's reedy voice teased.

"Mr. Frost, he doesn't partake of the evil weed," Herman said thickly, in what sounded to me like a TV announcer's voice. "Nor this heinous hooch."

"More for the wicked," Ben Frost said gamely.

"You're most charitable, sir," Herman said. There was a moment of quiet then and it looked like they were passing around a bottle.

"Ooooh, that's so warming," Dahlia half gasped. She caught her full breath. "And it's sweet, too."

"That's why it's called Southern Comfort, baby," Herman said. "Happy syrup makes happy people!"

"Can we please slip some to Mrs. Hahm?" Brenda said. "Maybe she'd lighten up on me. How am I supposed to dress in this heat? It's like she wants me to wear a turtleneck!"

"I think she'd prefer you in a minister's robe," Dahlia said.

"Maybe I would, too," Herman said, and they all laughed. They drank and smoked, laughing and joking more about how strict the reverend's wife was, even Ben Frost saying how she'd asked him to put on his shirt during a flag football game. But we all knew Brenda's figure from the thin cotton T-shirts she wore without a bra and the cutoff jeans shorts that rode so far up her thighs that they showed the hemispheres of her butt. She wasn't pretty like Dahlia, but she was flagrantly voluptuous, which of course a kid like David found especially energizing. He constantly referred to her as "stacked."

David whispered, "This is so cool."

"What is?" I whispered back.

"*Them*. They're like, being themselves."

"So?"

"Yeah, well, something might happen."

His meaning should have been instantly obvious but when he said those words I couldn't help but picture a frightening scenario: someone standing tall over someone else. A fist raised. Power and cruelty and humiliation.

We crouched there for a while. At some point Dahlia said she was tired and despite pleas from Brenda she got up to leave, Ben Frost going with her. Luckily, we'd been hiding beside a bush a few yards off the trail or they would have seen us when they passed, Dahlia leaning into Ben Frost's neck, his pale, muscled arm clasping her. I was so happy to see them like that. They were a beautiful couple, they strolled with such a lovely sway of languor and I think of them still whenever someone says *A match made in heaven*. Of course, that's just a dream. None of us is meant for a destined other, we are lucky or we are not, the fullest feelings of our lives drawn from the serial consequences of certain times and places.

After they passed us, I wanted to go back, too, but David cuffed me and had us creep closer to the pavilion, where it got very quiet. Then we could hear Herman and Brenda giggling, softly grunting, and once I realized that they were probably "making out" I inched closer to the entrance steps of the pavilion, resolved to see them. My mother and father would give each other quick pecks sometimes, I'd once seen my teacher kissing her boyfriend or husband in the parking lot after school, there were random amorous couples in the park, but that was it in real life, everything else I'd seen was on TV, where it seemed they were mostly pressing faces.

You could hear the creaking of the wooden benches.

"We're not going to, right?" Brenda said breathily.

"Sure . . . sure," Herman answered, his voice muffled. They kept moving and shifting, and breathing more heavily now, Herman or Brenda or both making hungry little snorts and sniffles.

"Hey, what are you doing?"

"It's fine," Herman murmured, "you'll see."

"Okay . . . oh . . . oh . . . are you sure about this . . . ?"

There was shuffling on the floorboards and then they got quiet again, and then not, until you could hear Brenda breathing but in a sharper register, like she was choking, and

I got panicked and thought of sprinting down the trail to get Ben Frost, but David pulled us forward to the opening and I shut my eyes, afraid of what might be happening to her. David tugged on my shirt and when I looked again it was quite dark, but I could see that they weren't kissing at all. Instead, Herman was on the floor of the pavilion, kneeling before her where she sat on the wall bench as if praying but with his head pushing into her lap, the way a too-friendly dog might nose between your legs. It looked like he was rooting for something, and I thought it might be the thing by her sandaled foot, some light-colored swatch now glowing in the weak moonlight.

"Whoa," David said in the softest whisper, his eyes afire. "Look at that. . . ."

Her foot had lifted and was pressed into his side and the thing dangled from her ankle while he pushed around some more anyway, when I realized it was her white underwear. The skirt she was wearing was pushed up high, showing most of her leg. His head kept moving in her lap and she was restless, too, or at least part of her was, though her arms were taut and outstretched on the railing of the pavilion like she was gripping it with all her strength. I felt aggrieved for her, and icy toward Herman, who was surely the opposite of Ben Frost with his smart-aleck comments, and how he craved attention for his guitar playing, how he was soft and unathletic. Suddenly she let out a deep-set, pained note and I thought this was it, but she drew him up to her and began kissing him all over his face. He kissed her back with the same fervor and I had the idea that maybe they had just fallen in love. He rose then in front of her, more than a bit wobbly, and I thought she was going to get up as well so they could hike to their tents like Dahlia and Ben Frost. But Brenda stayed sitting, her hands now fiddling with the belt of his shorts. They were both giggling as she kept fumbling, and finally he undid the buckle himself, letting them fall. He was standing there bare-assed, and I don't know if it was David or I who let out a gasp, but Brenda jumped up and screamed.

We bolted like spooked deer, not able to even turn on a flashlight. Herman was cursing into the dark, threatening to kill whoever was out there. Maybe he pulled up his shorts and tried to come after us but there was a heavy thud on the floor of the pavilion and more cursing and we ran even faster, crashing through branches on the edges of the trail. Somehow, we didn't trip or get poked in the eye, instinct shepherding us. By the time we got back we were huffing and panting and luckily the counselors' tents were set well away from ours. Sweating, we crept inside our tent and zipped into our sleeping bags and sweated some more, expecting to be rousted. But nobody came. Nobody awoke. It was very late, after all. Soon, the only sounds came from David, who had already fallen asleep, mewling fitfully in some disturbing dream, while I slowly sank into a chasmic, blank slumber.

The next morning, I couldn't stay still. I wasn't hungry, only strangely thirsty, drinking copious draughts of the powdered bug juice that was being continually mixed up during the day. I kept hiking back and forth to the primitive outhouse, which was up the hill from the pavilion. We weren't supposed to but most everyone was just peeing in the woods, plus holding in any poop for when we returned to our cabins. I kept waiting for David to pull me aside and school me from his store of carnal knowledge, but he seemed to be avoiding me, taking breakfast with a friend from another cabin, and then afterward enlisting the Sangs to be his partners for the chore of collecting kindling for the night's campfire. I even tried to join them and offered to help, but David shook his head and turned in the opposite direction while bearing a messy bundle of sticks and branches.

I couldn't help but find myself at the pavilion again. That scandalous stage. I was conflicted, part of me incredulous that David wouldn't share information and offended by his selfishness, part of me, like any child confronting adult realities, glad not to know anything more. The truth is that he was probably running through all kinds of notions about what we'd witnessed, hypotheses surely more informed than what little I had on hand but still amounting to baseless guesses. The image of Herman's head, though obscured by the night, was somehow growing ever clearer in my mind; I realized it was not his head so much as his face, and not quite resting there but instead settling and nudging in as you would into a pillow. What I kept snagging on as I stood in the very spot where he was kneeling was how Brenda's underwear had dropped all the way to her foot, meaning that she was exposed *down there*. A *down there* that must be like what I'd seen when I was still bathing with my sister and mother, something like Ella's straight dark slit or the more frilly hair-nested one of my mother. If Brenda was naked that meant Herman was nosed right up against her private parts, which didn't make any sense, for when I pulled down my underwear my own parts could sometimes stink sharply of dried urine and something worse, like a tiny zoo. Why would you want to be so close to that? Why, after being unsure at first, did she seem to want him to be? Naturally, I couldn't help but substitute other couples, my father and mother first, then Reverend and Mrs. Hahm, both scenarios more than a little nauseating, and then Ben Frost and Dahlia, who were fresh and bright and clean and weren't suitable at all; and finally myself, paired, surprisingly, not with my cherished Susan, but instead a scowling Katie Croker, from whom I knew intimately of the awkward and the weird.

Yet I understood I would do anything for Susan. She had hugged and kissed me in front of everyone, not caring about the opinions of others, she was firmly on my side of things, and suddenly there in the pavilion my shorts were down around my sandals and I found myself as bare as Herman was standing before Brenda. I wouldn't care if Susan were here. I wasn't afraid of her sparkling, fathoming eyes. I was naked before her in the damp warm air of the brightening day. My insides were rocketing, as if I'd been freed from an iron orbit.

"Whoa there, champ!"

At a light speed my hands wrenched up my shorts.

"I thought it was you heading up here." It was Ben Frost, on the first step of the pavilion, peering at me through his spectacles, his Jesus locks bandannaed as sportily as ever. He had a huge coil of thick rope hooped over one shoulder.

"Look, I realize it's a lot closer to go here than the outhouse, but come on, my man, do you have to go inside the pavilion?"

"Sorry."

"It's cool," he said, motioning for me to come down. He smiled wide, mussing my hair. "Nature always calls. But look how much there's around to take a whiz on. Right? I'll wait here for you."

"Uh-huh," I replied. I searched his face.

"Don't you have to go?"

I realized the tip of my penis was hurting, maybe raked by the zipper as I pulled up. I had a flush of panic that it was bleeding, and if it was bleeding whether the infirmary lady would have to put a bandage on it.

"You all right, J.-G.?"

"I don't really have to go anymore."

Ben Frost blinked. "Okay," he said, not quite convinced. "You still want to help me rig the Tarzan rope, right?"

He had mentioned me doing so on the hike up, having noticed that I had attached the loop of the skipping rope I had brought from home onto my rucksack, and he wondered if I was interested in learning about knots. I had told him I was, even though I despised knots, or at least the unintended ones, the snarls of which seemed to me the incarnation of how chaotic and frustrating and messy everything could sometimes get, and that made me crazy and aggressive and wanting not to untangle the strands calmly but to yank at them blindly, only making things worse. In truth I'd packed my little rope for what I envisioned would be some emergency, a desperate moment that would find me in sole possession of a literal lifeline.

I didn't admit this either to Ben Frost as we climbed the hill to the spot where the Tarzan rope was, chatting instead about my surprise birthday cake and how I would remember this one forever. My traction was poor because of my sandals but I was working harder not to seem slow. I asked about his eleventh birthday, and he said it was a memorable one, in fact, because he got a whole set of camping gear and tools.

"Did you go camping with your family?" I asked, trying to imagine my parents and Ella along with me and him, which would be both kind of perfect and completely wrong.

"We didn't have to camp out because we already kind of camped." He then described how his family lived in a couple of converted barns in the hills of northern Vermont along with a few other families, an arrangement where everybody worked together to keep house and grow vegetables and raise chickens and goats. It was one big family, he said, and mostly a happy one, but sometimes you wished you had your own private space, even as a kid. That's why his parents got him all his own gear.

"So I always camped by myself, at first right next to our house. Then I'd set up somewhere down in our valley, just for a night, then two, and after that a spot even farther away. I had to hump the gear and food and water I needed in a couple trips because I couldn't do it in one shot. Then I'd stay out for two days. One time, three."

"What about school?" I asked. "Didn't your parents worry about you?"

"They probably did but they never showed it. They homeschooled me, too, so the schedule was what we made of it," he said, going on to explain what being homeschooled was. From what he described it seemed like his parents had a whole library of books and just made him go through and read them, plus every so often do some math workbooks, which he could do when he camped out by himself. It sounded totally cool to me, except for at night, when bears or wolves could come sniffing around. I imagined him, a mini Ben Frost, with even smaller spectacles, sleeping with his hatchet.

"I bet you could have lived like that forever!"

"Very true, J.-G.," he said. We'd reached the massive, grand oak where there was already a rope hanging from a thick branch, though it was old and frayed. "My dad made furniture and wooden bowls to sell when they weren't tending to the animals and garden. My mom made quilts and also cheese. Then my dad died suddenly, and my mom moved us back with her parents. I went to a regular school after that."

"What did he die of?"

Ben Frost gave a little sigh. "Heart attack. You know what that is?"

"Something old people die of."

"That's right. But sometimes they're younger." He paused. "My dad was thirty-eight years old."

I was always forgetting my father's age, but I knew it was just around that, which seemed old to me but nowhere close to dying. I got scared thinking of his heart exploding inside him, this blood bomb going off, and how my mother would have to take us back to Korea where all our relations were and huddle with them in a stuffy room of a church and cry for what felt like days, which is what happened when a church family's mom had died in a car accident. I'd have to live in a neighborhood of real Korean kids who would have their own ways of organizing themselves and playing games and being kind and mean to one another, things I'd have to learn quickly.

"Looks even worse than I thought," Ben Frost said, once we'd reached the spot. He was surveying the old rope swing dangling from a high, thick limb. It was badly frayed down its whole length, at its end a dinner-plate-sized disc of wood bolstered underneath by a large knot that was crusted with dark mold. The limb itself was sturdy, as thick around as a telephone pole and reaching out into the air with its leafy branch tips upturned, as if to beckon the horizon. From where we stood beside the trunk of the massive tree it was just about the height of a basketball hoop (as measured from the base), high enough on its own to be daunting but even more so for how dramatically the ground fell away from us on either side, the tree rooted atop the rim of a natural mini amphitheater.

Ben Frost demonstrated the two kinds of knots he would be using, tying them on the branch of a smaller tree as he detailed each step. Then he had me do it, first the double bowline knot that would secure the rope swing on the limb. He guided me through each loop while outlining its various uses for boating and climbing and how the single bowline was a good knot, too, if not as secure. This doubled one, he explained, did best under "load," which is what we would provide when standing on the swing. I had a lot of trouble making it, trying and failing, and trying and failing again, but Ben Frost stood there calmly talking me through the operations until I got it right. When at last I cinched it tight we nodded saltily, seasoned comrades. Then I undid it and he had me make the much simpler, basic stopper knot that would brace the round piece of wood, which after he demonstrated I managed to do on my second try.

"Fine job," he said, as he untied the knot. "I can see you're a naturally curious kid. You know what my minister at home says? Those who keep learning about life and the world can't help but be good and generous people."

His words inflated me with the belief that it was true. But I already understood that my sense of curiosity—and in turn, my focus and effort—was selective at best, a character trait my parents saw as worrisome, and potentially hobbling, one that might well leave me with diminished options in life. What they didn't recognize was that I was most curious when it came to people, this whether I liked them or not, whether they liked me or not, some dark part of me automatically ascertaining whether it was best for me to engage them.

With Ben Frost, though, there was never a moment of determination. All I hoped for was for him to think that I was a good and decent boy.

"Now we're ready," he said, and stepped up to the tree and jumped to grab a big lower limb with both hands, swinging his legs up and righting himself in a continuous, powerful move. I was glad he had no intention of my helping him rig up the rope. He began climbing to the swing limb, the coil of new rope slung over his neck and shoulder, and from a mountain-climbing movie I'd seen (in which everybody except the hero ended up dead) I wondered if he would have some kind of special harness or clips on his utility belt to help him get out safely on that branch. But once he got there, he just sat on it and then shifted, hugging it from its underside with only his arms and legs. He crawled out with his back to the ground like a monkey, fifteen or so feet above the face of the grassy slope, which was maybe not a lethal height but certainly high enough to maim. When he reached the old rope, he let go with one arm to retrieve the utility knife from his belt. For a moment he couldn't get it out, tugging at it as he leaned far back, and I had to look away, watching instead his shadow playing on the slope while a prayer for him in Reverend Hahm's voice droned in my head: *Bless Your devoted servant, Lord, bless him with all Your Might.* I wasn't sure if I believed in God, but I knew Ben Frost did, and I'd say or do anything so that He might help him.

He must have gotten hold of his knife because soon enough I heard the rustle of the rope falling in the brush; when I looked up, he was resheathing the blade. He worked expertly after that, unwinding the new coil and then knotting it up on the thick branch just as he had me do, and once the bowline was in place he unhooked his legs and held himself with his hands locked around the branch, winding the dangling rope around his ankle. He then quickly grabbed the top of the rope and with hardly any apparent exertion smoothly lowered himself to the ground. There he removed the disc of wood from the old rope and gathered the end of the new one and hiked back up the slope to a leveled patch of ground that had been dug into the face, railroad ties serving as its retaining wall, and as I scooted there I could see that this is where you launched from, sending yourself out over the abyss and then back again like a pendant on a string. We took measure of the rope so it would just clear the edge, and then Ben Frost cut it before he had me attach the wood on the end with the stopper knot.

"Let's see how this thing feels," he said, about to hop onto the disc.

"Wait!" I pleaded, practically grabbing his shirt. "Don't you want to check it?"

"Have some faith in yourself, J.-G.! I was watching, though. You did fine work. Just like with last night's dinner." Before I could answer he sailed away, the limb creaking mightily. He reached his far point and then careered back, my heart pumping, and when he reached me we high-fived before he veered away again, crouching now to build momentum as he ticktocked higher, and higher; at one point I thought he might let himself go. Just fly. But he pendulumed back and then most casually released himself onto the dirt platform as if he were stepping off a commuter train. He truly was like Tarzan, whose hairstyle, it suddenly struck me, was very much like Jesus's. . . .

"Okay, my man, your turn."

I shook my head. I liked the dizzying, swervy amusement park rides but heights gave me a funny feeling, not straight-out fear so much as how it prompted a fearful fascination about dying like that, the world walloping you with its ground rush.

"You sure? When everyone else is here and you feel differently, you might have to wait."

He held out the rope with his wiry grapple of a hand, the very sight of which gave me courage. He was ushering me into a brotherhood, one of benevolence and gentility, one where we accomplished useful tasks and made things that brought joy to people and shaped our purposeful adventure each morning, whether clear sky or storm. If something happened to my parents, if they somehow never made it back to pick me up, I would want to finish out the rest of the summer at Charminster and then live with Ben Frost and his mother and grandmother, doing whatever chores they had for me and eating every last bite of food they prepared and be the boy he once was.

I took the rope. Grasping it, though, my hand felt prickly and feeble, as I realized that getting on wasn't as easy as Ben Frost had made it look; you couldn't simply stand on the piece of wood and then jump, as it didn't reach the ground. Rather, you had to hop up a little as you simultaneously pulled yourself free to launch over the now breathtaking chasm. Ben Frost saw my hesitation and made ready to gird me by holding the rope, but I nodded to say I was fine. I wasn't fine, nor was the whole setup of the Tarzan rope, which would never pass muster in terms of safety standards and liability now, or maybe even then. But I'm still here; my feet scrabbled on the smooth surface of the wood, and had I not squeezed the rope at that instant with all my strength I would have slipped off.

But I didn't, and I went, not so far and high, but after employing Ben Frost's crouch I started to gain altitude, bounding with fresh velocity, alternating between the delicious weightlessness of my apex and the loving tug of the earth. When I got back over the platform he pushed me, building my speed each time as I veered back and forth like a comet. I let go of everything then, I didn't understand how exhausting it was to hold so tightly on to things, and I alarmed Ben Frost when on my final approach I released myself, hurtling right at him.

"Whoa, my man!" he said, having to net me in his arms. "We should call you Evel Knievel!"

"Cool with me!" I gasped, caught between breaths. We gave each other five, then slapped an extra-hard high ten, my hands madly stinging like I'd fouled a ball off the end of the bat. But I didn't flinch; reveling in the good hurt, I realized there was a welling in my eyes, but I must have been beaming because Ben Frost was beaming, too.

We could hear chatter in the treetops, and the rest of the campers and counselors began appearing. The younger cabins arrived first and as always, a mostly orderly queue formed, at least of those who wanted a turn. Ben Frost showed everyone the rope and its disc of wood, explaining how they should get on and that he could hold the rope in place for them as well, and then without warning announced that I would demonstrate. I thought I sensed a murmur, like why is *that kid* the one he chose, but nothing was going to dissuade me, I stepped up and mounted the thing like it was my own pony, making sure not to swing too high or try any moves that seemed risky, not even when I noticed Susan and her cabin now joining the line. I had been entrusted by Ben Frost to do it right and so I did, with highest fidelity, perching steadfast on that piece of wood like it was the prow of the flagship SS *Charminster.*

It took a while to get through everybody, and in the end, I didn't take another turn. I didn't mind, as it was almost as entertaining to watch as it was to ride. Nobody fell off, though there were a few close calls; for some reason one girl wouldn't place her feet on the wood and instead held herself solely with her hands, everybody shouting madly for her to use the wood for support, and as she came back lost her grip just as she reached the earthen platform, tumbling badly but without any injury. One boy got the idea to climb the rope while it swung, which killed his momentum, and he had to drop himself into the arms of two counselors reaching up to him from the slope below. Jimmy Choi, being a jackass, got himself going too high and too fast, almost getting bucked off when he came down too straight on his drop. The rest rode smoothly while standing or sitting on the wood while the peanut gallery offered commentary about each kid's stance or style, oohing whenever someone looked particularly cool or relaxed. Nonchalance was the gold standard.

What I focused on was the cast of their faces, noting whether it was cowed or giddy, prayerful or in thrall, whether they were sorry they'd ever climbed on or wishing never to get off; I knew enough of them to be surprised by their expressions, which didn't always align with how I expected them to react. David, for one, was clay-faced and pale, looking a little nauseated, while soft-spoken Peter garishly showed his teeth while flashing the peace sign.

Of course, I locked in on every second of Dickens's turn, hoping he might somehow panic and embarrass himself, maybe his legs would quake, or he'd have to shut his eyes super tight, maybe he would try to showboat like Jimmy Choi and fall and break his ankle or arm and have to be ambulanced out of camp. But watching him along with everyone else, I had to admit that he made that rig of ours his own, building up speed with easeful flexings of his strong thighs until it seemed as though he were simply traveling with the rope and not because of it, his smooth, virtuous arcs causing the softest sighing of the double bowline knot as it tightened around the tree limb. The counselors watched him as raptly as we did, and when he finally got off—he'd ridden for far longer than anybody, though clearly no one cared—he passed the swing rope to Ben Frost, who in turn shook his hand.

I didn't blame Ben Frost, who was always and only fair and kind to all, but the sight of that speared me. There was no lingering, no exchange of words, but I could practically read the secret pact of their palms, that acknowledgment the physically gifted instantly share for the almost magical, if momentary, sway they can have over the world. I was athletic, agile and swift enough not to be left behind, but I knew I would never be one of them.

Others took their turns, including the counselors, but I didn't pay much attention. The only other camper I watched as intently was Susan. As she took hold of the rope, she looked uncertain, pursing her lips as she measured the crucial limb above and the sloped ground dropping away before her, but in the moment before Ben Frost released her, I caught her eye. She cracked a weak smile, it was the only instance I'd seen her be timid, and I made two fists and shook them up at my cheeks in solidarity, but I wasn't sure she'd seen me. She did fine, quickly relaxing herself, going back and forth a few times like any of the rest of us, keeping very still in her stance, but to me she was something majestic, like a beautiful owl gliding by you in a tranquil, comforting dream. When she was done, I went over to where she had left her canteen and was now taking a drink. I had nothing special to say. I wasn't seeking recognition for being supportive. I simply wanted to be near her.

But Dickens appeared, already a few yards ahead of me, and I started rooting behind a mound of blackberry bushes, pretending I'd dropped something. But neither of them was aware of me. He said brightly, "You looked good up there!"

Susan didn't reply; she was as thrown as I was by his tone. Dickens could be disarmingly neutral, inscrutably so; he was never cheery like that.

"I didn't think you were going to do it. But you weren't scared at all."

"It was okay," she murmured, looking unsettled. Then she said: "Maybe a little fun."

"Yeah," he said. There was an odd silence between them, a pause I didn't like. Then without asking he reached for her canteen, and she let him take it. He took a sip, and then a longer one. A kid from his crew called for him, saying they were heading back to the lake, and he handed the canteen to her. He started to leave but then stopped.

"You want to know something?"

Susan just stood there, a funny crimp in her mouth.

"You know you kinda look like a boy, right? If you had long hair like other girls, you'd be really pretty."

He reached out and brushed something from the point of her bare shoulder. I thought she would flinch, but she didn't shrink from him at all. He turned and hustled to catch up with his friends. I stayed where I was; she was tracking him as he made his way down through the woods with his crew, her eyes lowered, her fingers absently twisting the ends of her hair.

For the rest of the morning, I thought about what Dickens

had said to her. To me she was pretty already but now I was questioning it, picturing her repeatedly, from different angles, with this mane of flowing black hair. I naturally compared girls' and women's looks to my mother's, who I always considered to be the most beautiful person, and although Susan was still a girl there was something to the lilt at the corners of her eyes that my mother had, too, and that gave them both an elegant, and somehow sage, kind of loveliness.

Again, because of her hairstyle, I had first thought Susan looked like Speed Racer, but the more I thought about it the more I realized everyone in the show, whether boy or girl, looked a lot like him, and how they were all a perfect combination of boyish and girlish if you mentally removed their hair, which I began to do with not just Susan but also Peggy and Julie, and then Mickey and David and Recipe—Recipe being the most unfortunate boy/girl—and finally with Dickens, too, who could be a good-looking girl outright, if a daunting one like Katie Croker. It was confusing, so much so that I was glad we weren't back at the cabins because I would have been stuck staring in the bathroom mirror, running through all the weird possibilities.

I also kept turning over what Dickens had said to her, unpacking how his compliment was nested inside an insult, or maybe it was the other way around, and how it would be a disturbing thing for someone to hear regardless, especially when there was nothing you could do about it, like instantly grow hair. It was a trap, cruel as all traps are. I began to feel aggrieved for Susan, who after the Tarzan rope didn't take swim time with the rest of us. In the middle of it I got out of the water and wandered back to the tents and I spied her through the opened flap of hers; she was undoing the ends of a lanyard as she lay on her back, then rethreading them but having some trouble, and finally she dropped it onto her chest and laid an arm over her eyes, much like my mother might wearily do on the sofa after hollering at me and Ella for the umpteenth time in a day. Then she reached up and let down the flap. The tent was partly in shade, but it still must have been awfully hot and stuffy in there. I knew how you could punish yourself after somebody else punished you. He had made her miserable, or made her wish to be miserable. Possibly he had made her physically ill. And I grasped, finally, who and what Dickens was, this pointed and maybe unending draw on your energies, this drain of a person who swirled away any good feeling until there was nothing left except a parched sting in your mouth.

The rest of that day was the doldrums. I drifted from one activity to the next, participating in varying degrees but mostly occupying space as I rode the crests and shallows of my darkhearted thoughts. In truth I was not unhappy. I was not cross. There is an almost pleasurable enervation to that kind of gloom. It's like having a fever just debilitating enough to render you useless for anything more than wallowing in each pronounced sensation, their unlikely symphony a renewed summons to being fully alive. Susan appeared briefly, at lunch and then at the prayer meeting, both compulsory, but otherwise she laid low. I knew I should have gone to her, no matter if she wished to see me, no matter if she would ever kiss me again. But what could I say? She knew I hated him, too. More words would only signify more failure. What remained was to offer her something palpable, something undeniable, some small but radical alteration of our little realm.

Possibilities, I realized, abounded. There were a few propane-fueled lanterns around camp; one could be left too close to his tent. Yet there would be innocent others. There was swim time at the lake; I was clearly a stronger swimmer than he, I could dive with a knotted rope and snare his foot and try to drown him. But then I'd get caught for certain, and though Susan and others might be full of admiration and gratitude I had no interest in martyring myself. For him I wanted to pay no price. I decided that it had to be accidental, if not necessarily fatal, that if I could come upon him, say, riding the Tarzan rope and startle him so he'd slip, if I could anticipate his heading there and climb the limb beforehand to slash at the knot, if I could trigger a mishap and have him marked forever with something like a limp, such that every step he took he'd have to think about what he'd done to her and to me and to the numerous sorry others who'd ever crossed his gaze, I'd do so without pause.

Such was my resolve. I must have been acting funny because Recipe came up to me during the preparations for dinner—I had conspicuously excused myself from any participation—and said that he wanted to go skip stones in the lake. I shrugged but he pulled me along. Recipe was no good at throwing stones, or throwing anything else for that matter, essentially shot-putting instead of hurling, and I got so annoyed by the dull *phlunks* of his attempts that I ended up standing behind him and holding his wrist while I took him through the mechanics of the required submarining motion. I should have known that he was being willingly hopeless to divert me from my obviously rotten mood. Recipe was sensitive and kindly, replete with a soul already. His unbounded glee, I know now, was also a mask for sadness that would mark him always but never sour into bitterness.

He made a few decent throws, skipping his rock four times on his last turn. When I made five skips right after, he hailed me with a goofy jig like I was his eternal champion. What else was left to me but to raise my fists in triumph?

"So what are you going to do at home?" Recipe asked afterward. We were sharing a Snickers he'd brought, surely knowing it was my favorite. The end of our camp session, which no one had breathed a word of, was mere days away. Most of August loomed, as did the start of school, neither of which held any gleam. The kids back at the apartments, the kids at school, friends and rivals both, they seemed to me like comrades from a receded past, their faces still unblurred yet cold and academic. None of it mattered anymore.

"I don't want to go home," I said, "even though I sort of do."

"Right on!" Recipe chimed. "We're kind of stuck here, you know? It's like heaven, but it's like hell, too."

He was right in how mixed-up things were. I was thinking that if I could banish Dickens, this place would be a near-ideal world. I decided that I liked everyone here, no matter any faults, no matter any frictions, I decided that I liked them exactly as they were, the feeling of which gave me an ache, this heaviness in my marrow that made me feel older and more vulnerable and a little scared.

He said, "Do you think we could meet after camp? Maybe your parents can drive you to my apartment. Or mine can drive me to yours. We could invite Mickey and Peter. David, too. Even Jimmy Choi! Okay? It doesn't have to be just you and me . . ."

I said it was a great idea, lauding the part about including others, even though it didn't matter to me. Recipe, smiling, went with the flow. But he saw I was comforted by the notion that we could keep something of this place going and held out his hand and we shook on it, firm and hearty, like grown-ups who were confident they knew the future.

"And who knows, maybe we could also meet up with Susan," Recipe proposed, his wicked side widening his eyes.

"Not where I live," I said, picturing her peering up at the grimy, monotonous brickwork of our tenements. She'd described in detail for me her family's small house in Staten Island, a one-story cottage that was white with green shutters and a bed of roses in the front. "Maybe in your town?"

"Sure thing," Recipe said. "I know just the place. Right around the corner from our apartment. It's called Antonino's. She likes pizza, right?"

"I guess so?"

"Doesn't matter." He'd popped up to his feet, now assuming command. "They also have strombolis and calzones. If it's too crowded there's a little park nearby to eat. Wait, that's it! I can see it. A bench in the shade. Picnicking with your pizza and sodas. You'll have a *be-yooo-tiful* lunch."

"You won't be with us?"

"Next bench over, but with you-know-who. We won't be eating."

"Why not?"

"Too busy necking."

We hooted at that, Recipe frothing up with giddiness. He'd asked me several times in the first days what I thought of a girl named Minha and although I didn't have much of an opinion he kept pestering me and so I said she seemed pretty cool, if mostly so we could drop the subject. Now I expected him to paint this whole picture of him and Minha getting entangled on the park bench, but instead he got on to how my date with Susan would go, spinning ornate details such as how she'd dab some stray tomato sauce from my cheek with her pinkie and taste it, or share a straw with me from our fountain drink, or how we'd huddle close beneath a tree during a sudden downpour, scenarios that only fueled my own dreaming. I couldn't fathom then—nor perhaps yet could he—that his yarns were his way of subconsciously weaving himself into her place. It doesn't matter at all, but I must suppose Recipe ended up liking boys rather than girls. I just wish I could have told him he was important to me. Like certain other people all through my life, I should have cherished him in the moment much more than I did.

All those moments; they could have added up.

I can't remember what they made for dinner that last night of our campout. I was there, sitting on a log or rock among the rest of my cabinmates, we were no doubt eating and joking and jabbering away, but I was caught up in possibilities for meeting Susan in imagined spots around Recipe's city neighborhood, if in odd extrapolations. In one we had not aged a day but had graying hair and were dressed up in a church and inspecting a double casket to share for eternity, something I'd seen in a vampire movie. In another we had two crying babies who looked a lot like Ella that we pushed around in prams. Or we were sharing a strand of spaghetti at Antonino's like those lovey dogs in the animated movie, though never quite getting closer.

There was one, though, that discomfited. I hated to entertain it, but it kept flickering in my mind. It was of Susan, standing atop the bench in the little park looking just like herself, but completely unclothed. The strange thing was that her body, ghostly white in its glowing, had no private parts. She was statue smooth all over—so unlike my mother when I'd been with her in the shower, whose body had ample nubs and colorings, curves and hair—and yet I was desperate to shield her, I didn't want people to see her, my hands reaching and flailing to cover her up as she perched there, oblivious. And all the while there was a furious trembling in me down low, this sensation that I was simultaneously scraped empty and about to split open.

Yet I was purposefully not seeking her out. I stayed crouched in the huddle of us Antlers. I was afraid that if I saw her, that if I met her gaze, I would get too animated and do something stupid and awkward. I was going to play it easy, run it back cool the way Cleon might, or how Ben Frost would in his own laconic style. Dahlia and Brenda had announced that because of the full moon that night we were going to mark the end of the summer season with "moon water" and "moon dancing," terms they didn't further explain but that intrigued everyone, especially after Herman observed that we had finally landed on the "pagan side" of Camp Charminster. The counselors seemed to wink at one another, and we did, too, even though no one knew what *pagan* meant until a brainy girl named Un-Joo said it had something to do with Satan. This got everyone murmuring, and I turned immediately to Ben Frost, for whom, I knew, Jesus was an enduring guide. But he was just shaking his head and chuckling, so I knew that it was either Herman just being Herman or truly no big deal, Christ-wise.

At dusk they got one of the campfires closest to the lake stoked up high while Brenda gave the other counselors some lip pencils she'd brought along to face-paint us. You could get a peace sign or a five-pointed star or a crescent moon on your forehead or cheek. Like most of the boys I chose the star. Recipe and David went for peace signs, David's taking up his entire face. I let myself look around and I noticed Dahlia drawing a delicate crescent on Susan's cheek. Other girls got the same, but I thought its upturned hook complemented the sway of her hair and made her look especially impish, daring, even exotic. Yes, she was wonderful, yes, I was coveting her, but I was happy for her, too, maybe in thrall to her, I wanted people to know the jagged rent in my chest for how fantastic she was so that we could celebrate her simply being around us. It was the first time in my life that such an amplitude of feeling had nothing to do with me.

The festivities were unusual. First, Dahlia and Brenda had each of us fill a clear plastic cup with lake water and then place it in a spot that would fully catch the light of the moon. Someone asked if we would drink it and Dahlia mirthfully pleaded *Please don't* and explained that we were steeping the water with "spectral light," this infinitely ancient cosmic energy that would endow us with renewed strength and wisdom. This made complete sense to us, for whatever Dahlia believed or said or did in her beatific earth-maiden way was yet another blueprint for our future someday as merely semi-Korean people. Still, some kids couldn't help themselves and tasted it, though nothing like Susan had that first time we met when she quaffed deeply from the lake.

It was getting darker, and I couldn't be sure if Susan had taken a drink, just that like everyone else she and her cabin-mates had, as instructed, set their cups before themselves in anticipation of the moonrise. At some point Herman strummed a few chords to build the mood. Then Dahlia held her cup high so it could bask in the lunar glow, beginning a chant that went something like *Shur-u-ahm, Shur-u-eem, Shur-u-ohm,* then elaborating a different set of sounds before reprising the *Shurs*. She had us do it with her, explaining that it was a mantra to welcome the lunar cycle and help shed the negative thoughts and feelings we always bore, cleansing us of self-destructive forces so that we could embrace our in-born, beneficent selves.

"What frightens us most is to know how good we can be," Dahlia said after we finished. "Let's not be scared anymore. Let's not hold ourselves back." This provoked an extra-sharp hoot from Ben Frost, his outburst startling us.

Next Brenda demonstrated the moon dance with Herman accompanying her with a score of heavily syncopated riffs, her twists and shimmies and leaps making me think of the primitive tribal people in the Friday-night TV black-and-white monster movies I watched where the pith-helmeted explorer spies upon their frenzied ritual worship of the creature. Had we been a tad older, a little more jaded and knowing, her wild grasping at the bright soapy disc of the moon (and all the groovy exhortations from Dahlia) might have seemed risible, the gyrations and hair tosses bombastic and absurd, but instead we shadowed every one of their movements, we felt each pluck of Herman's mystical playing, we were acolytes of the unabashed reveling, an abandon we never saw from the adults in our lives.

I don't know how long it went on, but by the end we were slick with sweat, mosquitoes studding our steamy necks, clotting up our ears. Their bites hardly registered. We were inventing our own versions of berserk solo dancing, with me ending up, inexplicably, doing a few gym class squat thrusts; maybe it was the moon, or all the frenetic action around me, but I felt like I needed to burn off a dense lump of energy. Others were ballerina twirling, or jumping, or windmilling their arms as if swimming in place, Jimmy Choi shaking out his legs so crazily that one of his sneakers flew into the lake. Our odd array, individually distanced but still together, must have looked like some juvenile cult of the wood. Herman's strumming quickened and whatever each of us was doing we accelerated to match his tempo until he wound us up into a frenzy, and when he suddenly stopped, we somehow knew to collapse to the ground.

We lay staring up at the immensity of the moon, kids panting in the breezeless, sodden heat of the evening. The moon seemed only to grow the longer we looked at it. Dahlia asked us to spread our arms and legs as wide as we could. "Let's make ourselves sails for this kindest of energies. We're harnessing the greatest power of all, which is the power of forgiveness." Of course we had constant reminders of this at our home churches, and from Reverend Hahm and the youth pastor here at camp, the countless object lessons of Our Savior Jesus Christ, but then Dahlia added, "It's the power to forgive the world, my dear ones. And that means forgiving yourself, too."

I don't know if others were really listening, or could care less if they were, but for me a trapdoor opened, all my insides dropping away. You could theoretically figure out why you'd forgive those who'd crossed you, hurt you, made you anxious and scared, you'd be trying to show your enemies the ultimate futility of their armaments, but what Dahlia said jarred me into wondering why I was always so ready to be singled out, so ready to be wounded. I knew I wasn't a great person, or even a mostly good person, but maybe I wasn't such a detestable one, either. Maybe what she meant was that the world can turn you to become a certain way. A way that doesn't have to be you.

After a while Herman started playing again, singing one of his favorites, "The Sound of Silence." I didn't normally like his singing, his voice always too springy and bright, I thought he was a show-off who pretended not to be a show-off by making a play of showing-off, but this time he was singing softly, his register low and breathy, letting each phrase stand on its own. He was singing the song. I don't know if I realized how troubled and haunted the song's message was, but I surely felt it, and yet I wasn't afraid. I wasn't sad. Instead, I had receded into a kind of trance, for once not caring an iota for how people were perceiving me. The only thing close was when I sometimes woke very early on a weekend morning just before the light came up, when it seemed the entire universe was slumbering.

There was a nudge at my shoulder. It was Recipe, his broad face gleaming in the moonlight. But he looked pained. I asked what was up.

"Just come on," he insisted, tugging on my arm.

"Tell me first," I said, shaking him off. At this point kids were either still hanging about or had gravitated toward the one stoked-up campfire, where Herman was starting in on a camp song. Brenda and Dahlia and Ben Frost were getting everyone to sing along, which I didn't want to do. But I wasn't minding listening.

Recipe said, "I heard some kids were talking about sneaking up to the Ledges."

"So?" We'd been hearing chatter from certain big talkers like Jimmy Choi about going up there to fool around but no one much believed them.

"I think Minha was with them."

"Really? You saw her?"

"No, but she's not around here." He regarded me gravely. "And George isn't, either."

We were both aware of how George Lee had been hanging around Minha a lot on this campout; earlier I'd seen them playing gohng-gi off by themselves during swim time. I didn't think George was all that bad. He was a friendly, smart kid who knew a lot about Korean War fighter planes like the MiG-15 with its swept-back wing design, and we had a friendly debate about the merits of it versus the F-86 Sabre, so I liked him, though I never admitted that to Recipe.

"Okay," I told him. "Let's go."

Recipe already had his flashlight. We slunk away with it turned off, but we soon needed it, new banks of clouds intermittently shielding the moonlight. We moved quickly, going around the far side of Trench Lake to get on the main trail, which eventually led up, at times steeply, to the falls where we'd briefly dipped ourselves before. All this I still managed in my sandals, which at this point were getting ravaged. The Ledges were a short hike below the falls, at least going downhill, a more level section where there were depressions in the rocky ground and the falls water, when there was enough of it, collected in shallow, picturesque pools. Each cabin had gotten a chance to visit the falls properly, but the already meager flow had dwindled to almost nothing, and the pools of the Ledges had turned murky and brackish. But it was still a neat place to look for dragonflies and tadpoles.

"What are you going to do if we find them?" I asked.

"Don't you know?" Recipe asked, incredulous.

"Nope."

"I gonna kick that jive turkey's butt."

"Right," I muttered. He was hiking fast, and I kept nearly

tripping, his flashlight illuminating only the immediate patch of ground before him. "But what if George kicks *your* butt?"

"I don't care," he said. "I'm not afraid. He can give me a bloody lip. Shoot, maybe I'll even let him."

"Why would you do that?"

"So Minha can see. Girls need to know how much you care."

"Can't you just give her one of your candy bars?"

"Very funny. But I'll do that, too, when she comes to our tent to take care of me. I will be her brave soldier. She'll be my Florence Nightingale."

I was going to say he had a strange brain, but he already knew it, and he knew that I knew it, too.

"The most important thing is that I will tell her I love her."

I couldn't help scoffing, mortified by how he would undoubtedly express himself like some crazy character in a movie. But part of me was envious, always daunted by the prospect of professing such headlong passion myself.

"Anyway, you watch. Cuz heads gonna roll."

Soon we could hear voices. Recipe put his finger to his lips and switched off the flashlight. We crept up the rise. Moonlight had broken past the clouds and through the trees we could see them sitting on some small boulders. There was Minha, and Minha's best camp friend, a girl named Jackie, and indeed George, with another boy from his cabin whose name I had forgotten. Nobody was kissing or even hugging.

The girls giggled as George was lighting a match, or trying to, flicking it again and again. Finally, Minha said to give it, and she pulled a fresh match from the matchbook and in one stroke lit it and they all went *oooooh.* George's cabinmate leaned toward her, and I realized he had a cigarette in his mouth. I couldn't believe it. Minha lit it, the end of it glowing red as he inhaled. He started hacking and they all laughed some more and Jackie asked him where he'd gotten it, and he said from Herman's backpack.

"You stole it?"

"Yeah, two of them!" He passed it to George, who took a puff. He started coughing, too. Minha tried it and so did Jackie and when it was George's friend's turn, he drew on it gently and let out a fog-like gush, holding the cigarette to the side of his face like it was nothing.

Minha motioned for the cigarette. This time she took a longer drag and with her lips pursed she expelled a series of puffs, like from an old-style locomotive. "My uncle can make rings."

"So can my dad!" George said.

Each of them took a turn to see if they could make one but no one came close to succeeding, instead they just mostly coughed and giggled at one another. They finished the first and lit up the other, smoking now with less trouble. I thought it was all very cool, marveling at how transgressive other kids could be, even such well-adjusted, mannerly ones like Minha and George, the kind my mother would surely hold up to me as models. When I nudged Recipe to suggest that we should join them he shook his head vigorously. I badly wanted to try to smoke but it was more to smoke with them. That's when Minha gave a low groan.

"What's the matter?" George said.

Minha had curled up slightly, pulling up her knees.

"I feel funny."

"Like funny how?"

"I don't know," Minha said.

Jackie, sitting beside her, wrapped her arm around her friend. "Maybe we should go back."

"Not now!" George interjected. "We're still having fun."

"*She* isn't," Jackie said, giving him a glare. "Come on, George, let's go."

Minha nodded but said weakly, "I think I'll be okay. I need to get some air. . . ."

With Jackie's help she started to get up but was wobbly and turned her head and vomited into the shallow pool next to her. She threw up again, until it seemed like her whole dinner had come out, and maybe lunch, too. The boys were stunned silent and so was Jackie, and it was only Minha who was making any sound, a high, rapid wheezing. Then she started to dry heave as she bent at her waist, her head and neck getting bucked by her shoulders. Somehow, she couldn't stop. The boy who'd filched the cigarettes was now crying.

Jackie was berating him for his stupid idea. George stood there watching it all with his hands on his head.

I nudged us forward, but Recipe held me back.

"Can we just go?" he gasped.

"We should help her."

"I don't want her to know I was here."

"Why not?"

"I don't want to embarrass her," he said, wringing his hands. "*Please.*"

"Just be a man!" I hissed. He grimly nodded, but I could tell by his face that I'd said it in a way that hurt him.

When we showed ourselves, they momentarily shushed but saw we weren't counselors and started waving. Jackie asked us to help her get Minha to her feet, as she'd flopped down over her knees like a rag doll.

"We have to get her back to camp!" Jackie cried. "She's really sick!"

Recipe and I tried to lift her from beneath her shoulders. She was moaning awfully.

George stammered: "Is she gonna die?"

The very utterance panicked us, or at least it did the others. I would have been panicking, too, but suddenly remembered the very same thing happening back at our apartment playground to Salvatore Casagrande after he'd boasted about puffing through a half pack of his older sister's Virginia Slims, becoming so dizzy that he fell off the seesaw and badly sprained his wrist. He'd upchucked, too.

I recounted a version of this to everyone, one in which I split one of the butts with Sal and had warned him about smoking any more but that he did anyway because he could never control his voracious appetite (which was true), resulting in his getting too much of whatever it was in the smoke that could make you feel sick to your stomach. I'd been awed by his daring but cackled along with the rest of our gang when he toppled, laughing even after he got up, pretending he wasn't hurt. But now I assured everyone that the nauseated feeling would soon pass, just as it had for Sal. We just had to wait. This seemed to calm everyone down, particularly Minha, who was already feeling a little better.

"I hate throwing up," she said, wiping her face. "It always makes me cry."

"Me, too," I admitted. She nodded. The quiet gratitude with which she regarded me made me suddenly want to be chivalrous. Recipe and I were helping her get to her feet and I could now understand what he saw in her. She was dainty and girly, maybe prettier than I had realized, especially when she smiled.

"I think I'm okay now," she said, leaning more into my side.

Jackie said we should go back, and we agreed. The clouds were blotting the night sky again and it was darker, with the trail only wide enough for one. Jackie was taking the lead with her flashlight, the two other boys behind her. Because Recipe had his flashlight, he was naturally next. He tried to hand it to me, but Minha told him he should just go ahead of us and light the way. He said fine and then reached out a hand. She took it but she also extended a hand back to me, which Recipe saw. I could have easily brushed her away, let the two of them go as a pair and simply followed, but instead the three of us hiked in mincing steps on that descending brookside trail. I'd like to believe that I was guileless, that I was simply not conscious of Recipe, or even of Minha, that my chest was filling not with prideful vanity but with the piney tang of the night air, that a still young boy could savor simply being alive. I can recall the girl's warm, supple palm, the extra press of it whenever we had to take a tight turn, or step over a log, but now I feel her hand as if my hand were my friend's, each clench of hers a tiny pulse of his defeat.

The treetops swayed with a sudden, stout breeze. Stray droplets began ticking through the branches. Without a word we were trooping faster; we had to let go of one another. Eventually the trail became more level as it approached the lake, and you could see the campfire on the opposite shore, hunched silhouettes scampering to their tents.

"Come on, J.-G.," Recipe said. "You better keep up!"

Jackie and the boys were already out of sight. Minha had now retaken Recipe's hand, the beam of his flashlight jittery as they hustled. Soon Minha and Recipe were ahead of me, but the path was obvious, as it now followed the edge of the lake. The night sky rumbled directly above me, and I had an urge to run even in my slipping sandals, but I wouldn't let anything bother me. Let it rain. I could endure whatever I wished. I was my own person, maybe almost a man. Still, I had to control myself and slow my pace as the drops began to multiply, falling big and cold. But then it started to come down in sheets, and I could see by the ambered campfire light the frenzied surface of the lake. I knew that ahead of me was the utility hut, where gear like the deflated inner tubes was stored. I headed for it.

It didn't surprise me that they were already there, at the rear corner of the hut, sheltering beneath the eave. They were so close together that I felt a jab of envy; even Recipe would have his girl. But let him; I would be magnanimous. I was happy for him. I really was. Then I saw it was not his shape but a shape I knew. It was extremely confusing because it was suddenly Dickens and not my friend. I wanted to ask a question, I wanted somebody to explain how this had happened, to explain where he had come from, but there was only the full-throated holler of the rain. The bursting in my chest. For I had already realized it was Susan who was with him. She was wearing her embroidered Western-style shirt, the one I so liked. He was right up against her, and she was standing stiffly, so stiffly that she looked as if she were holding her breath. Yet she was facing him, unafraid. They weren't kissing. They weren't even moving, they were perfectly still, this awful statue, except his hand was pushing up her shirt. He was riding up the fabric, pushing it and bunching it, making it crimp in a grotesque, ugly way.

You think you can die only once.

What luck, if that's true. I was eleven years old, and I thought I knew everything.

I thought I knew how this life would be.

It was difficult for all that final night of the campout. Recipe was simply glad I'd made it back, for when I reached the campsite kids were standing around with their sleeping bags slung over their shoulders; most every tent had been flooded during the initial fury of the rainstorm. The counselors and some campers were trying to sweep out the water with whatever they could use, pieces of crating, their bare hands and feet, one kid frantically bailing with his baseball cap like he was on a sinking boat, but then the rain came again, this time steady and droning, rendering those efforts futile.

Herman proposed that we hike back to Charminster, but Ben Frost immediately shot that down: the trail would be slick and at points too dangerous, especially in the dark. We would have to try to shelter inside the tents, which we did, sitting atop our sodden batting-filled sleeping bags because it was too wet to lie down. In ours we took turns using flashlights as a lantern until David ordered it turned off, because nobody was in the mood to play cards or look at one another anyway. Shivering in the dark, the soaked canvas panels emitting a fresh stink of mildew, my mates were probably as miserable as they had ever been in their lives.

They could not know my state of being. It was easy enough to wallow with them, to grunt and sigh. To dwindle into a grim silence in that dank, sagging box. Eventually they fell asleep, but I never did. I wasn't thinking or feeling; I was not replaying any scenario.

All I remember was that I was breathing, I was acutely aware of my lungs, that this was what I was, just a thing that took in air and expelled air, no matter how foul. And it was foul, with all the soaked gear, our soiled clothes, the boys serially burping and then farting as they slumbered, rasping through their many days' unbrushed teeth. Normally I was sensitive to strong smells, I would have been bracing myself or already escaped to crouch under a tree, but the creature of me didn't flinch, inhaling deep, and then deeper, in the hope that it might poison itself.

But it didn't. It was still there. Just before daybreak, I crept outside, standing alone among the tents. There was no sun, just a gray illumination diffused through a low-hanging mist. The rain had ceased but you could hear the drops petaling down from the trees. Everything was soddened, the ground saturated, how right and good it smelled, of plain wet earth, of scoured stones and clean bark, the world made fresh again. Only I was rank, my still-damp shorts dingy and mud-stained, my shirt drier but soured with sweat. I could catch, as my mother regularly would, the meaty odor of my own scalp. She would say it was time, that I was a filthy boy.

Suddenly I craved hearing her voice. I hadn't realized how much I missed her.

By the lakeside, I kicked off my sandals. I wanted to strip down, but I thought I should keep my clothes on, to wash them. As I stepped into the water I flinched; it was much chillier now from all the rain. And inky; I couldn't see my feet as they squished into the muck. It was not frightening, even when the bottom sloped steeply away and I had to tread water, it seemed, with extra effort. Maybe it was the clothing weighing me down, but I had to start swimming to stay afloat. Soon I realized I was as far out as we'd gone with the inner tubes, to the spot where it was legendarily deep. I could feel the ribbons of a much sharper cold reaching up to lick at my feet, and for a couple seconds, I panicked. But then I stopped flailing, my limbs working rhythmically again, and although I wasn't tired, I wanted to stop treading, I wanted to bob there in the middle of the dark, deep little lake. Again, it was difficult, it was too much effort to float, so I took a big breath and then another and then at last I exhaled and let myself sink.

It was such a strange, comforting cold. To be enveloped by that gentle, frigid flume. I was aware that I could die. I gave myself over, not like to a bully, not like ceding yourself to nothingness, but so I could tap something of its vast, secret power. I sank far enough down that my ears began to hurt, my lungs pushing up into my throat. My feet went numb, and then the rest of me, too.

I thought: *I can open my mouth.*

How I surfaced I'm still not sure; it must have been my legs, suddenly tasked to save me. At some point I trudged onto the shore and lay on my back. The grounded mist had dissipated but there was still no sky, and I closed my eyes to the darkening pall.

Some rain on my face woke me. Or it was drops from the bill of Dahlia's straw cowboy hat, which was actually Ben Frost's.

"What are you doing out here, sweetie?" Dahlia said, wiping my brow. Ben Frost was beside her and he helped me sit up, shielding me with a side of his plastic hiker's poncho, which every one of us had but that I wasn't wearing. It was raining only lightly.

"Don't tell me you slept out all night," Ben Frost said.

"I guess so," I muttered.

"But why?" asked Dahlia.

I said something about it being stuffy in the tent.

"Okay," Ben Frost said, somewhat flummoxed. "You better change into drier clothes. We have to break down the tents and hike back to Charminster. It looks like it's going to rain all day, and maybe even thundershower."

They walked me back to my tent, where Recipe and David and Peter were just waking. They didn't notice that I was changing out of completely soaked clothes. Nobody was in the mood. Our other cabinmates, as with the rest of the campers, were getting roused by the counselors, and when we emerged you could see kids slowly climbing out from under the flaps shivering and frowning at the rain. It had been an awful night and now it was no better, and maybe worse, as there were the many tents to be broken down and stacked for later pickup by the staff, not to mention the long hike back to our cabins. Some kid asked if the camp would send a bus for us but apparently the dirt road to get here was too steep in parts for even a pickup truck to manage when it was this wet, much less anything as large as a bus. There weren't enough vehicles anyway to retrieve us all. It was the trail for us, which everyone knew would be muddy, sloppy, and very slow, especially the parts where you had to climb or shimmy down through rock formations. For breakfast you had to run over to where Herman and Brenda were quickly making peanut butter sandwiches—to start a cooking fire was pointless—and eat one before it got wet. I saw Julie take a bite of hers and then flip it into the woods like a Frisbee. There was only stale canteen water to drink, no time for any bug juice to be mixed up.

It started to drizzle, and most everyone took cover beneath the trees. You never saw such a wretched collection of kids, save maybe on the evening news, these scrawny Oriental children staring out listlessly as if in the aftermath of some natural disaster. Wondering how it had all come to this.

I was not among them. I stayed out in the rain with a handful of other campers helping the counselors dismantle the remaining tents; somehow, I even began directing other kids on the best order of operations, as I knew every step of how we'd put them together. When a patch of heavier rain came, they, too, wanted to bail, but I didn't flinch, I wasn't registering it the way they were, I'd been flooded already, and as one boy and I carried a folded tent to the pile, I stuck out my tongue to catch the drops. The rain was fresh and almost sweet, like from the deepest, purest well, and I tilted my head to taste some more, the kid eyeing me like I was a freak. Normally I would have made a joke of it, or tried to ignore him, but instead I found myself staring back at him, not to test him, or defy him, but because I couldn't help but take the full measure of his apartness. For a strange feeling had arisen in me, or around me, that this random kid, this incessant rain, this present arrangement of life, was existing only on the periphery. It was real, for sure, but it was happening out there, repelled to arm's length by some reversed magnetic field.

And yes, I was conscious of where *she* was.

And yes, of where *he* was.

They weren't anywhere near each other, nor seemed in the least to want to be, and yet they might as well have been slinging away from me into orbit, bright enough but ever receding.

Once all the tents got stacked, Ben Frost announced that we should retrieve our backpacks from where they'd been piled beneath two large tarps. It was time to go. We shook the water off our ponchos. Unlike on the way here there was no intention to the column, everyone grabbing their rucksacks and trailing whoever was in front of them, and closely, as the counselors had advised. The cabins didn't much matter anymore, just making it through what would be a drenching, difficult hike. Only the counselors took certain positions, Dahlia leading the way and the others distributing themselves along the line at regular intervals, with Ben Frost in the middle and Herman in the rear.

I ended up in the last third or so. The rain had paused, and resumed, and then paused again, this before we had even reached the main trailhead on the far side of the lake. And now we were already stopped; a girl had slipped on the path, the whole side of her muddied, including most of her hair. The path was very narrow at that point where it just skirted the lake, and Brenda was helping her. The girl was crying, and Brenda had to calm her down and the rain was starting again, and you could hear some grousing up and down the line. There was a tap on my arm, and it was Mickey, who'd come up from behind.

"It's messing you up, huh?"

He pointed at my feet. I'd retrieved my ruined hiking boots and pulled them on after Ben Frost saw my feet and told me there was no way I could hike back all the way in sandals. At first, they'd seemed to work, for I'd laced them up extra tight, and the going was slow enough that it wasn't bothering me. But now the fire-deformed sole of my left boot made it impossible for me not to walk without obviously lurching.

I shrugged, half grinning.

"We can switch boots after a while," he offered. "I think we have the same size."

This wasn't true, and Mickey knew it. My feet were smaller than his. Wearing my boots would be painful for him, if not outright torture.

I told him it was okay.

"Well, just tell me if you want to."

"I will," I assured him, though I knew that I wouldn't. He had been constantly looking after me, just as he'd promised my parents on the first day, and while I liked every one of my cabinmates, including, I had to admit, Jimmy Choi, Mickey was my favorite. He was the last person I should ever want to cause trouble for, which was why it was difficult for me to accept that I had casually patted his neck with my poison oak–laced palm after I brag-fibbed about Cleon being my best friend back home. I assumed that like me he wouldn't be affected, that he'd suffer at most a mild rash and not a full-blown allergic reaction that resulted in weeping, post-burn-like boils, the scabby remnants of which still marked the underside of his jaw.

I kept thinking how he had played sports and swum and taken his meals through the worst of the affliction, how he'd never once complained about the itching and the aching, the discomfort of which must have been terrible. It lasted nearly a week, whereas I would have been ceaseless in my carping, railing on about my bad luck when I wasn't trying to blame somebody for having somehow tainted me.

I kept thinking how in a certain way the world was made up of people like Mickey and people like me, and how unfair it was that the people who lied, who cheated, who did terrible secret things, knew more about the truth of it all than those who simply went about their good and decent way.

I kept thinking how if it were left to me, if I were the ruler of Earth, or God, or some powerful magician, I would call out and expose every one of us before our family and friends, to force us either to change ourselves or to go away forever.

The fallen girl was consoled enough that she finally got moving, and so did the rest of us. Mickey stayed up with me, but I made him go in front so that he wouldn't have to keep watching my sorry limp. I was happy that I could do that at least. Our column trudged forward, the footing getting muckier with each step for those of us toward the back. But I realized that I had to watch Mickey now, I had to keep seeing the patch of healed but rough skin on his neck and that he was reflexively pawing at it still. He kept touching it and I thought I should chide him like my mother did me when I would claw at mosquito bites until they bled, warn him he might only make it worse. Yet his hand wouldn't rest, every few steps it went up like a gate arm, suspending for a half breath, before giving, like the hind leg of a dog, a quick strum of a scratch. I realized that this in fact had been his reflex since he first broke out in the rash. I alone had caused him to suffer this odd, pathetic-looking habit.

Finally, I asked him if it still itched and he grumbled, *Why would it*, his tone suddenly distant in a way that unsettled me. I shut up after that. But as we slogged along the west shore of Trench Lake, I couldn't help but feel the rippling on his skin as if it were my own. Even in that complete dampness, the rain coming down steadily again, I could feel the flaky scaling, the once-angry nubs surely healed but harboring an incessant, phantom itch. I wanted to rid him of this pestilence, I wanted to pitch my fingernails at a furious angle like I would do to myself and deliver that wonderful, if excruciating, relief.

I was reaching for him when well ahead of us Jimmy Choi wailed, "C'mon, man, are we really doing this?" It was because the clouds had let loose, the surface of the lake seething, and you could almost hear the shared thought along the line that we were at the very beginning of what could only be an endless, dreadful day. Dahlia and some kids at the head of the group—was Dickens among them?—had just reached the trailhead and were now scrambling past one another up the rise to get beneath the trees. Jimmy Choi broke rank and bulled his way forward, drawing others to follow, and the column pretty much collapsed, kids pushing and crowding the narrow path until Herman and even Ben Frost were shouting for people to get back in line. But I didn't try to get under cover any faster, nor did Mickey, who was berating Jimmy Choi for again doing his part to make things more difficult, though I'm sure Jimmy Choi couldn't hear him, or care if he did.

For me the troubling thing was my one ruined boot. Where the ground wasn't as mushy it was causing my foot to jam hard to one side, each step like I was half turning my ankle. Inside the soaked sock I could feel the abrasions gaining against the edge of my foot and heel. I thought I could easily withstand it—I wanted to withstand it—but as we made our slow way toward the trailhead, the footing, though still slippery in spots, was only getting firmer, perhaps from the eons of rocks migrating down the hill, perhaps only in my imagination. Mickey, head tipped against the pelting, was getting farther ahead of me. I tried to keep up. But the two girls behind me scooted past, then a few others, until I was being regularly overtaken, even by Herman, who gave a thumbs-up to check if I was okay but didn't wait for an answer. Again, I didn't care about the downpour. I was biting my lip with each buckle of my foot. Yet it seemed to me that this was what I deserved, which was all these people passing me by with little pity, passing me by like someone they should forsake.

I had made a grave error. From the start of camp, from the very first day, it had been a profound mistake. I should have been another J.-G. This one part of the gang, for sure, though a J.-G. maybe more like Peter, who nicely tagged along, who sported the mildest grin and rarely extended an opinion or asked for anything, settling in the mid-ground in his fine, clean clothes. This J.-G. would sprint in the race but with no special fury; he would wait in line at the campout with his paper plate and eat whatever some conceited kid believed he could cook; he would decline any offer to drink lake water, however eccentric and endearing; he would play the decoy, making a strong run but never aiming himself to capture the flag.

This is the J.-G. I should have been, because this is the J.-G. I was.

I was sure of it.

I was sure of it.

I was sure of it.

That's when Susan came even with me, sidling her way past me like anyone else. But then she realized it was my sorry self and stopped.

"Did you get hurt?" She was shouting through the heavy rain.

"It's my foot!" I could yell, still, for her.

"Yeah!" She nodded, waiting for something less apparent. "What happened?"

"I don't know!" I blurted, intending to explain in detail how the ground conditions were affecting my messed-up boot. But it was all I could utter, stopped dead by her wonderful face.

"Wait!" she cried.

I thought she was going to wave one of the counselors over, but instead she hooked her arm into mine. We got going. I was determined not to slow her down, or force her to tug me, so I made myself keep pace. But moving at this speed hurt, it was surprising how much, my ankle feeling like it would fail at any moment. Plus, now there was a searing on the side of my foot, which I could tell was the water-logged skin beginning to be flayed.

"You're okay," she said, but I barely heard her. The shock of each step seemed to feed the next shock, and the next, until the pain was a frantic singing in my ears. The only thing saving me was the soft, bared interlock of her elbow and mine. Here was a momentary reprieve. If I could be yoked to her like this, I'd promise to forget what I'd seen, I'd never ask her to recount it, I'd march until my ankle shattered and my foot rotted to mush. I was crying, crying I thought with the smashing dream of it and not the physical torment, but the torment was so great that I pulled back the hoodie of my poncho and let the skies shower my face, so she wouldn't know.

Somehow, we got to the trees. I let go of her and tipped back against a large, thick tree, sliding down to its soaked, mossy roots. We'd made it just a few yards into the woods, but I had to stop. Those before us had hiked up only a little farther, to a relatively open area of ground beneath the dense canopy, where at least it wasn't pouring. The rest behind us had now settled in, too, wherever they could find drier ground or a felled tree trunk, some simply crouching, everyone covering up whenever the wind shook sprays of rainwater from the treetops.

All the counselors were huddled at the first crest of the rise. It seemed they were debating again whether to keep going or sit tight, and you could hear Herman raise his voice to try to make a point and then they were arguing hotly until Ben Frost whistled sharply in the way he could between his fingers to calm things down. They were all fed up and miserable, too, though clearly not Ben Frost, who was gesturing up the trail and giving instructions to another male counselor, a counselor in training whose name I can't remember, who had now pulled on his backpack. He and the C.I.T. now started hiking again. I didn't like seeing Ben Frost go but I heard someone say they were checking the trail ahead for us and would be back.

Susan was still breathing hard, from having dealt with me. She must have been as miserable as anyone else, her short hair plastered flat on her head, her shins and knees completely mud splattered (no doubt from the rough slogging with me). And what had been her white canvas Keds low-tops were now these odd, fudgy paws. But there I was, numbed by too much pain, seeing her only as bent over me, concern creasing her eyes.

"Check it out," someone said. It was one of the Coyotes, laughing and pointing at Susan's feet. He was with another kid, and then Dickens, too, who wasn't laughing. His baseball cap was pulled close to his eyes, and his head was angled up slightly and I could see he was staring at Susan, not at her feet but at her directly. I was going to tell him to stop when I realized she was meeting his eyes right back. It was just for a second, they were communicating only to each other, but then Dickens tapped his buddy and said, "Come on."

They walked off. Susan had turned away from me now. At first, I thought she was clawing at the ground. Then I saw that she was wiping mud from her sneakers, and from her ankles and shins, she was trying to clean the dirty splatters on her skin, but she was making it worse. It was frightening to see her like his because this is what I would do, to make it wrong, to unfix the fixable, this is why my near-finished scale models ended up smashed, why my bug bites had to bloat and fester, why the minor knot in a rope became a snarl of a garrote with which I would strangle the world.

"I'll help you," I said, already up on my feet.

She didn't answer.

"We can go back out in the rain, to clean you."

Nothing again.

"I can go on you," I mumbled. I was trying to undo the waist button of my shorts.

"What?"

"I can go on you."

She could not have understood what I was offering. Yet I would never see such a revulsion again.

I watched her hurry away.

I was alone then. There were the others around me, I could see who was talking, I could hear what they were saying to one another and to me, and whatever I said back. But I was alone. I'd had the feeling before but now it was stronger, squaring in my chest, not a pressure exactly, not even a hurting, more like a force of its own, this bolus of momentum that was turning and turning but had nowhere to go, like the toy gyroscope I had back home.

Kids were pulling on their backpacks. Ben Frost and the C.I.T. had returned from checking the trail sections up by the falls and it was decided we should continue. I ended up someplace toward the rear of the line. I was unaware of who was around me, just keeping pace with the backpack in front, marking the alternation of the sludgy heels of their shoes with the sludgy tips of mine. As much as my foot was hurting, I kept moving, abhorring any attention, abhorring any relief.

Soon it was harder ground, which was worse for me, we were hiking up the rise, slick patches of stone outcroppings to step gingerly on, and over. The natural chute that ran to the side and below the level of the trail, which days before had been a trickling sluice, was now a mini rapids, its bolted waters splashing up against what had been stranded rocks and downed branches. The trail then narrowed as it wended through some denser brush, veering away and then turning back to track alongside the chute again. It got steeper, the trooping slower. There was no singing now, no camp cheers, no call-and-response chanting like on the hike in. Nobody was talking to anyone else or making any noise.

Then you could just catch it. The breathy rasp of the falls. I had been dragging, the gap between me and the backpack widening, but now I was right up on the kid. I had to hold myself back a little. We climbed, and climbed some more, until we reached the now overflowing pools and then the sound was full, drowning out the rain, the wind, the swaying trees. This beautiful cascade. The whole line of us had to stop and take it in. The falls wasn't immense, it wasn't grand, but it was broad enough and high enough that you could feel in your chest the hard smacking of its waters on the basins below, the spray fine and stony smelling, almost alive.

One of the counselors reminded everyone that nearly the entire hike back remained. We got going, treading the path again in our lengthy line. I tasted something funny and when I touched my mouth there was blood; I was biting my own bottom lip. We took a looping offshoot of the trail we had come in on because of the severe steepness of the path beside the stone formation. The trail led away through the woods, and then up a gradual rise until it came out onto a sparsely treed plateau at the top of the falls. There was a section of the bank that jutted out and despite the rain kids were lingering again, pausing and bunching as they marveled at the thigh-deep water streaming over the broad ledge in a smooth, riverlike flow. I was blocked from a clear view, and I pushed forward enough to glimpse the sheer drop, the sight of which made me trip over my own breath.

A gap opened between people. I could see the running water, how fast it was falling off. It all seemed right. Yes, the sky was spitting, and the air was chilled, and my ruined foot was begging, roaring, shouting for its life, but the sharpest notes were blunted enough that I could filter out what the world was saying, and only to me.

Yes.

It's okay.

Yes.

I barged forward, wanting the precipice, because every precipice is of consequence.

I launched myself, leaping straight through the opening. But then I saw the boy and he was standing there and I had no thought. Then he was in the stream.

He could have stood. He should have stood. But the flow was too strong.

It was taking him away.

Someone jumped in, reaching for him. It was Ben Frost. He had him and was hugging him but then he lost his footing and together they slipped. I tried to call out, to warn him they were still moving.

They went over.

It was still raining when my father and mother arrived. They'd left Ella with Mrs. Fredericks. This was the day before the official pickup day, when cars would again crowd the lot and everything would happen in reverse, parents and siblings packing up the footlockers and rolling up sleeping bags and carrying totes of laundry down the front steps of the cabins while their campers exchanged mailing addresses and their final teary or stoic or sobbing goodbyes, before stopping for the grand send-off by their counselor, who'd wrap them in a full bear hug or raise their hands for a palm-stinging, double high five.

See you next summer! would be the cry, the hard promise, whether you wanted to see them again or not.

My cabin was empty when my parents walked in with Reverend Hahm. Herman had already come by with his campers to accompany the other Antlers to the dining hall for lunch.

I was sitting on my cot, all my things ready to go. Recipe had insisted on helping me. In fact, he did most of the packing, as I was moving very slowly, or hardly moving at all. The others had been steering well clear, avoiding even looking at me, save for Mickey, who stood just outside the door and regarded me with wary, grown-up eyes. I didn't try to engage him. There was nothing to say.

Recipe was the last to leave and nudged me on the shoulder.

I kept my head bowed, staring at the burnished old flooring. The planks were slightly cupped in parts, some risen edges frayed with little splinters that had over the session gotten most of us. Even in this dusty cabin we went shoeless. We'd had to help one another pull them out. I so craved to sweep my hand over it, make it perfectly smooth.

"It'll all be okay, J.-G. You'll see."

He hugged me, tightly, with empathy and love, any flickers of which I was desperate for. But what I did was become the stone; it would take a thousand years of hard rain and ice to pierce me.

He left, too.

I can't remember if Reverend Hahm carried something, or if it was just my father and me bearing my things, but I can still see my mother trying to hold an umbrella over the reverend as we made our way out in the light rain. She couldn't quite maneuver herself into the right position, once nearly tripping him up. Finally, he grunted, *Please, that's fine.* She retracted it and we walked to our station wagon, the lone vehicle in the field.

We loaded the back of the wagon, and my father told me to get in the car. I sat in the rear seat, leaning against the window. It was stuffy inside and smelled faintly of vomit from our many car trips, and I had to roll down the window a few inches. I shut my eyes, hearing their voices as they stood at the back of the car. It was mostly Reverend Hahm talking, and they were getting wet in the rain, and although I wasn't trying or wanting to listen, I was hearing everything they were saying.

I drifted in and out then. I had not slept the night before, when our campout group eventually got back to Charminster. The car ride home seemed to take all day. I don't remember my parents saying a word. My mother kept silent, turning her gaze to the side, and my father just drove. I woke intermittently to the trees rushing by on the parkway, to the storefronts of different but same-looking Hudson River towns, to the circuitous, slow last stretch of road along the Sound that led to our apartment complex. In the parking lot we unloaded and after my father handed me my rucksack, he put his hand on my neck and for a second I was certain he was going to choke me. Instead, he grasped the back of my head and pulled me hard to his chest and I cried, I cried harder than I ever had before or have since, my mother behind me tightly clutching the rolled sleeping bag and crying, too.

I shared a bedroom with Ella but for quite a few nights I stayed in my parents' room, sleeping between them in their bed. Ella wanted to be with us, too, but a part of her understood that something was amiss that she should probably not ask about and so she made the best of it, setting up her colored paper cutting and dolls on my bedspread. It didn't bother me. I was avoiding my own things, not touching the toys or games in my bin or the scale models on my desk. Without prompting I brushed my teeth and dressed myself in the morning. After breakfast, and after my father left for work, I stuck close to my mother. If I could be useful and not a hindrance I helped her with the chores. I wasn't trying to be good. I wasn't trying to make amends. I only wanted there to be an order to things. When we went to the supermarket I carefully pushed around the cart with Ella in the plastic seat and responded to my mother's usual queries about what we should have for the next few dinners with an unusual surety that she noticed but didn't remark on. If they were her usual homey dishes, I didn't care, I wanted whatever I could anticipate the taste of, that I could count on not to surprise.

I stayed inside, mostly. The start of school was a couple weeks away, and my apartment friends should have figured that I was back, and yet I didn't hear anyone calling up to my window from the playground. Nobody rang the doorbell. Somehow, they sensed things were different. Sometimes I looked out the window and could see some of them playing Running Bases or going headfirst down the slide and I'd have the urge to sprint down the stairwell and run out there but the thought of hanging around with them in close quarters laughing and joking about the usual stuff made me shrink. Certain days, when it was nearing dinnertime, I'd tell my mother I was going out for a bit and she wouldn't protest, hoping surely that I was meeting friends, but I knew the playground would have already emptied out except maybe for Cleon's older brothers and their crew smoking and drinking beer on the benches, who wouldn't bother acknowledging my presence. Instead of sitting I would stand on the belt of the swing and get myself going not like Ella would but high enough to pendulum for a while, to feel that good gravity again. But the feeling would be too much, and I let my momentum dwindle, waiting out the last excruciating seconds when I was hardly moving, or not moving at all, until I was dead stopped.

One night, after our dinner, after I showered and put on my pajamas, after we watched a variety show together during which Ella, as always, fell asleep, my mother wondered aloud to me whether I'd like to sleep again in my own bed. She was massaging my ankle, as she had been doing nightly since we'd returned from camp. The ruptured skin on the side of my foot was finally healing. I said I did. No doubt she believed it was I who was ready to sleep by myself again.

She didn't know that I was staying in their bed because I sensed that she needed me to, that she was desperate to see and feel and cradle her son and convince herself that he was like any other boy. It was the first time in my life that I understood the power I had over her, over them both, and that I should do whatever I could to ease their anguish.

For what Reverend Hahm told my mother and father that day must have been devastating. They're both long gone now, and my memories of them are full, but that moment is one that I think about when I think of them together. What makes the recollection keep rippling outward is that I didn't see them, I was in the rear seat of our station wagon, eyes shut in exhaustion, in a fugue, my heart marking the meter of the reverend's calm, grim voice.

He said that while the incident was determined by the local police to be an accident, it was best for all that they take me home. My father asked how it could be deemed otherwise. Your son may well have tripped, he said, and was falling in himself, but a camper informed her counselor that she saw him knock the boy into the water. But why? my mother said. Had they been fighting? The boy said no, the reverend said. And your son wouldn't say.

He described the rest of what happened, how a counselor jumped in to retrieve him, but the force of the waters swept them up and they both went over the falls. The drop was more than twenty feet. Given where the group was, and the poor condition of the roads because of the weather, the emergency workers could not reach them for almost two hours. The boy was in the local hospital, with a broken shoulder and arm. His injuries would have been much worse had it not been for the counselor, who had protected him with his own body. The counselor, however, was in a much graver state and had to be sent to the regional hospital. It was a true blessing, he said, that they had both survived.

Reverend Hahm then had them pray with him, right there beside the car, for the welfare of the injured ones and for the welfare of their son and for the mercy and glory of God, but all I could think of was how he had kept referring to me as their *ah-deul.*

Ah-deul, ah-deul.

Your son, your son.

I hated his saying that. I wanted him to use my name, to say it over and over until it grew profane, so that my mother and father might somehow see me for what I was, that I was my own form, my own creation, that I was no longer theirs.

But inevitably, I was. I slept in my own bed again, listening to my sister's feathery breathing. I started playing a little with my friends, then more so once the school year began, when we'd gather after the last-period bell and choose sides for one of our usual, furious games. My parents went about the exertions of their days, my father leaving early in the morning and returning just as my mother was setting dinner on the table, with Ella and me vying to pry the cap from his bottle of beer. If it had been a difficult day, he'd have one more, and my sister and I would tangle again. I was eleven years old, but I might as well have been six. My mother kept everything in motion and in an acceptable state of order with her cajoling and berating and fretting, though perhaps she was dialed back a half notch. Sometimes it seemed she regarded us from afar, without ardor, and I'd move to her and tuck myself in her side, breaking the spell.

The one marked change was that we were going to church every week, when before it might be twice a month, and although the autumn was mild, I didn't join the kids playing in the parking lot after the service, and my parents didn't push me to do so. Once the weather cooled it was better anyway staying in the basement with the adults and the snacks and juice and tea. One Sunday, as the baskets were passed down the pews, Reverend Hahm announced that all the offerings that week, not just from this church but the others in our tri-state church association, would help pay for the next round of surgeries and continuing rehabilitation for a counselor who had suffered a terrible accident while at our summer camp. His selfless action had likely saved the life of one of our campers, he said. The young man was a hero. Reverend Hahm thanked everyone for their generosity, not once looking in our direction, but I saw my parents eye each other and when it came around to us my mother held the velvet-lined basket for my father while he put every bill from his wallet into it. It was the only time that we'd driven back across the Whitestone Bridge with an empty station wagon, having had to skip our post-church shopping at the Korean grocery.

We went to church the following week, but not the week after; there was freezing rain, and the roadways were slick and dangerous. Soon our attendance began reverting to the former frequency, and then grew spottier, until by the time the school year was ending, we had almost stopped going, missing, among other things, the announcement about the coming Charminster session. My parents, as noted, were not devout people; they valued the fellowship and social life of the church but in their ever-dwindling free time, you could see that their neighborhood interactions were growing in number and importance to them. The circle of our family was expanding. There were errands and chores to do on Saturdays but on Sundays my parents arranged other appointments, we were going to family picnics, to the municipal swimming pool, to potluck dinners at people's apartments, my parents hosting turns at ours. For the first time, not every person was Korean. My father took me into the city for a baseball game, and the whole family for the circus. A Pan-Asian grocery opened in the next town, which, though not ideal, we could shop at any time, though most often did so on Sundays. We attended church one more time that year, at Christmas, but then never again.

You could think it had nothing to do with me.

We moved on, far afield, propelled, like most everyone else, by circumstance and necessity. Time kept happening. My parents, who never got rich, provided enough of everything so we could make something of ourselves, and that we'd know we'd failed had we not. Ella grew up to be a brilliant geneticist, as renowned as someone like that can get.

Once, in Boston, I saw a young woman wearing a T-shirt with Ella's face silkscreened on it. I couldn't help but ask; it turned out she was a post-doc in the same field. She wondered how I knew Ella, and I responded that we were old friends. I don't know why I lied, maybe it was the sparkle of excitement in her eyes, but suddenly it felt burdensome to have to acknowledge our siblinghood.

I made my usual lighthearted escape.

And what of me? I've failed many more times than not, which is nothing special. I've done fine, in the end, although it's not quite the end. I wish only that my parents, who weren't very long-lived, could have experienced fewer of my dips, my shallows; no matter my crawling out, they were always worried about me. One evening, a few weeks before she died, my mother kept hold of my hand after I'd helped her into bed and asked if I could forgive them. My father had died several years before, but she always spoke as if they were still together.

For what? I said.

Modeun-geos, she said. *Everything.*

I told her I had no idea what she was talking about. But that broke my heart.

Sometimes, it arises. I can still hear the last thing Reverend Hahm said to my parents that day. *Ask your son to tell you what really happened*, he advised them, *for your sake as well as his. What God already knows should be brought to light. Otherwise, it will raze you all from within.*

For the following week, the following month, veritable years, I kept expecting them to confront me. Have me tell it aloud. I don't know what I would have said to them. I had readied all the versions.

But they never did.

I've not gone back to any of the old places. Not the apartments and the playground, not the elementary school, not, even if they allowed it, the youth centers, the therapists' offices, the penitentiary. Not Camp Charminster.

Once, though, I went to the church. When I was first working and living in Manhattan, a striving, struggling young man, I'd sometimes take the subway on the weekend to eat at a run-down gomtang place in Flushing. It was cheap and good. I needed the succor of that simple bone soup. That springtime Sunday, I took an indirect route; I walked by the church on Roosevelt Avenue, its dark red stone cladding still cold, oddly uninviting. The information marquee for the services was in Chinese rather than Korean, and scores of well-dressed congregants and their children were coming out from the nave and down the main steps, like so many fish streaming down the chute of a river. They were so colorful, alive, warmly greeting one another in their language and shaking hands as they overflowed around me onto the tiny patch of front lawn and onto the sidewalk, their swaying, merry-sounding talk filling the air.

It could have been wonderful.

I waded in.

About the Author

Chang-rae Lee is the author of six other novels, including *Native Speaker*, winner of the Hemingway Foundation/PEN Award for first fiction, and *The Surrendered*, winner of the Dayton Peace Prize and a finalist for the Pulitzer Prize. A 2021 winner of the Award of Merit for the Novel from the American Academy of Arts and Letters, Chang-rae Lee teaches writing at Stanford University.